WHISPERWORLD

ARON CHRISTENSEN & ERICA LINDQUIST

LOOSE LEAF
STORIES

Cover by Damonza.com
Edited by Hache L. Jones, Cedar LaBrie, Lacey Waymire,
Amber Presley, Kathy Lindquist and Mara Van De Rostyne

————

This is a work of fiction.
All characters, organizations, places and events portrayed in this book
are either the product of the authors' imagination or are used fictitiously.

————

Find more of our books at LLStories.com

For Leon and Torrin
Fly high and dream big

I UNSLUNG my crossbow and put my back against the cracked concrete wall. These raids didn't usually end in violence, but people got emotional, and emotional people did stupid things. I worked the lever on my steel 'bow and slid a bolt into place. On the other side of the door, Zach did the same with his own weapon.

When my partner was ready, he nodded. I banged on the wall with my fist.

"Greenguard!" I shouted. "Open up!"

People seemed slightly less threatened by a woman's voice than by Zach's big booming one and we needed the advantage. I hated these jobs even when they went smoothly.

There was a burst of activity from inside the apartment. Furniture scraped and voices whispered harshly.

"It's the Greenguard, Sam. The Blackthumbs are here!"

"Quiet! Go and hide!" hissed a second voice. A baby began to cry, but was quickly silenced.

My hands were full of crossbow and I couldn't punch the wall. So I banged my head against it instead. *Blackthumb* meant someone dangerous – usually one of the Greenguard – and that really wasn't how I wanted this to go down.

Shit.

Zach frowned until I finished my temper tantrum and then cocked his head at the door. No one drew the curtain. The apartment had a computerized polymer door, of course, but the power that operated it had failed a long time ago. Now it was pried and propped open, covered by a mat of woven agave fibers.

Not for long. Zach grabbed a fistful of cloth and gave it a sharp yank. The hanging tore away with a snarl of ripping fabric and I stepped through. I kept my crossbow tucked against my shoulder but the bolt pointed down at the floor. Zach came in right behind me. A middle-aged man with thinning brown curls was herding a pair of children away and all three of them jumped as I charged into the room.

"Where's the baby, Garza?" I asked.

Sam Garza pulled his children protectively behind him. One was a girl of nine or ten with her father's thick brown hair. Her brother was a few years younger. They stared at me with wide eyes, at Zach and then up at their father. Sam's lined face was pale and his kids began to cry.

"These... these are my children," said Sam. "Gabby and little Samuel."

"Where's the other one?" Zach asked.

"These are my children," Sam repeated. "Two's the limit. We would never break the Gardeners' law."

I glanced around the Garzas' apartment. We were up on the tenth story, high enough that Zach and I had to climb two ladders and then a crooked set of stairs that would probably collapse before the end of the year. No one lived this far off the ground that didn't have to. The highest floors were always the first to collapse. They were a long climb and a dangerous fall from the busy streets and markets below.

But Sam's clothes and those of his children were linen – not cheap cotton or agave weave – and dyed a deep, vibrant blue that I didn't see very often. A copper water pitcher sat on the counter, polished and well cared for. Dinner was still on the table and looked like a nice fat gopher snake, not the grainy gray crickmeal I expected from a highriser.

"You're a dyer, Sam, and you obviously bring in good barter," I said, nodding to the table. "What's a man of your means doing up this high if not for privacy?"

Sam tightened his shaking blue-tinged fingers on his children's shoulders. Zach moved to the doorway where Sam had been taking them. My partner stopped and brushed aside the curtain that hung across it, leaning inside. He motioned with his crossbow and then stood back.

A woman emerged from the doorway. She hung her head, dark hair falling over her face and the baby she cradled to her chest. She shifted the child in her arms and her breast popped out of its mouth. The baby fussed until Sam's wife resettled it against her.

Zach shook his head. "Two children, Garza. You know the law. The Whisperward is already straining to protect us all. A third baby means another mouth to feed and someone else goes hungry."

"Please, don't take her!" the woman begged.

"Mary, be quiet!" Sam hissed, but then took up his wife's plea. "Please, sir, we didn't mean to. Surely she was a gift from God!"

"The Gardeners speak for God," Zach said without hesitation. "Two children. No more. You know what happens to the extras."

Mary cried even harder and the other two kids clustered around their mother. Sam stepped forward and I tightened sweating hands on my crossbow. The weapon was suddenly heavy in my arms. If things went stormy, this was when it would happen. This was always when the parents did something stupid. Sometimes they tried to bribe us. Sometimes they came at us with a kitchen knife. One hysterical woman even threw a potted cactus at Zach a few months back.

Don't be stupid, Sam.

He was.

"Don't give her to the storms," Sam pleaded. "Take me instead! Leave my children and take me. I'll go willing!"

"And leave your wife on her own to raise three children?" Zach asked. "You're the tradesman, Sam. Do you want your family to starve without you?"

Sam hung his head and his whole body shook with bitter sobs. He was breaking down now and I didn't think he would do anything violent. Sam had taken his only shot and missed. I couldn't help feeling sorry for the guy. There's nothing like birth control duty to make me hate my job.

Zach looked away from the family. I doubted that the mourning Garzas could see it, but I knew Zach well enough to read the turmoil beneath his steely expression. This was different than killing the dangerous mutants that strayed into the Whisperward, different than hunting down thieves or dreameaters. He hated this just as much as I did.

"Zee, do we have to...?" I said, but Zach was already speaking.

"The Gardeners have read from the Book of Law, and you have broken that law." Zach's jaw was clenched and sweat beaded along his dark brow. "So here is what we're going to do. Julia and I are going to leave now. But we're coming back tomorrow. And when we do, we're only going to find two children. Rosy?"

Sam and Mary looked up hopefully, but Zach kept his expression stern and his crossbow leveled at the family. With his dark eyes and square jaw, he did *stern* way better than I ever could.

"Two children," Zach repeated. "You find a way, or we have to do it ours."

"There are refugee families who have lost their own children–" Sam began.

Zach held up one big hand. "Shut it. I don't want to know. Just make sure your family's the right size when we come back here tomorrow."

We hurried out of there before the Garzas could blubber their thanks too much. I didn't like this job nearly enough to enjoy being thanked for it. And I really didn't want any of it getting back to Gregory. Being chewed out by the boss wasn't as bad as birth control, but it still wasn't fun.

It was a long climb back down to the street and not much easier than going up. Some of the buildings in Angel City had ropes and pulleys running through the old elevator shafts, but the one in the Garzas' highrise was choked with rubble that no one had ever managed to clear out. The upper stories probably only had a generation or two left before they crumbled, anyway.

When we reached the sixth floor, Zach and I climbed down a series of ladders braced against the outside walls that led to lower rooftops nearby. From around our necks, we pulled bandanas up over our mouths. Zach settled his wide-brimmed hat low over his brow, but I left my goggles up in my hair. The dust wasn't so bad today and the view from up here looked out all across Angel City.

Angel City was the largest Whisperward in the west and second only to Apple City far in the east. There used to be other cities besides the walled Whisperwards, but that was a long time ago. Now we were all that was left of civilization.

From this high, I couldn't see all the cracked walls and rusting bits of exposed rebar. Harsh white daylight was giving way to sunset's flaming colors and shadows softened the city's sharp edges. A dozen other ancient buildings rose up around us, apartments just like the Garzas' stacked high into the sky. The top stories were all long gone, crumbled away decades or maybe even centuries before my birth. Their remains crowned each highrise in jagged angles of broken concrete and shattered glass that threw back the bright sunset glow until the buildings shone like huge torches.

Below us spread the patchwork of houses and markets, cactus fields and scale farms built from ruined old buildings. One of those farms was likely where Sam picked up his nice little dinner. As the long day darkened toward night, the lizards crawled over one another to find the warmest spots on the cracked cement while the night herders waved off black clouds of evening insects. I wondered if the prices down there were any better than with Harrison, my usual scale farmer.

From the center of Angel City rose the huge, dark shape of the Stormsphere. The shiny black dome was perfect and impervious, never dulled by dust or damage. It reflected the sunset's fire all along the smooth western curve. Haloed in red and gold, I could almost believe the Stormsphere really *was* the Tear of God that the Gardeners claimed.

I slipped on a rung of the ladder and Zach scolded me for daydreaming.

Again.

"You've got the sharpest mind I've ever seen, Julia, but you let it wander way too much," he said.

Zach sounded like my mother. *Let your mind drift and a dream-eater will gobble it up!*

Maybe Zach thought that he needed to father me a little. God knew I was the malcontent child of the Greenguard. I began to answer, but my bandana slipped and the wind whipped the tip of my auburn braid up into my mouth. I spat it out again.

"Eat thorns, Zee," I said.

I think Zach scowled at me beneath his own bandana, but I doubted he meant it any more than I did.

The lowest levels of the apartment building were better patched and cared for than up high where the Garzas lived. Down here was where the rich and important people lived, where the foundations were strong. Zach always said that I should be grateful that I had one of those lower-level apartments now. We had both grown up in poor families, but making it into the Greenguard was the next best thing to being an actual Gardener. We had privilege and power and all that good shit.

Sometimes I missed my mother's eighteenth-story apartment, but by the time we were on the ground again, my legs ached and I was glad for my neat, clean little second-story home. Now I just had to get back to it.

A group of children ran around the corner, all laughing and shrieking as they chased each other. In the distance, I heard some poor parent's shout, trying in vain to summon them back for dinner. The kids pulled up short at the sight of me and Zach. In our olive drab fatigues, big black boots and carrying our steel crossbows, they knew exactly what we were: Greenguard. Blackthumbs.

Our uniforms were made of something the Gardeners called *carbon microfiber*, though I guess there weren't any carbon plants left and nothing that grew in the Whisperwards made cloth like that anymore. It was stain-resistant, repelled the dust, and was next to impossible to tear or cut.

The children skidded to a halt, all crashing into each other, and eyed us warily.

"Evening," said Zach. He touched the brim of his hat in salute.

"Good evening, sir," they chorused.

I remembered how I used to look up at the Greenguard when I was a little girl, with a confusing mixture of fear and respect. The Greenguard practiced birth control and took away the extra children, but they also fought off dangerous mutants from beyond the walls and protected us from dreameaters and Whitefingers. I never wanted to be one of the Greenguard when I grew up, but they were heroes.

Still, it was hard to forget that at the end of the day, our job was to kill. Our official name was *Greenguard*, but just about everyone in Angel City called us *Blackthumbs* – violent death-dealers that they counted lucky to have on their side and prayed that the Gardeners never sent against them.

But not even our oiled metal crossbows or the knives sheathed on our hips could hold the children's attention for long. As soon as we passed, they leapt into motion once more, continuing whatever game we had interrupted.

"Hey, Zee," I said.

"What?"

"Thanks for what you did back there. With the Garza girl... I really didn't want to give her to a storm."

Zach shrugged his big, broad shoulders. Like me, he was one of few Blackthumbs not born to a Greenguard family. He'd grown up like the Garzas. A lot worse, probably. Zach's lantern jaw worked for a second before he spoke.

"They're our people. I was only doing my job," he said.

"I doubt Gregory would see it that way."

"We're not Whitefingers, Julia. We don't worship the storms. We don't breed dreameaters to hunt innocent souls. And we don't kill people we don't have to. As long as we can count only two Garza children tomorrow, then the law of the Whisperward is preserved and we don't have to execute a baby girl."

"What if the Gardeners ever change the law?" I asked. "Only one child?"

With all of the refugees from Sun City and now Bridge City, too, the Whisperward was filling up. Fast. If Angel City wasn't already at its limit to support them, it soon would be. And more people were arriving at the city gates every day, tired and hungry after month-long treks across the endless desert that separated the Whisperwards.

"I don't know," Zach said.

"Do you think there will be a pruning?" I asked. "Even the Gardeners would never order that, right?"

Zach shrugged again. But I could tell he worried about it, too.

SUNSET'S GOLD and orange had turned into deep red and purple by the time we made it through the crowded streets of Angel City to the Greenguard base. Zach had hung his hat down his back by the cord and he pulled his bandana off again to breathe in the cooling night air. Just a few more minutes, then we could make our report and finally be on our way home.

Even at this hour, Men and women in pale linen worked busily along the road outside the Greenguard base, carefully raking the gravel streets smooth. They swept the patched sidewalks clean of the day's dust and sand, keeping the roads of the Whisperward clear and passable. Blackthumbs – like me and Zach – returned to the base after a day out in the city, passing other Greenguard on their way to the city walls or streets to make their evening rounds.

I followed Zach along a chain-link fence topped in spiraling razor wire that wrapped around the base to an open gate. On the other side, we headed toward the nearest building. The Greenguard base was a blocky complex of steel and concrete, sturdy and better built than almost anything else in Angel City. The centuries since God's Wrath had hardly touched the building at all. The base's huge gray bulk reared up over the Whisperward, dwarfed only by the Stormsphere itself; a stern knight kneeling at the foot of his great obsidian queen.

We made our way through two sets of reinforced metal doors and it was even cooler inside. The base was one of the few places in Angel City that still had power. Bright blue-white lights glowed in the ceiling without coal or oil, and there was a cold breeze inside created by something the Gardeners called *ay-see*.

As a child, I had demanded explanations from the Sunday school teacher. He told me that *AC* were letters, not words, though he claimed not to know what they stood for. I decided on my own that they meant *air-cooling*. It seemed accurate.

Yeah, that's the sort of kid I was. And, if I was honest with myself, the kind of woman I am now. I ask a lot of questions. I don't let up until I have answers and I'm not particularly polite about getting them.

I used to think that was why the Gardeners made me a Blackthumb. They say that anyone can learn any trade, if you can just find a master willing to teach you. But parents tend to apprentice their own children or close relatives. Gardeners were the sons and daughters of other Gardeners. Most Blackthumbs were the sons and daughters of older Blackthumbs, and so on.

But I ask questions and I'm good at finding the answers. So when I was offered an apprenticeship under a real Greenguard, I felt sure that I knew why. But now I was starting to think that the Gardeners preferred their Blackthumbs a little bit dimmer, a little more obedient than me. A little more like robots.

I've never been able to shut my mouth, though. Maybe the Gardeners figured that they should keep me close, where I would enforce their laws instead of break them. I wondered if the Gardeners ever regretted that decision. I sure as hell did.

Most of the Greenguard base was built down underground, with the floors above the surface taken up by our lockers and ready rooms. There was also an extensive armory, and a smithy where the crossbows were cared for, where new arrowheads were poured and honed to deadly gleaming points.

Zach and I exchanged greetings with a few other Blackthumbs, but being born outside the Greenguard, neither of us were particularly popular. We were smarter than the rest of the Blackthumbs, too, and Zach could outfight any of them.

Hey, that's only my opinion. I'm entitled to one.

It was just my luck that one of the Greenguard who *did* like us caught up before we could report in with the watch commander.

"Hey, Reed, Dias! Wait up," Woods called.

I'm Reed. Julia Reed. Zach's last name was Dias.

Woods was twenty-one and had been a Blackthumb for just a few years. The only things he had going for him were a Greenguard mother and a Gardener father of middling rank. Woods liked me, though that seemed to be based more on the fit of my fatigues than out of any genuine interest in my sparkling personality or obvious brilliance.

We paused in the hallway under one of the rectangular lights. The glare was harsh. There was a buzzing sound and an occasional flicker from the tubes. Even in the base, the old things didn't last forever.

"Gardener Gregory wants to see you both right away," Woods said. "He's been asking for you all afternoon."

"It was just birth control," I told him. "We got it sorted. Nothing for Gregory to get cracked over."

"We'd better go see him, Julia," said Zach.

I glared. Traitor. But I shrugged and we moved on, turning right at the intersection of hallways instead of left toward the watch commander's station. Woods trotted after us.

"Hey, Reed?"

I looked back over my shoulder but kept walking. Briskly.

"What?" I asked.

"I've got an apple. I was wondering if you wanted to share it with me tonight?"

Damn. I had never eaten an apple before. Angel City had only two apple trees and barter for their fruit was steep. There weren't many besides the Gardeners who had ever tasted an apple. Trust Woods to be able to get his grabby little hands on one.

I was tempted to take him up on the offer, at least long enough to eat half an apple before backing out of whatever else he had in mind. But I wasn't sure I could endure Woods' company that long.

"Sorry, Woods," I said. "Gregory needs to see us right away, remember? Got to go!"

I picked up my pace and Zach lengthened his stride to keep up.

"Why doesn't he get that he's not my type?" I complained when we had put some distance between Woods and ourselves.

"No guys are your type," Zach pointed out with a smile.

I silently took back the *traitor* thing. Zach understood me. If I liked men that way, I'd like Zach.

"At least I have this stupid meeting with Gregory as an excuse," I said.

"The meeting isn't stupid, Julia," Zach chided me. "You don't even know what it's about. It could be important."

Shit, I'd gotten on his bad side again. Zach was a nice guy and a great Blackthumb. The only way that Woods would ever have a true black thumb was if he smashed it with a brick. Which seemed likely... But Zach was the real thing, an actual badass. His parents had been well diggers, so an apprenticeship with the Greenguard was a dream come true.

But Zach had worked his ass off for it. When the kids in his neighborhood were playing handball for fun, he played to train. He couldn't convince a Greenguard to teach him how to shoot, so he practiced throwing rocks until his aim was good. Zach learned to win fights by getting into them. In the end, the Blackthumbs didn't have much choice but to apprentice him.

Zach was the best of the Greenguard. You may have picked up my thoughts on that. But he took the job *way* too seriously.

"Zee, you know Gregory just repeats whatever Thorn tells him," I said before I could stop myself. "He's as empty as an old saguaro boot."

"Gregory is a Gardener, Julia," Zach said. He had his stern face back on. "Chosen by God to tend the garden in His absence. They care for the Tears of God that protect the Whisperwards. Even if Gregory is only an extension of High Gardener Thorn, you should have respect. Thorn is a great man."

One of these days, I would doubt the Gardeners or God a little too much and Zach was going to play handball with my head. Would that be today?

"You know that the Stormspheres can't actually be God's tears, right?" I said. "It's only a nickname, like when people call us *Black-thumbs*. The Stormspheres were built with old science. They must have been."

"God works in mysterious ways."

I wasn't really trying to shake Zach's faith in God, though I wasn't His biggest fan. Were we supposed to be grateful that after destroying the entire world, He cried a few tears that fell to Earth to protect us few survivors? If He wanted to protect us, then why destroy everything in the first place? Yeah, the hubris of man and all that. I remembered my Sunday school lessons at the Gardeners' feet.

It was just a fun challenge to try to poke at Zach's rock-solid conviction. Fun like punching a twenty-ton slab of concrete, maybe, but still fun.

Challenge accepted. I guess I'm a glutton for punishment.

But Zach was right about one thing. High Gardener Thorn *was* a great man, or at least a powerful one. He pretty much ran Angel City single-handedly. The Gardeners in charge of the greenhouses, the schools, the Greenguard and every other aspect of Whisperward life were hand-picked by Thorn. They were all like Gregory, chosen for their obedience more than their wits.

Some said – and for all his reverence, at least Zach wasn't one of them – that the Thorn family name meant he was anointed by God Himself to rule. Thorn, Gardener, get it? More skeptical people tended to believe that the Thorn family simply named itself after their high position among the Gardeners.

I had my own theory: I thought his name was Thorn because he's a giant prick.

But I let Zach win the argument this time and we walked on in silence. We took the north stairwell down a couple of floors, but to get into the deepest levels, we had to cross the hangar and use the east stairs.

There were only a few lights in the hangar, casting pale columns of radiance in the close, menacing gloom. Zach and I walked cautiously along the clear path down the middle. Our footsteps echoed on the hard concrete floor, resounding unevenly as they bounced off the hangar's contents.

Robots loomed tall and still in silent ranks, filling the darkness with the burnt scent of ozone and standing at mute attention between massive gray supports. Dim light glinted off metal bodies, illuminating angled limbs and chassis and the muzzles of strange weapons that looked nothing like my crossbow.

The Gardeners said that at any moment, all of the ancient robots could be activated and ordered into action. They reminded the people of the Whisperwards that they were protected... and that the Gardeners held that power. Only Gregory and Thorn had the codes to activate the mysterious mechanical warriors.

I had seen a robot in action once. It was eleven years ago, when I was fifteen. Just before I apprenticed as a Blackthumb. A particularly nasty storm had driven every mutant out of the Pacific Desert and up against the city walls. The Stormsphere projected the vast invisible barrier that shielded all of Angel City from billowing, boiling clouds of scouring sands, but it couldn't keep a hundred ravenous three-foot-long locusts from jumping over the walls. The Greenguard were fighting them off, but they were dying, too, and the mutants threatened to swarm the city.

Then this robot comes marching out of the base. I remember thinking that it was like a storm itself, an angel of thunder and lightning. It cleared the street in a few seconds and strode through the gates, fighting against the backdrop of sand and lightning. I was one of the rebellious kids who climbed up onto the wall to watch. Bright light and fire had streaked out from the robot and chopped mutant bugs in half, or just burned them down to ash. The locusts went wild, swarming all over the robot, but none of them could do any damage before being blown to pieces.

I had cheered along with the Blackthumbs on the wall as the robot exterminated the mutants. It was all over in less than five minutes. With its job done, the robot turned around and began marching back through the sand and charred corpses. But then it shuddered and stopped. It started up again a few seconds later, but ground to a halt almost as quickly. All of its shiny metal limbs drooped and the lights went out, one by one.

And it just sat there. After the storm passed, a dozen Greenguard hauled it back through the gates. The robot disappeared into the base once more.

Maybe that particular robot was even still down here somewhere, one of these silent sentinels. I doubted the Gardeners' claim that they all worked, though. We had a lot of bits left over from the world before the Wrath, but the ones that used power only had so much. When it was gone, it was gone. We didn't know how to give them more. And if the robots or anything else broke, we were shit out of luck then, too.

So the Gardeners never handed out any tool that wasn't urgently needed. Even our uniforms. They're tough and strong – like the Greenguard themselves, in theory – but there are only so many to go around. It would have been nice to dress everyone in resilient carbon microfiber, but we couldn't. There were more than twenty thousand people in Angel City – with more arriving every day – and never enough for everyone. Not robots or clothes or apples.

Gardener Gregory was all worked up by the time we reached his office. He paced behind his desk, nervously smoothing his hands down the front of his black robes. Some Gardeners exchanged the robes of their order for the fatigues worn by the rest of the Greenguard. Gregory's predecessor, Sidra, had been one of those – a real Blackthumb. Gregory looked the part, to be sure, with a prominent nose, strong chin and thick brown hair silvering impressively at the temples. But the head of the Greenguard constantly undermined himself with a dozen nervous habits and a tendency to quote Thorn in every conversation.

"There you are!" Gregory said when we walked into his office. "Where have you been all day?"

He ran his hands over his robes again and I barely stifled the urge to shout at him that it was *fine*, that his clothes were, in fact, still there. Gregory sat down at his desk, a huge block of actual wood covered in curling sheaves of pale green and brown paper. Behind him stood a row of metal filing cabinets and an immense, hand-drawn map of the Whisperward. Gregory steepled his fingers and cleared his throat.

"It was just routine birth control," I started.

Gregory cut me off with a perfunctory wave of his hand. Did he already know that we hadn't staked the Garza baby out for the storms? How?

"This has nothing to do with your regular duties," Gregory said. "I have a special assignment for you two. This comes down from Thorn himself."

Big surprise. Our boss tapped his fingertips together.

"Something happened last night," he said.

"What is it, sir?" Zach asked, all respect.

Now seemed like as terrible a time as any to trade out my worries that Gregory had somehow found out about the Garzas – or the vain hope that Zach could bring himself to lie to a Gardener about it if asked – for some brand new anxiety. Gregory might only be good for repeating Thorn, but the High Gardener *was* smart.

"Thorn wants to speak to you himself. He asked for my best," Gregory said. He brushed at the front of his robes again and must have seen the utter shock on my face because he elaborated. "That is, those Greenguard best suited to... hmm... complex and curious issues."

The implications were pretty clear. I was hardly a model Blackthumb, but even Gregory couldn't deny that when it came down to piecing together information, Zach and I were the best. I liked to think that we were the best at running down criminals and killing mutants, too.

Well, *Zach* was good at those things, but we're a team, right? I deserved some of the credit.

"You're to report to the Houses at once," Gregory ordered. "The High Gardener will explain what he needs from you."

"What? Now?" I blurted. "We just got back!"

"I'm aware of that, Reed, but this task is of the highest priority. It comes from Thorn himself," Gregory reminded me, in case I had missed this all-important point the first time.

"That's bugshit!" I said, glaring at my commander. "We've been climbing up and down the city all day. If you really think we're going to go running off to the Houses just because–"

"Yes, sir," Zach interrupted. "We're on our way."

He grabbed my shoulder and hauled me out of Gregory's office before I could stick my other boot in my mouth, too.

DESPITE MY PROTESTS, the Houses weren't very far from the base and I was a little curious about them. I'd seen the Houses from a distance, but never worked any closer to them than the Greenguard base. While going to the Houses wasn't actually forbidden, I'd never had an excuse to visit them before.

Houses was short for *Greenhouses*. Sometimes people just can't be bothered with three syllables. Except for the Stormsphere itself, the Houses were the most important place in the Whisperward. There were more wells here than in any other district of Angel City and I wondered how many more people the Whisperward could support if all that water went out to the rest of the city.

The greenhouses were arranged in glittering rows at the base of the Stormsphere's black immensity, an area painstakingly cleared of ancient rubble so the plants inside could get as much sun as possible. At midday, hundreds of carefully protected and polished panes of glass reflected a blinding light that the Gardeners liked to think of as a symbol of their divine right to rule.

But it was twilight now and I could barely see into the greenhouses. There were the delicate, shadowy shapes and bright colors of orchids, violets, hibiscus and zinnias, plus a handful of flowers I

didn't know the names for. They taught us in school, I think, but memorizing a bunch of flowers didn't seem that interesting to young Julia Reed – and it was no more interesting now.

There were orchards behind the glass, too, little pieces of Eden where people like Woods and the Gardeners picked apples and other juicy delicacies. I wondered what it smelled like inside.

This was the world of the Gardeners and even at night, robed men walked through the greenhouses, carrying lanterns and carefully checking every leaf for signs of blight or delicately pollinating the blooms with small brushes. Though Blackthumbs patrolled the rows between Houses with crossbows cocked and loaded, that had never been one of my duties. My talents would have been a little wasted standing guard over a bunch of plants.

Maybe Gregory wasn't quite as stupid as I thought. He must have known that if I ever got too bored, I would become a lot more trouble than I was worth.

Someday I *would* end up here, though. Eventually, everyone died and we all went to feed the plants. As a Greenguard, I would have the honor of being buried in the orchards instead of the cactus patches like the common folk, but we're still not good enough to be buried with the flowers. Only the Gardeners lived among the colorful, sweet-smelling blooms and that's where they stayed even after death.

As Zach and I made our way between the glass greenhouses and closer to the smooth dome of the Stormsphere, the Whispers began. At first, they were just a wordless babbling at the edge of my hearing. There was a reason the last cities were called Whisperwards, after all. The sound was always quiet, a strange little rasp at the back of your mind like rustling pages or wind-rippled cloth, but there was something *almost* like words in it.

As you got closer to the Stormsphere, the Whispers were never louder, but they became... clearer. That was the only way I could ever describe it. The Whispers were sharper and harder to ignore, but never any easier to make out. If there were words, I could never understand them. I would have blocked the Whispers out if I could, but covering my ears was useless – the sound didn't come through there.

It was in my mind.

In Sunday school, the Gardeners told us that the Whispers were the voices of angels, though not even they claim to comprehend what those voices said. But they came from the Tear of God and were proof that He still loved and cared for us. Apparently.

Now I did my best to ignore the Whispers as we made our way through the Houses. They reminded me way too much of what the dreameaters did.

The Gardeners made their homes in a row of large yellow and brown adobe houses. There were no leaning tenements here, and at the end of the line stood another ancient building. The Gardeners' headquarters had power, too, and lights glowed steadily in the windows after dark. But it looked nothing like our stern old base.

The Gardeners' building was a graceful white presence, much smaller than the Greenguard complex. It was skirted in columns and marble stairs that led inside to bright electric lights and humming machines. I wondered if it had been an important place even before the Wrath.

Two silhouettes stood in a window at the very top. One of them must have been Thorn. The highest floor of *this* building wasn't reserved for the poor and dirty. The Gardeners' headquarters weren't going to fall down any time soon. And it had something none of the highrisers and even our base did – a working elevator.

───────

Zach and I dropped gratefully into chairs with soft red seats outside Thorn's office. As it turned out, the elevator was reserved for Gardeners.

But I convinced myself that I was only a little disappointed. When I was young, another girl in my building climbed into a broken elevator to hide during some game we were playing. She managed to shut the doors behind her, but her terrified parents could never get them open again. I wasn't *that* eager to step into an elevator, even one that still had power.

Another dark-robed Gardener informed us that Thorn was in a meeting and we would have to wait. He, too, bustled on to something more interesting before I could ask any questions. I griped to Zach about the hurry-up-and-wait, but he wasn't very sympathetic.

"People wait for weeks to get a minute of the High Gardener's time," Zach said. "We'll manage."

We sat in a wide hallway with stone floors and bright red carpet running down the center. The polished wooden door of Thorn's office was slightly ajar. The shiny brass latch hadn't quite engaged and I could hear him talking to someone, the other silhouette I had seen in the window from the street outside. It was only partially out of boredom that I stood and crept closer.

"Julia, what are you doing?" Zach whispered sharply.

"Shh," I said.

"They'll hear you!"

"They'll hear *you* if you keep hissing at me. Shut it!"

Zach couldn't do much more without shouting at me and I knew he wouldn't risk that, so he would have to physically grab me and pull me away or else let me satisfy my curiosity.

I slipped out of arm's reach, just in case.

"How long did it take?" That was Thorn's deep voice.

"Maybe a year," said another man. He had the crisp, educated diction of a Gardener, but I didn't recognize the voice. "We didn't realize what was happening until it was too late. Jacob thought it might even have begun three or four years ago. But by the time we noticed the Tear's perimeter shrinking, things were already degenerating too fast."

Thorn again: "How quickly?"

"At first, it was no more than a yard. Still outside Bridge City's walls," said the other Gardener. "But the next month, it was five yards. And then it was shrinking that much each day. The storms were pulling apart the walls and the outer districts. We had to leave. Only about ten percent of us made it here."

"I grieve for your loss, Matthew," Thorn said, and sounded like he meant it. "Did the Whitefingers sabotage the Tear of God?"

"We have no idea. There was no sign of damage to the Stormsphere itself. Our Greenguard protected it right up until the end, but they saw nothing."

"The greenhouses, then?" Thorn asked.

"I don't *know* how they did it," Matthew said. His voice rose and even Zach sat up straight, listening. "But the Whitefingers were there, Thorn! I saw them."

"When?"

"When we were leaving the Whisperward. One of the robots carrying our seeds and plants was malfunctioning. Jacob and I were trying to get it moving again and fell behind. That's when we saw them sneaking into Bridge City!"

There was a pause before Thorn answered. "And you're sure it was Whitefingers?"

"Yes," Matthew insisted. I heard footsteps coming toward the door and tensed, but then they retreated again. The angry Bridge City Gardener was pacing. "I saw those damned sneaks heading right for the Tear."

"Scavengers, perhaps..." Thorn said. "But... perhaps not. What happened to the Stormsphere?"

"The Whispers had already fallen silent. We couldn't uproot all the trees, but we picked them clean before leaving. We took every flower that survived transplant, and gathered every seed. I'm sure that we left a little food behind. Some of the cactus fields weathered the last storms. Nothing of significance, though."

"If the Whitefingers weren't scavenging, then what did they want?" Thorn asked. "I'm sorry, Matthew, this can wait. You've traveled a long way and lost many of your people on the journey. Go and rest."

I beat a hasty retreat to my chair as Matthew finally emerged from Thorn's office. He was a short, round man with even rounder glasses and spectacularly receding gray hair. His black robes were dusty and worn. The Gardener glanced at us and I tried not to look too elaborately innocent. Matthew nodded once and then waddled off down the hall. A moment later, Thorn appeared at his office door and motioned me and Zach inside.

High Gardener Thorn's office was a greenhouse in miniature. There were shelves and tables full of flowerpots. Every surface was covered in bright colors and delicate petals. Tall windows would have let in sunlight during the day, but for now, they just looked out across the shiny pewter angles of the Houses. There were even paintings on the walls, bright and expensive pigments depicting plants that I had never seen. That probably didn't exist anymore.

Not a cactus in sight. There were no thorns in Thorn's office. I snorted and Zach shot me a warning glance.

Thorn stood behind his desk without any of Gregory's twitching or fidgeting. He was even taller than Zach, but as thin as a flower stalk. Thorn was far from physically imposing, but somehow still dominated the room. He was in command. Of himself, of the Gardeners, of the whole Whisperward and he damned well knew it.

"You must be Julia Reed and Zachary Dias," said Thorn.

"Yes, sir," I responded at once.

I didn't really mean to say *sir*, but the powerful High Gardener sort of startled it out of me. Zach echoed my response, inclining his head respectfully.

"I asked Gregory to send me his brightest Greenguard," Thorn said. "Apparently, you two have a reputation for tracking down the most difficult problems. Now I would like to apply your skills to solving a special murder."

"A murder? Who died?" I asked.

"A Gardener. His name was Daniel Byron. I believe a dream-eater is responsible for his death."

"There are lots of ways to kill someone. You don't have to be psychic," I pointed out. "Sir."

"You haven't seen the destruction," Thorn said. "But you will."

"A dreameater could have come into the Whisperward with the Bridge or Sun City refugees," Zach suggested. "Or maybe a local one slipped through our routine screenings. There are so many people in Angel City these days. It's getting too crowded to monitor them all properly. But I'm sure we can pick up the trail and find your killer, sir."

Thorn smiled at Zach. I think he liked my partner a lot more than he liked me. Well, I could hardly blame the High Gardener for that. I'm a pain in the ass.

"We all use the gifts God gave us," Thorn said. "So I leave the investigation to you. Find this murderer with all possible speed."

"When was Byron killed?" I asked.

"Early this morning, before sunrise," Thorn answered.

"Where?"

"In the Houses. I will have one of my aides show you the exact place. He was the one to discover the bodies."

"Bodies, sir?" Zach asked.

Thorn nodded. "Yes. Two Greenguard were found dead along-side Byron."

"Were there any witnesses to the crime?" Zach asked.

"As far as I know, only the guards," Thorn answered. "But with them dead, I'm afraid there are no living witnesses."

"Except the killer," I said.

Thorn's aide was a moon-faced teenage boy named Martin. We met him downstairs in the polished lobby and I liked the kid at once – after all, he had brought us a special present. Martin held out something wrapped in padded cloth.

"This was sent up from the Greenguard armory for you," he told us.

I took the bundle carefully. I knew what was inside: a Halo, a relic from before the Wrath. But I opened it anyway. I didn't get to play with the old tech very often.

The Halo was a ring of pearlescent white polymer that snapped closed around my wrist like a bracelet. There was a slightly recessed button on one side and when I pressed it, the halo-gram appeared in the air above my wrist. I wasn't scanning anything, though, so it just shimmered and the words *system ready* glowed in transparent green letters.

Gregory didn't let these things out of the armory very often, and I shut off swiftly. Their batteries were finite, and when they ran out, the Halo would be nothing more than a useless piece of jewelry. And if a hapless Blackthumb actually broke one while using it, then God help him. Or her.

"Do you want to carry it?" I asked Zach.

He shook his head briskly, so I wrapped up the Halo again and secured it away in one of my pockets. Zach turned to Martin, who had been watching in fascination. Not me, I suspected, but the Halo that I now carried.

"Please show us where Byron was killed," Zach told him.

We followed Martin out of the Gardeners' brightly lit building and back into the dark night. The round-faced young Gardener retrieved a glowing lantern mounted on a hooked pole, then led us back out into the rows of glass greenhouses. More Blackthumbs patrolled the Houses, crossbows loaded and held ready, or stood at attention at the shiny intersections. A pair of them nodded to us and our Gardener escort as we approached.

"This is it," Martin said. "I heard the glass breaking and then screams. When it was done, I found Gardener Byron here. He and the Greenguard were already dead."

It would have been easy to find the crime scene even without Martin. There was broken glass everywhere, shining as our guide gestured with his lantern: huge, glittering blades, finger-sized shards and uncountable tiny splinters that shone in the lamplight. Someone had already removed the bodies to begin burial preparations, but they had poured a white chalk outline around where each one had laid. Zach crossed his arms, inspecting the damage.

"No wonder Thorn suspects a dreameater of doing this," he said. "Look..."

Splashes of blood had seeped into the earth all around the chalked body outlines and dried black during the day. I pulled Martin's lantern down and held it close to the ground. The closest pieces of glass were covered in blood. And dust. And footprints. I growled.

"What the hell is all this?" I said, pointing to the ground. The dirt on top was dry, not sticky with blood. All of this foot traffic happened *after* the killing. "Was there a parade or something?"

"The Gardeners had to move the milkweed," Martin said. Not very apologetically, I thought. "With all of the glass broken out, the greenhouse is useless. Anyone or anything could just walk right in."

Milkweed? I had to think for a moment, but I remembered that particular flower from Sunday school. It was useless. Worse than useless – milkweed was poisonous. But it was a flower and so it was the Gardeners' sacred duty to protect it. And now they had trampled my crime scene to save a toxic weed.

"Those aren't the only tracks," Zach announced, interrupting my irritation. He squatted down beside the other chalk outline. "The dirt's kicked up under the blood spatter. From before Byron died. And this man, at least, got his knife out."

One of the dead Greenguard silhouettes did indeed have a bladed shape at the end of his arm.

"But this was sloppy work," I said. "Why didn't he use his crossbow?"

"Maybe he did, but then didn't have the time to reload," Zach suggested.

We went inside the ruined greenhouse. With the glass broken, all that remained was the welded metal frame. It was like walking through the bones of some long-dead but still mighty creature. Martin followed us carefully between boxy flowerbeds and empty shelves. There was even more broken glass in here. I winced as a piece snapped sharply beneath my boot.

"Over here," Martin said. He held his lamp out above another pool of blood and powdery white outline.

I knelt to inspect the scene. This must have been Byron, inside the greenhouse while the Blackthumbs patrolled outside. I scanned the shelves and now-empty flowerbeds. There was blood and glass everywhere. Delicately, I picked up a large triangular shard. It was dark with blood, covered on every surface. Not just drops, bled on after the fact.

"I think this was the murder weapon," I said.

"What?" Zach asked. "So our killer grabbed a piece of glass and stabbed the Gardener and Greenguard? Slit their throats, maybe?"

"No." I pointed to the bloodstains on the greenhouse floor. "I don't think so. This isn't a pool of blood. Look at the edges. There were multiple blood sprays. Byron wasn't stabbed and then left. He must have been bleeding from a dozen wounds or more."

I looked to Martin for confirmation. The boy was nodding.

"They were all sliced up," he agreed. "It was horrible."

"I think Thorn's right. This had to be a dreameater," I concluded reluctantly. I could practically hear Zach aching to say *I told you so*. He restrained himself... for now. "Look at the walls and ceiling. There isn't a pound of glass left in the whole frame. This wasn't just someone throwing pots or stones through the walls. Something shattered the *entire* greenhouse, but I don't see or smell any sign of an explosion. It had to be psionics."

"A dreameater pulled this whole place to pieces and flung the shards at Byron and the Blackthumbs. That's not a quiet way to kill," Zach said. He squinted out through the broken walls. "Maybe he was surprised. Dreameaters are jumpy, unpredictable. I don't think this was planned."

"Then why did it happen?" I asked. "What was a dreameater doing in the Houses if not to kill Byron?"

"I'm not sure yet, Julia."

I stood and walked slowly around the small crime scene. Martin followed with the lantern.

"Zee," I said.

I pointed to one of the steel framing struts. A scrap of lace was caught on a jagged tooth of glass like a cobweb. Lace wasn't easy to make and I'd never seen much of it. This particular piece looked old and frayed, stained by dust but still delicate and beautiful.

"From our killer?" Zach asked.

"Well, we don't wear any of this stuff on our uniforms, Zee. Do you think Byron was big on lace?"

"Probably not."

I pocketed the lace for the moment. If it had been part of our killer's clothing, it might help us find him.

"I've got something here, too," Zach said.

He pointed down to another black spatter of blood. He ducked through the broken greenhouse to another one in the street. It was at least fifty feet away from the outline of Byron's body or those of his two dead Greenguard.

"More blood," I said.

"Not as much as around the bodies, though. I think it belongs to our dreameater. It's not a full trail, but he definitely hurt himself."

"One of the Blackthumbs might have shot him," I pointed out.

Zach shook his head. "Bolts do internal damage, but they tend not to bleed a whole lot. I think our suspect not only wasn't planning on killing anyone, but was startled and managed to cut himself when he attacked."

"Maybe," I said. "It's getting late and I want to go the fuck to bed. Let's see the bodies, Martin."

———

DANIEL BYRON WAS LAID out in the tool shed, a large building that housed the sacred implements of the Gardeners' trade. It was also where the dead – at least Greenguard and Gardeners – were prepared for burial. Luckily, the Gardeners had been more worried about their precious milkweed than their deceased brother, so no one had changed Byron out of his clothes yet or removed the glass from his body.

The two Blackthumbs lay motionless on tables nearby. Bright white bulbs glowed overhead, casting stark spotlights across the shed that swung wildly when Zach bumped into one.

"Be careful," Martin snapped.

"Of course," Zach said. He removed his hat and held it to his chest. "Sorry."

"Martin, who was Byron?" I asked. "What was he doing in the Houses after dark? The plants sure weren't up to anything exciting at that hour."

"Gardener Byron was probably checking the night bloomers," Martin answered. "He tended the Houses day and night. He was breeding the flowers for better nectar."

"Why?" I asked.

Thorn's aide blinked and then answered carefully. "Are you saying the God-given duties of the Gardeners have any bearing on your investigation?"

"Probably not," said Zach. "I doubt a dreameater would kill Byron over flower nectar, even accidentally."

Martin nodded stiffly. I really wanted to pry, but didn't think that I was going to get anywhere with Martin clenching up and Zach backing him, so I busied myself examining the body.

In life, Byron had been tall – almost as tall as Thorn – but with a workman's muscular build. The dead Gardener seemed to be somewhere in his late thirties or early forties, with the darkened skin and ruddy complexion of someone who spent a lot of time in the sun. He had large, capable hands with dirt and green plant material crusted deep beneath the nails.

Cuts covered Byron's face and hands. Most of them were shallow. His palms and forearms, particularly, were studded with shards of glass. Defensive wounds, I suspected, as he raised his arms to protect his face from the storm of glass. It hadn't done him much good, though. There was a sliver the length of my small finger buried in Byron's left eye. It would have been painful as hell, but not for long. Another larger piece of glass stuck out of the side of his neck. I inspected the wound. It had sliced the artery clean through. Even with glass blocking the flow of blood, he must have bled to death in a matter of seconds.

I told Zach what I'd found and he said that the two Black-thumbs were pretty much the same. Both men were riddled with glass. Somewhat less of it had been able to penetrate the tough Greenguard fatigues, but still enough to kill them.

"It's all about the same size as the pieces in Byron. One blast hit all three of our guys," I guessed.

"That's a powerful dreameater," said Zach.

I pulled away the stiff black collar of Byron's robes and found a thin red line below the dagger of glass that had taken his life. This wasn't a cut, but a narrow abrasion ran along the back and sides of his neck.

"Take a look at this," I told Zach. "He wore something around his neck."

"Something that's not there anymore. Maybe the dreameater took it."

"Martin?" I asked. "Do you know anything about this?"

Thorn's aide fidgeted and didn't immediately answer. I fixed him with my best authoritative stare. Strictly speaking, Martin out-ranked the hell out of me, but I hoped that I was invested with a little of Thorn's authority in this investigation. Either I was right or else I was getting to be as intimidating as Zach.

"Gardener Byron was a keybearer," Martin said at last.

"Is that a ceremonial title or was he actually carrying a key?" I asked.

"There was a key," the young Gardener admitted.

"To what?"

Martin turned red this time and bristled like a prickly pear.

"Something important," was his short reply.

Zach put a hand on my arm before I could start shouting. Why ask us to investigate this murder if the Gardeners wouldn't tell us what we needed to know to solve it? Maybe I should have been a Gardener instead of a Blackthumb. They seemed to have all the answers and maybe my curiosity wouldn't go so often unsatisfied.

"The Gardeners manage and care for the Houses," Martin told us. "But there were a few other workers this morning, sweepers and water boys and the like. They've all been collected and are under guard until you clear them."

The workers were being held, but I noticed that Martin said nothing about the Gardeners. Of course not. The Gardeners were above reproach.

"We'll test them tomorrow," said Zach. "We know our killer is a dreameater and that he's injured. That narrows it down. If we can clear all of the greenhouse personnel, we'll move out into the rest of Angel City."

Gently, I patted the Halo in my pocket. "We'll find the bastard. And then he's going to answer my questions."

I was grateful to finally get away from the Whispers. They faded not long after leaving the Houses, and by the time I made it back to my street, they had fallen silent. No, I corrected myself. Just gone, not silent. I remembered Matthew, the Gardener from Bridge City to the north. Their Whispers had gone silent and when they did, the Stormsphere stopped working. Its barrier crumbled and the Whisperward failed.

Storms gathered quickly in the vast deserts year round, and could engulf a Whisperward for days at a time. Winds churned and blew sand hard enough to strip away skin and do lethal damage to an unprotected traveler within hours. Constant lightning strikes melted sand and dirt down into glass, which relentless winds tore apart and added to the deadly shrapnel of the storm. If the lightning didn't kill you, the glass sand would finish the job. It wasn't pretty.

But the Tears of God protected us from all of that. I didn't make a big secret of doubting all the Sunday school stories, but even I couldn't deny the power of the Stormspheres. About five hundred yards outside the walls of the Whisperward, the sandstorms just hit an invisible wall of force and flowed around it. That invisible wall was projected and maintained by the Stormsphere in the heart of the Whisperward.

From the top of the city wall, you can still see bits of old Angel City outside, worn down to dust and skeletal ruins by centuries of storms. Without the Stormsphere, we'd all be dead. It had happened in Bridge City, and I supposed that was what happened to Sun City, too, since refugees were coming to us from the east. I wondered if some of them were moving north to Boulder City or Wind City, maybe even further east to Apple City... If those far-off Whisperwards weren't having the same problems that Matthew told Thorn about.

What about Angel City? The storms still seemed to part around us like the mythical Red Sea and nothing more dangerous than dust made it over the walls. We were safe here.

Our apartment building loomed suddenly out of the dark night. Zach and I trudged up the stairs, but stopped at the second floor. This building was mostly Blackthumbs, though there were some homes for well diggers and sweepers up on the highest levels. Zach grunted a weary goodnight and turned down another coal-lit hallway. I stumbled toward my own door.

A few doors down, a curtain twitched aside and a pale woman poked her head out into the hall.

"Reed, are you only now getting in?" she asked.

"Yeah, Silva. Just got off."

Diane Silva usually worked nights patrolling the greenhouses, so she was still awake at this ridiculously late hour, even on her day of rest.

"Did someone really murder a Gardener?" she asked.

Rumors must have been flying.

I nodded. "A pair of Blackthumbs, too."

"Why would anyone kill a Gardener? They care for the flowers," Silva said. She sketched a teardrop shape over her heart with one finger. "They care for us all. It was a mutant, wasn't it? Or maybe a Whitefinger?"

"We don't know yet," I told her. "But Zach and I will find out."

I pushed through my curtain and left Silva to go back inside or anywhere else. I was way too tired for her piety.

I stumbled around my apartment until I could light a lamp, then checked the cool box for dinner. There were a couple of grass snakes and barrel cactus fruit, but I didn't have the energy to cook up the snake. I grabbed a few fruits and ate clumsily while I undressed. When I was done, I placed my crossbow on its wall hook, dropped bonelessly into my bed and tucked the Halo under my pillow for safekeeping. Lumpy, but luckily, I'm a deep sleeper.

I blew out the lamp and pulled the covers over my head. Tomorrow, Zach and I might be sifting through hundreds or thousands of people for a single dreameater – unless there had been more than one. In any case, it was going to be a long day and I wanted a few hours of sleep.

Except that sleep cared what I wanted about as much as a rock did. I lay awake in the darkness, inhaling the scents of dust and old plastic. I needed a candle or some of that expensive flower oil.

Silva's question kept echoing through my mind. A Whitefinger? It was possible. While Greenguard hunted dreameaters as treacherous abominations in a world already full of dangerous mutants, the Whitefingers welcomed them with open arms. Some said that they even bred psychic animals out there in the wastes.

So our psychic killer *could* have been a Whitefinger. They occasionally scaled the city walls and prowled into Angel City. The Whitefingers stole food and clothes, sometimes weapons or other supplies, but they rarely hurt anyone. Searching out the wastelanders and catching them was a Greenguard's job. It was a damned sight better than birth control duty, and Zach and I were both good at it. Whitefingers fought like scorpions when cornered, but they were more thieves than murderers.

Which amounted to the same thing, I supposed, with supplies stretched so thin. Still...

That key Martin had refused to tell us about was gone. Maybe theft *was* the motive for Byron's murder. Or was there some strange dreameater reason? Did they read something in Byron's thoughts? Or was there something in his head that they wanted to find?

What about the flowers...? Martin seemed to dismiss Byron's breeding program as a potential motive, though, and not even my overactive imagination could manage anything that made sense. The Gardeners tended greenhouses full of trees and flowers, but most of the citizens of the Whisperward lived on cactus, crickmeal and lizards. I could hardly see even a Whitefinger killing Byron over some new flower breed.

What if someone wanted access to the Houses and the orchards inside? I remembered Woods and his damned apple. Despite my dinner, my mouth watered. I'd never eaten an apple and I would seriously consider killing to taste one. Or at least consider killing Woods. What would a Whitefinger born and raised in the Pacific Desert be willing to do?

So did the stolen key open the greenhouses? I thought back to the evening's investigation. I didn't recall any locks on the greenhouse doors, but I resolved to check next time. Still, the walls there were only glass and our dreameater – potentially a Whitefinger one – had made spectacularly short work of them. What did he need a key for? Maybe he wanted to keep the greenhouses intact? Zach had guessed that the destruction was accidental, after all.

I wished that Zach would let me grill Martin a little more. But he just didn't share my skepticism of the Gardeners. Zach was grateful for his job and strove every day to prove himself worthy of the uniform.

But Zach didn't blindly obey the Gardeners' every order – I needed only remember the Garza girl to know that. He really did care about the Whisperward and its people. My partner did a good job and was suitably rewarded. It seemed like a fair enough deal. So why did I always feel like I was being punished instead of blessed?

I finally dropped off to sleep with the sky already beginning to pale outside. I dreamed of the Whispers, but even in my dreams, they told me nothing.

THE BRIGHT SUNLIGHT woke me a few hours later. I had left my curtains open last night so this would happen. I didn't want to over-sleep when there was an important investigation to work on.

Fuck you, me from last night.

But there were people waiting to be tested with the Halo, to be cleared of suspicion so they could finally go home. They had been waiting since yesterday morning and probably gotten even less sleep than me. So I clawed my way up out of the sheets and dressed, pocketing the Halo once more. I strapped my crossbow into place on my back and after a moment's consideration, tucked the piece of lace from the greenhouse into another pocket. Maybe I could match it to someone's clothes.

When I stepped outside onto the street, the sun momentarily blinded me again before I could fumble my goggles down over my eyes. The lenses flickered and then darkened to blunt the worst of the glare. The sky was still brilliant white, but to the northwest, I could see patches of yellow-green light and the air tingled. There was a storm coming.

Builders were already hard at work shoring up the cracks in the sides of buildings and the people living there pulled down loose hangings or anything else light enough to blow away. The Tear deflected the storms, but even with its miraculous and mysterious blunting effect, winds in the Whisperward could be stiff.

Most of the refugees hadn't been settled yet and scrambled to find shelter. They were being slowly herded up into highrise apartments, but there were so many that the Blackthumbs hadn't found space for them all yet. Homeless families with dust in their hair stood in the streets and spilled into the ladder- and bridge-filled alleys between buildings. It wouldn't be a fun day, but so long as the Stormsphere held, they should be safe enough.

I resettled the heavy steel bulk of my crossbow on my back and wondered what it was like out at the city walls, with refugees pouring through the gates and into the protection of the Whisperward. What about those still making the long journey from Bridge City? How many of them would take refuge in the outlying ruins? How much shelter was there to be found outside Angel City's walls? Not much, I knew... But the Whitefingers survived out there, somehow. I could only hope that the people escaping the failing Whisperwards could manage it, too. At least long enough to reach us.

Zach waited for me outside our building, holding a pair of roasted fence lizards skewered on long thorns. He held one out, garnished with a *good morning* slightly garbled by his own breakfast. I accepted the meat and took a huge, grateful bite. Last night's snack hardly qualified as a meal and I was glad for some protein before setting out to test a bunch of frightened people for psionic power. I probably wouldn't get a chance to eat again until late tonight.

We set a brisk pace out toward the greenhouses to begin our work. With any luck, we could finish before the storm hit. A dozen Greenguard had established a cordon around the Houses and were questioning everyone coming or going from the area. Except the Gardeners, of course. I wondered if it ever occurred to them that one of the Gardeners might be a dreameater. Anyone could be a psychic, and that was part of what made them so dangerous.

But there was no point in asking – it would only the Black-thumbs suspicious of *me*, not the Gardeners who employed them.

Not that any Gardeners were crossing the cordon line this morning. They all worked and lived inside the Houses and their duties didn't often force them out into the rest of Angel City. If our psychic murderer *were* a Gardener, then we had no chance at all of finding them.

I just had to hope we were luckier than that.

It wasn't just the Greenguard and Gardeners who made their livings here in the Houses. There were street sweepers, too, and cleaners who kept the greenhouse glass sparkling clear. Water carriers hauled buckets from the wells to the plants and couriers ferried messages between the important people of the Whisper-ward. There were freighters who carted meat in from the scale farms, as well as cloth and other supplies that couldn't be grown or made in the Houses.

The Blackthumbs had roused and gathered up the workers who had been in the Houses yesterday morning. They stood together in the broad street in front of the Gardeners' white headquarters, yawning and pacing as they worked the stiffness out of their joints. Everyone milled impatiently and waited fearfully for their turn while the street rakers grumbled about the damage we were doing to their precious roads.

We checked in with Captain Davis, the stocky Blackthumb in charge of the roundup, who gave us the numbers: seventy-three potential suspects. And this was only the beginning. I didn't think it likely that Byron's killer was someone who worked for him. It was too easy.

"Has anyone talked to the wall commander?" I asked Davis.

The other Blackthumb nodded. "Jameson just got back from the base. No one's been seen leaving Angel City."

"Not through the city gates, at least," I grumbled. "That doesn't mean no one scaled the walls and slipped out into the desert."

"One thing at a time, Julia," Zach told me. "Let's start with these people. Then we'll move out into the city. If the Halo still can't find our guy, we can figure our next move from there."

"Let's get to it, then."

I unwrapped the shiny Halo and snapped it on around my wrist. When I pressed its power button, the little device made a quiet chime as it powered up. Zach waved the nearest cleaner forward.

"Kneel," he instructed.

Zach motioned with his crossbow, cocked and loaded. If we found a dreameater, things could get very ugly very fast. My mother always said a psychic could hollow out your head and dance your empty body around like a puppet. I'd never seen that, but my own experience was no less chilling.

Two years ago, a routine screening went stormy and a terrified young dreameater ripped up a shattered chunk of concrete foundation with her mind. It was twenty feet from corner to corner, but she flung it like I might throw a pebble. She killed seventeen people before Zach managed to put a bolt in her eye. We don't fuck around with psychics.

I walked behind the kneeling cleaner. His brown hair was going gray at the sides and his skin was coated in muddy grit and dirt. He bowed his neck as though in prayer and his shoulders shook. I placed my hand on the top of his head. The floating *system ready* halo-gram flashed and then vanished, replaced by a glowing image of the cleaner's brain. It was divided in two down the center and covered in convolutions like writhing snakes, just like every other one I'd ever seen on the halo-gram. I wondered what my own brain looked like, but even apart from the difficulty of reading the display with my hand up on my own head, wasting the Halo's power was enough of an offense to blunt even my curiosity.

A little.

Rings of light danced over the glowing image and the halo-gram flickered. Maybe this Halo was almost at the end of its long life...

But after a tense moment, the ancient device gave a disappointed-sounding beep and flashed green around my wrist.

"You're clear," Zach said.

He extended his big, rough hand and smiled as he helped the cleaner to his feet. Zach patted the man on the shoulder as he walked on shaking legs past the Greenguard and away. Zach picked one of the other workers and hooked his finger authoritatively.

"You. Kneel."

And so it went for the next two hours. Men and women knelt before me and I placed my hand on their head, scanning. When I was done, Zach told each one that they weren't a dreameater and helped relieved Angel City citizens back to their feet. I had moved the Halo to my other wrist, but by now, both of my arms ached.

"Want to trade, Zee?" I asked. "You've got bigger arms, anyway."

"Sure. One more and we'll switch for the rest," Zach said and then pointed again. "You. You're next."

A sweeper covered in dust she had removed from the Houses' roads stood slowly on obviously stiff legs. So it made sense when a teenage boy just to her right thought that Zach was pointing to him. The kid shuffled back several steps, pushing against the crowd of people waiting their turn. He was probably a water boy, to judge by his bruised and scabbed knuckles. Those buckets were damned heavy. His sandy hair was lank with sweat and there was an oozing red gash along his left forearm. I stared at him for a long moment before I realized why. Something glittered in the rolled cuff of his pants. Broken glass.

"Zee," I hissed under my breath, but the boy had seen me staring. Or maybe sensed it.

He sprang into motion and Zach leapt after him. I was right on his heels, but we were shoving our way through confused and frightened people. Davis shouted and the Blackthumbs closed in, hemming in the scattering crowd too late and making our job ten times harder. The blond boy had already cleared the Greenguard perimeter. He was young and setting a pounding pace, vanishing rapidly into the shiny glass of the Houses.

"Move it!" Zach ordered.

He slammed into the crowd, using his greater bulk and strength to clear a path. People shouted and threw themselves down to the road in their haste to get out of Zach's way. He shoved the rest aside and we burst through the cordon. There didn't seem to be any more broken glass – or broken Greenguard – so the kid hadn't started killing again. Not yet.

My crossbow bounced between my shoulder blades, bruising my spine, but I stretched out my legs and ran. Zach was good in a sprint, but he's a solid son of a bitch. I was half his size and twice his speed. The boy shot a terrified look back over his shoulder and almost smashed into the corner of a greenhouse as he darted down a side path.

He clipped the glass with one elbow and cracks shot through the pane. I flinched, waiting for blade-edged shards to fly out at me. But nothing happened, so I poured on the speed.

His head start and my momentary flinch were all that my water boy suspect had going for him. For now... Running through the rows of greenhouses meant that I could see every turn he took right through the glass. He was nearing the edge of the Houses, though, and when he got out into the streets of Angel City, there would be a lot more people and solid walls. That meant Zach and me questioning hundreds of people in the thin hope that someone had seen the kid or would turn him in. It could take days and by the time we uncovered a lead, he would be long gone.

The panicked water boy jumped over a compost pile that I barely cleared. My boots scraped through drying human waste and the smell chased after me. I heard Zach's heavier feet thump, but he was falling swiftly behind. He would have his crossbow in hand by now, I knew, sighting down the bolt and ready to fire if it looked like our suspect was about to get away.

Not yet, damn it! I couldn't get answers out of a corpse.

The boy angled toward a line of concrete wells. Familiar territory, maybe. Wrong move, kid. I sucked down a hot, dry breath.

"Greenguard!" I shouted. "Get out of the way!"

Other well dippers and water boys scrambled to clear the road without spilling any of their precious buckets. My suspect dashed around one of the wells, but I went over it. I jumped up onto the ledge, risking the coiled rope and a long fall, and leapt across. I felt cool, wet air wash over me, sprang off the far rim and then came down on top of my suspect, bearing him heavily to the ground.

All the breath and fight whooshed out of the kid as we slammed together against the ground. He pressed his face into the dirt and sobbed.

"I didn't do it!" he cried. "I swear to God, I didn't do it!"

I yanked the boy's thin, wiry arms up behind his back and latched a pair of handcuffs around his wrists. "By divine sanction of the Gardeners, you are our prisoner. You will be tried and convicted according to the Book of Law. Is there any sin you wish to confess before sentence is passed?"

"I didn't do it!" he shouted again.

"Keep at your business," Zach said to the staring crowd of well dippers as he caught up. He motioned with his crossbow. "Go on. The Gardeners need you."

I climbed off the boy and hauled him up to his knees.

"I didn't do it!" he screamed.

"I heard you the first three times. What's your name?" I asked.

He hesitated, panting and coughing, before answering. "Liam... Liam Fox. But I didn't hurt anyone!"

"He doesn't look much like a killer," I said to Zach.

The big Blackthumb shrugged. "They never do. Test him, Julia."

Zach was right – you didn't need to look like a killer to be a dreameater. No one knew where the psychics came from or when their power might manifest.

The Gardeners told us that they were cursed, like Caine. Cursed to live off of dreams, eating thoughts like I ate lizards and cactus. But the dreameaters looked just like normal people. Short of an impressive display of power, the only way to uncover one was with the Halo. I checked my wrist and let out a sigh of relief. The shiny white polymer was a little dusty, but it seemed to be intact even after throwing myself on top of Liam.

I pressed the button and placed my hand on the boy's head. Zach stepped to one side so he would have a clear shot. Cursed by God though dreameaters may have been, their mental powers were damned impressive. Destructive and deadly, as Byron could have attested if he were still alive. If Liam made the slightest move – or if anything around him did – Zach would put a bolt in Liam's skull.

The halo-gram flickered into glowing brilliance above Liam's head like a summoned ghost. The rings of light passed over the squiggly projection of the boy's brain, moving back and forth as the Halo scanned. Bright red light appeared across the image, outlining several sections of the scan as though they were burning.

Fuck.

"Positive," I barely managed to blurt instead of the other word. "He's a dreameater!"

I leapt away from Liam and the halo-gram vanished. Shaking, I unslung my crossbow and brought it up to point at our prisoner. Zach kicked Liam's shoulder and knocked the boy down to the ground. He held his crossbow with one hand while he worked at the knot of his bandana with the other. Awkwardly, Zach tied it across Liam's eyes, blindfolding him. There wasn't much that could protect us from a dreameater's mental powers, but blindfolding one made it a lot harder for him to hurl shit at you. I had no idea if it hindered their ability to read minds, but I sure hoped so.

"I didn't do it," Liam kept sobbing. "Please, I didn't hurt anyone!"

"Julia, look here," said Zach.

He pointed down at the water boy's bound hands. There was blood and the colorful remains of flower petals ground under his fingernails. A water boy had no business even touching a flower, to say nothing of the blood.

Carefully, I retrieved the shard of glass from Liam's pant cuff. It was thick and shined clear, well cared for and clean. Greenhouse glass. Liam had been there when Byron died. Zach hauled the boy to his feet and began dragging him away.

"Liam Fox," Zach said. "You have been found guilty of murder and possession of psionic power. You are hereby sentenced to be given to the storms."

————

WE MARCHED Liam through the Whisperward, past two more Blackthumbs standing guard at the edge of the Houses. They stared and I twirled my finger next to my ear, the hand signal for *dream-eater*, then gestured to Liam. One of them made the sign of the teardrop to protect himself, but they fell obediently into step beside us. There were four crossbows pointed at the blindfolded psychic kid now.

Everyone watched as we passed, curious and frightened. Zach and I gave them our best reassuring smiles. The Greenguard had done its job again, caught the bad guy and all that good shit. The refugees – crowded into the spaces between buildings and wherever else they could find room – watched even more avidly. Maybe their Greenguard did things a little differently in Bridge City, but they all stood back to let us pass.

Liam cried through the entire half-hour hike across the city and Zach's bandana was swiftly soaked in tears. Out here, the buildings were encrusted with sand, and all of the sharp corners were wind-worn and rough. If our Stormsphere ever fell silent, these neighborhoods would be the first to feel the full wrath of the storms. There would usually have been only a few scattered families living out this far from the comforting black dome and wordless Whispers of the Tear of God, but with the constant stream of refugees from the fallen Whisperwards, they filled every house up to the highest remaining floors.

The city walls loomed up into the darkening sky, a tall but lumpy amalgamation of long-still automobiles all covered in a thick layer of concrete and adobe. Greenguard were hurrying another straggling group of tired, dusty people through the gates and into Angel City. The new refugees had wrapped themselves in all the clothes they owned, just like Whitefingers, to protect themselves from the stinging wind. They staggered wearily into the Whisperward, each clutching bundles containing all that was left of their worldly possessions. Even the children carried some small burden. Were they the last out of Bridge City? The other Whisperward was hundreds of miles away. Anyone still out there had to find shelter soon or they would die.

Like Liam.

The dreameater boy hung his head. He still couldn't see, but he must have sensed that we were approaching the edge of the Whisperward and his feet dragged through the dust. I couldn't blame him – I wouldn't exactly have a spring in my step walking to my own execution, either.

"I didn't do it," Liam said for the hundredth time. "I swear it wasn't me!"

It was starting to bug the shit out of me. Not the monotonous mantra – I had heard that before – but the nagging feeling that the kid was telling the truth. The blood and the flower petals, the cut on his arm, the glass in his pants… It all placed Liam at our murder scene. And he *was* a dreameater.

But why would a water boy – probably working in the Houses since he was old enough to carry a bucket – suddenly kill a Gardener? Was Liam just another natural malcontent like me? It didn't seem likely. Other than Zach, I didn't have many friends, and there was a good reason for that. I wasn't like most people.

Had Liam recently discovered his psionics? When a dream-eater's power emerged, it was sudden and usually messy. Young psychics often panicked and lashed out, not knowing what they were doing and unable to control themselves. These new dream-eaters were almost as dangerous as the ones trained by White-fingers to hunt and kill with their cursed powers.

Maybe Liam had killed Gardener Byron by accident. But what about the missing key? It could have simply gotten lost in the chaos, but I doubted it. This key seemed far too important to the Gardeners to just be overlooked. Zach had searched Liam, though, and found nothing.

The Greenguard had started shouldering the city gates closed behind the refugees, but they saw us coming and heaved the big steel plates open once more. Wind was beginning to howl outside Angel City like a demon.

"Best hurry, Dias," one of the Blackthumbs shouted to Zach. "That storm's coming in fast!"

It was. The sky had turned from threatening gray to a diseased-looking green-black. The western horizon was gone and the ruins of the old city vanished swiftly behind a seething wall of sand. Flashes of yellow-green lightning crackled through the midnight clouds bearing down on us. By unspoken agreement, we all broke into a run.

"No!" Liam screamed.

He dug his heels into the ground. Zach and one of the other Blackthumbs grabbed the boy's arms. They dragged him through the gates and toward an ominous row of thick metal spikes driven into the earth just beyond the storm line. Steel chains dangled from each post, clanking as the rising wind pulled at them. When the storm hit, it was going to be a tossup whether the sands would flay

Liam or if a lightning strike to the pole would burn him first. Zach hurriedly chained the boy to the nearest pole.

"God rest your soul, Liam Fox," he shouted out over the rising shriek of the storm.

The other two Blackthumbs were already dashing for the gate. Zach gave the chains a yank to make sure they were secure as Liam pulled against them, still screaming his innocence.

"Come on," Zach called to me.

"Wait," I yelled back. Sand swirled around my feet and the air actually crackled with energy. "I don't like this, Zee. This whole thing... It was just too easy."

"You call this easy, Julia? We chased that boy all through the Houses!"

"I'm going to question him."

"What?" Zach had reclaimed his bandana and tied the wet cloth across his mouth. He pulled his battered leather hat low over his goggles. "Julia, the storm's almost on us. We've got to get back into the city!"

"Why did he kill Byron?" I shouted. "Why didn't he attack us? There's too much we don't know, Zee!"

"He's a dreameater, Julia. He'll twist your mind!"

"I have to be sure!"

I turned away from Zach. He could go back to the Whisperward if he wanted, but I couldn't leave until I had answers.

"Liam, you say that you didn't kill Byron," I said. "But you were there. Why?"

"I didn't kill the Gardener!" Liam screamed. The boy wasn't looking at me. His bulging eyes were fixed on the colossal, flickering mass of the sandstorm boiling up toward us. "I was there, but it wasn't me!"

"What were you doing, then?" I asked. "Were you working?"

"No, I... It was the Tear of God. I had to see it. They... they asked me to come. I was going to the Tear!"

I could barely hear Liam. The storm hissed and boomed with thunder. The air seethed with heat and violent potential.

"Bugshit," I said. "No one called you there. Only the Gardeners are allowed that close to the Stormsphere."

"Not them. The Whispers...!"

Wind whipped away the rest. I leaned in until I was almost within kissing distance of the condemned boy.

"If you didn't kill Byron, who did?" I asked.

"Whitefingers!" Liam gasped.

"Whitefingers?" Zach asked. "Every murderer says that the Whitefingers did it, Julia. This is a waste of time. We have to go!"

I could tease Zach about getting drawn back in long after he said that we had to go, but later. I held up my hand to silence my partner.

"What did you see?" I asked Liam.

"Someone short, all cloaked and white with salt. They were sneaking up behind Byron and I shouted. I warned him! Byron saw the Whitefinger and they fought. The Blackthumbs were running to help him and then the greenhouse just... exploded. Glass flew everywhere."

My heart pounded. "Did you see anything else?"

"The Whitefinger was cut up, but I guess he was alright enough to run. He took something off Byron. A white rectangle on a chain, but thin like... like paper and shiny like the Halo. Please, don't give me to the storm! I didn't do anything wrong! I tried to help Byron after the Whitefinger left."

That explained the blood and flower petals under Liam's nails. The glass and the cut, too. What about the white plastic card? Was that the key that Martin said was missing from around Byron's neck...? A greenish bolt of lightning snaked through the seething, boiling sky and I tried to blink away the spots floating in front of my eyes.

"Why didn't you come forward? Why didn't you tell us?" I asked.

"I'm a dreameater," Liam cried. "You would have killed me just for being like this... I didn't mean to be! It only started a few days ago. I hear the Whispers wherever I go, even when I'm not in the Houses. And then I began hearing other things... Things people were thinking. I don't mean to, and I never hurt anyone. I swear it to God!"

"Julia!" Zach grabbed me by the arm and started dragging me away. "We're out of time. Get back to the city!"

"Don't leave me out here!" Liam shouted. "I didn't hurt anyone!"

Liam strained against his chains. His short blond hair was beginning to stand up on end as the charged air swirled around him. Sand scoured Liam's skin and opened a shallow gash along the boy's cheek. Bright red blood oozed from the wound.

"Zee...?" I asked.

"Even if he didn't kill Byron," Zach said, "he's a dreameater. You know the sentence for that, Julia!"

Zach pulled me back toward the city walls. My mouth was full of grit and the wind had torn most of my hair free of its braid. I pulled my bandana up onto my face and goggles down over my stinging, streaming eyes. The howl of the wind was deafening and my ears rang as Zach hauled me away.

We ran toward the city, out of the screaming wind and once more into the protection of the Stormsphere. Zach pounded on the gates. Behind us, the storm churned up over Liam and the row of iron rods, then slammed into the Stormsphere's invisible barrier. Thunder boomed and nearly knocked me off my feet.

"Open up!" Zach shouted.

The Blackthumbs shoved the gates open a few feet and we staggered through. I yanked my bandana down and coughed sand and mud out into the street.

Clouds of dust whipped up over the top of the craggy walls, but nothing else passed through the Stormsphere's perimeter. Refugees huddled together in the alleys, fighting for space out of the wind.

They were frightened. The Stormspheres in Bridge City and Sun City had failed, letting the storms in to ravage their Whisperwards. Were they afraid it would happen here?

"What the hell was that? You closed the gates on us!" Zach shouted at the Greenguard. "The Tear will stop the storm a hundred yards off!"

"Sorry, Dias," said the other Blackthumb. "It's been getting closer. We didn't want–"

Zach let loose one of his rare strings of profanity as I slumped against the wall. I swore that the wind still carried the sound of Liam's screams.

ZACH and I returned to the base, but Gregory insisted that we report immediately to Thorn's office.

"The High Gardener will want to know what you've discovered," Gregory said. "Good work, you two. Less than two days and you found your man."

"We still don't know–" I started to object, but our boss was already leading Zach and me out the door, brushing his hands excitedly down his robes.

"Very good work, Reed," Gregory insisted.

He led us out of the base, intent on being present when Thorn received the good news. We strode briskly through the ranks of dark and silent robots, back up into the dim greenish daylight and across the base lot toward the Houses.

This close to the Stormsphere, there wasn't even a breeze to mark the sandstorm raging beyond its protection. But the western sky glowed in pale flashes of lightning and illuminated dark clouds of billowing dust. Liam had to be dead by now, scoured away by the sharp sands and winds or charred to bones.

The boy wasn't a murderer, but he *was* a dreameater. Psychics were dangerous. I had seen that first hand. Just last year, I put a crossbow bolt through the skull of a psychic man holding two other Blackthumbs in the air with nothing but the power of his rage. I'd felt damned good about the shot, too.

But that had been a grown man. He was psychotic, not begging for his life.

This sick, heavy weight in the pit of my stomach was more like what I felt during birth control jobs. As far as I knew, no one chose to be a dreameater. It just... happened. The Gardeners said that God cursed those he judged guilty, whether we mortal creatures understood their sins or not. Did God see a difference between the penitent ones, like Liam, and those like the Whitefingers, who cultivated their curse?

Gregory hesitated in the polished lobby of the Gardeners' white building, nervous eyes flicking between the stairs and elevator.

"Come with me," he decided, and pressed a button on the wall marked with an arrowhead. It lit up.

Zach looked at me and gave a restrained grin. To him, this was a treat. I nodded back with a smile that I hoped was convincing.

I was edging closer to the stairs when there was a noise like a tiny bell. The elevator doors opened, not swinging in or out, but sliding into the walls instead. The science of the old world was amazing, but I didn't quite see the point. What was wrong with hinges? Actual doors instead of curtains seemed luxury enough and there was no shortage of space for them in here.

We all climbed in and Gregory pressed another button inside the elevator. There were a dozen of them arranged in rows along a shiny metal panel, each with different numbers and symbols engraved on them. The elevator doors slid closed with a hiss and I gasped as I felt the floor move under me. Was it going to fall? Even Zach reached out and grabbed the handrail around the tiny room's edge. But Gregory just swayed with the soft lurch and checked his reflection in the polished surface of the sliding doors. He smoothed his robes several times and went to work on his hair.

There was another bob and dip as the elevator settled to a stop a moment later, but this time I was prepared for it and didn't do anything embarrassing. With another bell tone, the doors opened and I found myself looking down a different hallway. We were on the top floor already.

Thorn's office was still a lush paradise. The air was sweet with the smell of flowers and I couldn't help but take several deep, sweet-scented breaths. Greenguard weren't allowed to enter the greenhouses any more than the water boys or glass polishers. We were paid in luxuries like fruits and vegetables from the gardens, but flowers were the sacred, God-given province of the Gardeners – and the Gardeners alone.

"High Gardener Thorn," Gregory announced, sketching a little bow. "I wanted to personally inform you that Daniel Byron's killer has been found and executed. My Greenguard, Reed and Dias, caught and sentenced him earlier today."

"His name was Liam Fox," I said.

Thorn stood in front of his expansive windows. Beyond Angel City, the storm filled the sky with churning black and flashes of yellow-green lightning.

"What about the key?" Thorn asked. "Was it recovered?"

Gregory shifted nervously, perhaps regretting not debriefing us before marching us over to his superior. "Um... I'm not sure..."

"What did you find?" asked Thorn.

He directed the question at Zach. Gregory fell silent, excluded for the moment.

"We found a water boy who had been injured by the glass that killed Gardener Byron," Zach said. His voice was steady. I wondered if mine would be, too. "The Halo scanned him red, a dreameater, so we sentenced him to the storm."

"But he said there was a Whitefinger in the greenhouse," I interrupted. "Liam swore that he tried to warn Byron, not kill him. That the Whitefinger actually killed your Gardener."

Gregory puffed up and waved his hands. "Come now, Reed. If I had an orchid for every time a criminal said a Whitefinger did it, I'd have my own greenhouse."

I took a deep breath and started digging a grave for my career.

"I don't think the boy was your killer, Thorn," I said. "If he was powerful enough to kill a Gardener and two Greenguard, then why didn't he use his psionics to escape us today?"

One of Thorn's thick brows shot up. He considered that for a moment.

"When a dreameater's abilities first awaken, they are often confused. Out of control," the High Gardener said slowly. "Liam may not have been able to summon that power when he needed it. Do you have any other reason to doubt his guilt?"

"Yeah, actually," I answered. "We found something at the crime scene that doesn't fit."

I produced the piece of lace from my pocket and held it out. Thorn took the scrap and inspected it, then handed it to Gregory, who made a show of examining the lace closely.

"Unless you recognize that," I said, "we still don't know where it came from. It was snagged on a piece of glass, which means that it was caught or placed there *after* the greenhouse was shattered. We haven't been able to match it to anything."

"That's true, sir," Zach agreed. My hero. "Liam also said that the Whitefinger took something from around Byron's neck, a piece of white plastic on a chain. I searched Liam, but he didn't have anything like that on him."

"The key," Gregory said slowly. "He could have hidden it or thrown it away, I suppose."

"Key?" I asked. Zach gave me another warning glance, but my curiosity was seldom bound by good sense. "That was the key?"

"Yes," Thorn said.

He reached into his robes and withdrew a chain from around his neck. A small plastic rectangle dangled from it, a bit thicker than a sheet of paper. It was shiny and white, just like Liam had said, with a black stripe running down one side. There were faded markings on the other side that looked like letters and maybe a winged shape. A bird?

"What does it open?" I asked.

"This is a very special kind of key," Thorn said and Gregory began nodding along with him. "An ancient key that opens only one door in the Whisperward."

"Which door?"

"The door of the Tear of God."

YESTERDAY, I didn't even know that the Stormsphere had a door and today, Zach and I were in charge of protecting it. Thorn took my story of a Whitefinger killer seriously enough to double the guard on the Stormsphere and tasked us with organizing the defense. Zach and I now found ourselves reporting directly to the High Gardener.

"Someone has that key. And they may attempt to use it," Thorn had said.

"Why?" Zach asked. "What could a Whitefinger want with the Tear of God?"

"Nothing good for the Whisperward, my child."

I slept like shit that night. It took hours to fall asleep and when I finally did, I dreamed about the Whispers telling me that Liam was blameless. That I was guilty. That I had killed an innocent boy.

I was still tired when I hauled myself up out of bed the next morning and chewed listlessly on a couple of red pitayas. My eyes felt full of storm sand. I pulled on my Greenguard fatigues, combed and braided my hair, and then got ready for the most boring assignment in the world. I didn't want to guard the Stormsphere. I wanted to be out *there*, hunting down that Whitefinger.

Not that I thought Thorn was wrong. For once, I actually agreed with Angel City's biggest prick. The Whitefinger thief would likely try to use his stolen key at the earliest opportunity. Zach pointed out that this was our best chance to nab the thief, but until then, it was just a waiting game and I've never been very good at those. I preferred to be more proactive. Or hyperactive and impatient, as Zach more accurately liked to put it.

"How are you, Julia?" he asked when I showed up at the base.

"Rosy," I said with a smile that I figured looked fake as hell. "Slept like a baby."

Zach knew me. He knew it was all bugshit, but he smiled back and patted my shoulder. He checked the bolt on his crossbow and then led the way. Gregory had given us a list of Greenguard we could order out for extra protection. I was dismayed to see Woods' name on the list, but there were some useful ones, too.

We picked up our new Greenguard from the base's training yard and then marched them out to the Stormsphere. The Whispers were inaudible at first, but started as soon as we were within sight of the shiny glass Houses. I strained to make out words, but unlike my dream, I heard no accusations, no mantras of innocence or guilt.

"Good morning, Reed," Woods said. He smiled broadly at me and then bade a belated good morning to Zach, as well. "If you're free sometime soon, I could get my hands on another apple."

I knew what he wanted to get his hands on, alright. If Woods had been a dreameater, then he could have read my mind and known it was a lost cause. And then I could have shot him.

"Zach and I are in charge of the Stormsphere's security. Day and night," I said. "Sorry."

I still wasn't looking forward to it, but at least the boring guard duty had this thin silver lining. I ordered Woods away to the first guard post Zach and I had picked out.

We stationed the rest of the Blackthumbs at seven other points all around the Stormsphere. Each pair was within sight of the next to provide backup and covered every approach to the Tear. Zach and I circled the Stormsphere to make sure that everyone was in place and that we didn't leave any major gaps. When we had double-checked our work, we reported to a tall Gardener with dark skin and an intensely curling gray beard. His face was deeply lined, as if he'd been carved that way instead of naturally aged. He kept his hands tucked into the sleeves of his robes just to drive home the image of a keeper of the Gardeners' secrets.

"I'm Gardener Torres," he said. "You'll want to know what you're protecting. Thorn tells me I am to show you the Door."

I could hear the capital D on that last word. Maybe this *wouldn't* be the most boring job ever.

"Julia Reed. This is my partner, Zachary Dias," I said, nodding as respectfully as I could manage.

Given five uninterrupted minutes, I could probably have pissed Torres off enough to get myself kicked from the assignment, maybe even get Gregory to put me back out on the streets. But Zach was right – this was our best chance to catch Byron's real killer. I owed it to Liam to find that Whitefinger.

And I owed it to myself, or at least my curiosity, to get a look at this Door.

We followed Torres around the dark curve of the Stormsphere. It rose up out of the dusty concrete ground, utterly smooth and utterly black. White daylight reflected from the surface, but even that couldn't seem to stick and appeared to hover a fraction of an inch up off the polished blackness. I knew that the Tear was huge, but close enough now to touch it – which I didn't do – I could appreciate its true scale. There were taller buildings in Angel City: the Stormsphere was only about two hundred feet tall, but twice that wide. It was the biggest thing in the entire Whisperward.

"Hey, why is it called a Stormsphere?" I asked Torres. "I mean, it's only half a sphere, isn't it? Why not a Storm-hemisphere... or Storm-dome?"

The old Gardener actually laughed. "It *is* a sphere, Reed. You simply can't see it from up here. The Tear extends as far beneath the earth as above."

Rosy... That thing really was huge. And at this range, the Whispers were loud inside my skull, demanding attention as they rustled through my mind. I shook my head, but that didn't help, of course.

Refugees gathered around the dome at a respectful distance, huddling in pairs or groups and looking to the Tear of God and the Gardeners for deliverance. For protection. Some prayed aloud, a susurrate murmur like an earthly echo of the Whispers. Others simply closed their eyes and listened. Could they hear something I didn't?

Torres frowned and Zach paused to shoo the praying refugees back from the Tear. They withdrew quietly – this probably wasn't the first time they had been told to disperse – but went no further than Zach ordered. By the time we were moving on along the Tear's huge curve, they were creeping closer once more.

"They're frightened," said Torres. "The Whispers give them comfort and I'm glad... But we can't let them interfere with the Tear of God."

There was one building near the Stormsphere. It was a small, windowless thing, blocky and ugly. Someone had painted it with images of plants, but the decorations utterly failed to hide the bleak gray walls. Not this close to the immense, pristine glassy black of the Stormsphere.

This was the shrine where the Gardeners made offerings to God in thanks for His continued protection. Or so Torres told us as we approached. A pair of Blackthumbs stood at attention beside the entrance, the ones Zach had hand-picked as our best. Well, next to the two of us, at least.

Torres motioned us inside. I guess it was an offering day. Gardeners worked at tables with baskets of milkweed – bundles of small flowers, red and pink and star-shaped – and heavy-looking plastic jugs full of something liquid.

"What's that?" I asked Torres, pointing.

"It comes from the flowers," he answered, but didn't offer any more details.

Zach shook his head when I opened my mouth to ask. I quieted, but stuck my tongue out at him. Zach smirked.

The milkweed was being carefully spread out in shallow metal trays and Gardeners poured the contents of the jugs into small bowls. It looked thick, syrupy like agave nectar and smelled sweet. Flower nectar, perhaps? I knew the milkweed was poisonous, but maybe the other flowers were edible.

The Gardeners bowed to Torres, then lined up in two rows with trays of milkweed on one side and dishes of nectar on the other. Torres dug into the pockets of his robes and produced a plastic key just like Thorn's. He made his way solemnly to the back of the shrine and pushed open the doors there. He didn't use the strange key, though, so I guess the show wasn't over yet.

Beyond what I already thought of as the sorting room, I expected a temple with a big statue of God and burning flower oil or something. I was completely taken aback by the simple concrete staircase leading down. Torres motioned for Zach and me to follow, and we walked slowly behind him. The twin rows of Gardeners trailed behind, carrying their offerings.

I was beyond curious, but the air of mystery and tradition hung so thick down here that even I didn't dare disturb it. Besides, I wasn't even sure what questions to ask. *What the hell is all this?* just didn't seem to cover it.

The only sound was the Whispers, rustling ceaselessly in the back of my mind. Long tubes of electric light glowed over the stairs. A few of them sputtered and one or two were dark, but the passage down into the ground was well lit and kept just as clean as Thorn's office.

And there were paintings here, too. The walls were covered in intricate murals that surrounded us with painted fields of milkweed. Tall green stalks and clusters of flowers rippled in an invisible breeze. As we went down the stairs, though, the milkweed gave way to broad plains and mountains so that walking down the stairs felt like a long trek across a world that no longer existed. From Angel City to Apple City, God had left his children only miles of harsh desert.

The murals had been repaired. More than repaired, actually. Large patches of the scene had been entirely repainted – mostly swathes of blue sky and white clouds in paint decades or maybe even centuries old, but obviously still newer than the ancient mural beneath. I wanted to stop for a closer look, but the inexorable procession of Gardeners descending the stairs kept us moving.

Toward the bottom, the mural was full of painted trees. They were tall and slender, with leaves that looked like cactus spines. I had never seen anything like them before. I craned my head and squinted as we passed. The trunks of the strange trees had been repainted at some point, too.

Something else finally caught my attention. We had reached the end of the stairs and the passage terminated abruptly in a shining black wall that curved away to either side. It took me a moment to realize that we were looking at the Stormsphere – an underground section of the slick black skin. The Whispers were still quiet down here, but somehow... deafening. They filled my head like something soft yet vast, crowding out all other thought. I half raised my hands to cover my ears before stopping, knowing it was useless. Zach looked like he was engaged in the same internal struggle and I patted one big arm, trying to reassure both of us.

Torres stepped up to the surface of the sphere. It wasn't perfectly unbroken down here – there was a large inset rectangle with softly rounded corners to match the curve of the Stormsphere.

The Door.

Torres held up the white plastic card he wore chained around his neck. There was a small protrusion beside the door, marring the smooth perfection of the sphere. It was black like the rest, but lacked that impossibly shiny sheen. A slot ran down the center, with a tiny red light glowing like an ember on one side. Torres placed the rectangular plastic key into the slot at the top – dark stripe first – and then slid it through, never losing his solemn, ritual grace.

The pinprick of light turned from red to green. A low mechanical growl sounded from beyond the door and I held my breath. This was a little closer to religion than I really wanted to get. Normally, I preferred it when God stayed up behind the clouds. He had done enough already, in my opinion. I was caught between curiosity and – frankly – abject terror. For the first time since leaving my mother's house, I made the teardrop sign over my heart with one finger. I shrank back against the painted concrete walls.

The Whispers stirred, their murmur swept up like dust in a wind as the door opened. The shiny black surface sank back into the sphere and then slid away to one side. From my vantage point, I could make out only a narrow slice of the interior. It wasn't black inside, but white. Blindingly white and clean. Even the twin rows of proud Gardeners looked dusty and haggard as they stepped forward into the Stormsphere with their offerings. With another swipe of his strange ancient key, Torres sealed the Stormsphere behind them again.

"This is what we protect," he said. "The Door."

I had no idea what we'd just seen, but I nodded my head dumbly. For once, I had nothing to say.

———

THAT WAS the only time we saw the Door that we were guarding. Yeah, it deserved the capital D.

Zach and I stationed ourselves right outside the sorting shrine. I tried to talk to Zach about what we had seen, about the murals and the strange plants, the toxic milkweed and sweet nectar offerings, the Door into the Stormsphere... But Zach didn't want to discuss any of it.

"I'm not sure I want to know God's mysteries, Julia," he said. "It's enough that God gave us His Tears and they protect us. We're here to guard the Stormsphere and, if we can, catch that Whitefinger. That's our job."

I sighed. At least Zach believed that there was someone else to catch. He may not have believed Liam, but he believed in me.

We managed the rotation of the Greenguard to keep the Stormsphere protected day and night. We were up at odd hours and I had a lot more contact with Woods than I wanted. And after the initial awe of witnessing the Door, I grew swiftly bored again. Bored and agitated.

When I went home at night, I kept dreaming of Liam screaming as the storm tore him apart, and would wake with the torn piece of lace from the greenhouse clutched in my hand. Silva came running to my door once, but I told her that I was fine. She finally left, promising to pray for me.

I found myself tracing my fingers over the lace in quiet moments afterward. Just what the hell was it doing at our crime scene? I was sure that it was connected to our killer somehow. I was impatient to catch the Whitefinger and execute him for Byron's death. Maybe some real justice would chase Liam out of my dreams.

The next morning, I leaned against the sorting shrine's painted exterior, watching Zach and Myers chase off another group of faithful. More refugees, to judge by their tattered clothes and desperate expressions.

Would catching the Whitefinger *be* real justice? All of our evidence pointed to Byron's death being an accident. Liam's warning had surprised the Whitefinger and alerted the Gardener. It was the ensuing scuffle that forced the Whitefinger to kill Byron and the two Greenguard, injuring Liam. If the boy hadn't been creeping through the Houses that night, maybe the Whitefinger would have completed his robbery without bloodshed.

Of course, then we might not have had any idea that he was trying to get into the Stormsphere. Even in death, Byron had protected the Gardeners' charge. I couldn't help a little grudging respect for the dead man. I readjusted the weight of my crossbow and nodded to Zach as he came trotting back to his post.

"Nice work," I commented dryly. "How old was that littlest one? Five? Did she put up a terrible fight?"

"I feared for my life," Zach answered with a perfectly straight face. "You must be bored, Julia. You're sense of humor is usually sharper than that."

"Eat thorns."

"Well, it *is* about lunch time. Let's go grab a bite."

————

THE WHITEFINGER WAS MUCH MORE patient than I was. For a long and tedious week, I stood outside the shrine doors, trading lame jokes with Zach and avoiding Woods. The most interesting part was when Thorn himself came down to lead the offering procession through the Door and check on our progress.

"Nothing yet, sir," Zach said.

His lantern jaw was tight. I don't think he liked having to admit failure any more than Gregory did.

"Stay sharp," Thorn told us, then vanished inside.

"Thanks," I murmured once the High Gardener was safely out of earshot. "Wouldn't have thought of that, sir."

"It was encouragement, not an order," said Zach. He seemed a little bolstered by Thorn's visit, at least.

And with that, the exciting bit was over.

Another party of refugees arrived at the gates that afternoon and bled slowly into the overcrowded Whisperward. These were from Sun City, Woods informed me, not Bridge. I hadn't asked, but I frowned at the news. How many other Whisperwards were failing out there?

Half of the newcomers made straight for the big black Tear, maybe because they had seen storms out in the deserts and gained new appreciation for its power, or perhaps just to give thanks for their safe arrival. The crowds were restless, though. A few had taken it into their heads to make offerings. The Gardeners did it daily and I could hardly fault the relieved travelers for making the attempt. But it was still our job to wave them off when they tried to place bits of concrete carved with names or other small, precious keepsakes at the foot of the shrine.

"Move back," Meyers called out. "Step away from the Tear!"

"We'd better help him," Zach said.

It was nearing the end of our shift and we were in the middle of the handoff to Ericson and Hollinger. But if this got any stormier, we weren't going anywhere. Why did things always get worse when I was about to go home? I glared thorns at Zach and looked back at the growing crowd of refugees. He was probably right...

"Wait," I whispered. "There!"

Someone was pushing through the crowd, ignoring the Greenguard's instructions. They were wrapped in layers despite the heat, with a cloak thrown around their shoulders. Short, like Liam said, and his gloved hands were white with salt. A Whitefinger.

He was making for the front of the crowd, to where the pair of our Blackthumbs was trying to maintain the perimeter. I hissed another warning to Zach and we trotted forward, toward the crowd and the cloaked Whitefinger. I reached for my crossbow when I felt Zach's hand on my arm.

"Not until we get closer," he said. "Do you want to skewer one of these people?"

But then the Whitefinger was suddenly up at the front of the throng while Zach and I were still yards off. I brought my crossbow up and fired. Zach's hands were a blur and his bolt was only half a heartbeat behind mine. One of them missed entirely, but the other shot – I wasn't sure if it was mine or Zach's – went right through the Whitefinger's cloak and buried itself three inches into the dirt.

I charged toward the Whitefinger. My hands went automatically through the motions of cocking and reloading my crossbow, then aimed again. The crowd tore apart, scattering and screaming.

"Whitefinger!"

"Blackthumbs!"

"God help us!"

There were people everywhere, running and scrambling over each other to get away. The rest of the Greenguard leapt into action, aiming and firing more steel crossbows. The Whitefinger crouched and threw out his salt-stained hands. Our shots smashed into something invisible and spun harmlessly off through the air... just like a storm rebounding off the Whisperward perimeter.

"Oh, shit," I said.

The Whitefinger was leaping back now, trying to vanish into the crowd, but they had pulled too far apart. I yanked my knife out of the sheath and held it up to keep from accidentally stabbing myself or an innocent refugee in the chaos. The crowd had identified the outsider and every time the Whitefinger tried to lose himself in them, they retreated again. I sprinted to close the distance between us.

"Stop!" Zach shouted at the Whitefinger. He swore and began running, too.

My legs pumped hard as I ran after the fleeing figure, but he swept his white-encrusted cloak in a backward motion. Sand billowed up from the ground into a thick, dirty cloud. I squeezed my eyes shut, felt the dirt against my face and spat it out of my mouth. I swiped the grit away and opened my stinging eyes again.

While we were blinded, the Whitefinger had fled down the road, running toward the market. The crowds there were even larger there and would have no idea what had happened at the shrine. He would have little trouble hiding. I yanked my goggles down over my eyes in case the Whitefinger tried that dust trick again and kept running.

"Julia!" Zach shouted.

I heard the warning note in his voice and dodged to the right. Zach's arrow flew past me and just over the shoulder of the retreating Whitefinger. He stumbled, ducking the sharp whizzing noise and I closed a few more yards. We were coming to the top of the road, where it dropped down a hill and past the farming patches, and I finally managed to grab the wastelander's cloak. The cloth was rough and faintly sticky in my hand. I didn't have a very good grip, but I jerked as hard as I could to break his stride.

The Whitefinger leapt back, yanking his cloak out of my grasp and I charged in. I slashed at him with my knife and he slithered away, as quick as a snake, but I kept on my attack. Zach was right behind me with his big crossbow and deadly bolts. All I had to do was hold the Whitefinger's attention for a few more seconds. And hope he was too distracted to use more of his dreameater powers.

The little bastard wasn't unarmed, though. He reached under his faded cloak and whipped out an arm's length of metal tubing. He swung it at me and I ducked, recovered and jumped in once more with my knife. I had to leap away again as the Whitefinger jabbed his weapon at me. The damned pipe had a sharpened head on it – a spear, albeit a short one.

I faked off to the right and then lunged left, grabbing for the Whitefinger's wrist with my free hand. I got another handful of cloak instead, more of the cloth than before, and pulled hard. The Whitefinger stumbled and the cloak's fastening snapped. The hood fell back. A bandana – not unlike my own – was tugged down around the Whitefinger's neck, probably dislodged by our battle, and I finally saw my Whitefinger suspect.

She had a delicate face, with a pointed chin and fine, high cheekbones. The girl's eyes were angular and a deep, earthy brown. Her shoulder-length hair was straight and as dark a brunette as you can get before giving up and calling it black. She was beautiful.

Wow... Not at all what I expected.

I almost caught her spear in the guts while I was staring, but I twisted and grabbed the shaft of her weapon. I threw an overhand stab that the Whitefinger ducked, pulling on her spear, but the girl was five feet tall – if I was feeling generous – and wasn't going to recover it by strength alone. Her lovely face was hard.

Something I couldn't see slammed into my chest and I flew back. Oh, right. She was a dreameater. She didn't have to rely on brute force. Though I might have changed my mind and called the force that hit me pretty damned brutal. I lost my grip on the short spear and dropped my knife as I hit the ground. I felt bruised from shoulder to waist and struggled to suck air down into my lungs.

I heard the sharp twang of a bowstring and a bolt flickered over my head. The Whitefinger cried out sharply, but I looked up just in time to see her turn and sprint away into the city once more. I coughed and forced myself to stand, with or without breath. Zach stopped and crouched by my side. He dropped another bolt into his cocked crossbow and scanned the street.

"Did we lose her?" I managed to wheeze.

"Her? It's a girl? No, we didn't lose her. Not yet." Zach pointed a few yards away, where the dust was busily soaking up a spatter of bright red blood. "I hit her."

I reloaded my crossbow and we followed the road down into the market at a brisk trot. Thousands of people, Angel City natives and refugees from Sun and Bridge Cities, argued and haggled at the scale farms and cactus fields. The musky smell of reptiles competed with the odor of hot concrete and sweat. Stands selling roast fence lizards and baked snake offered a more pleasant scent, but shoppers moving through the square stirred up the dust and stomped our evidence into the dirt.

Zach and I moved forward in a low crouch, scanning the road until we found a lucky spot of blood on a corner of concrete. A hundred yards off, there was a commotion more frantic than the usual marketplace barter. A bugmonger shouted and pointed.

"Stop! Stop her!" he cried, alternating between gesturing at a running figure and panicking about the cage of fresh crickets that had been knocked over. The insects scattered across the street, squeaking and hopping.

The Whitefinger girl had pulled up her hood once more and replaced her bandana. But she was limping from Zach's shot and even her cloak couldn't entirely conceal the salt ground into her clothes.

"That's her," I told Zach.

We broke into a run again, right through the spreading swarm of crickets and past their shouting seller. The Whitefinger was bolting down the main street toward the city's edge. My lungs burned and my legs ached from the chase. Zach brought his crossbow up again, but people were shrieking in terror and scattering across the road. He couldn't get a clean shot.

"Shit!" Zach shouted. "Shut the gates!"

The Whitefinger was closing quickly on Angel City's northern gate. I was right on her tail, but more refugees were sifting into the city and at least one of them must have been a Gardener or someone else important – most of the Greenguard stood off to the side, all gathered around a pair of robed men and offering up their canteens.

The Blackthumbs jumped when they heard Zach's shout, but they reacted too slowly. The Whitefinger had reached the refugees at the gate, who were all staring out at Angel City, at their new home. By the time the Greenguard got to the gates, our suspect had already slipped through the crowd and bolted out into the sandy wastes beyond.

I staggered to a panting stop as the other Blackthumbs closed the city gates in my reddened face.

"Not now, you idiots," I gasped. "Open up!"

The two men in brown and green patchwork fatigues started and then heaved the huge doors open once more. I stared at the empty husks of ancient Angel City, bits of the old world protected by the Stormsphere, but outside the walls of the Whisperward. Nothing but mutant bugs and lizards lived out there. In the distance were the stark black slashes of more iron stakes. Not the ones where we had taken Liam – those were at the west gate – but those dark spars had doubtlessly taken their own unfair share of lives.

There was a flicker of motion beyond the row of tall iron rods and their tangled chains. It might just have been heat shimmer or a swirling dust devil... or a cloaked girl on the run. Blood spattered the ground at my feet. The Whitefinger was still bleeding. If we moved quickly and if we stayed right on her heels, she wouldn't have time to stop and bind the wound.

"Julia," Zach said, staggering to a halt beside me. "She got away. I'm sorry."

"She's out there, Zach! We have a trail. Let's go find her!"

"There's nothing out there but mutants and Whitefingers," Zach panted. "And the storms."

"Whitefingers get through the storms somehow. And we've got thousands of refugees who survived the march!"

"Julia, one in ten made it here from Sun City. One in twelve from Bridge," Zach said. He looked up. "And I don't like the color of that sky."

The blank white sky had a dangerously greenish tinge on the western horizon. But the Whitefinger was out there. Our killer. Our answers. I checked my canteen and felt the weight of water sloshing around inside. I had barely touched it today. I could make it last.

"I'm not going to let a storm steal our answers again, Zee," I said. "I'm going after her. Tell Thorn I'm finishing this."

Zach groaned and hefted his own canteen. "You can tell him yourself when we get back."

I grinned at Zach. We pulled bandanas up over our mouths and Zach settled his hat down low on his brow. We started off into the sand-buried ruins of old Angel City, following the Whitefinger's blood trail.

THE BLOOD WAS QUICKLY GETTING hard to follow through the sandy rubble. Zach hadn't hit anything vital with his last shot, otherwise we would have a dead – or at least unconscious – Whitefinger on the ground back in the Whisperward instead of one capable of sprinting like a frilled lizard across the desert.

The darkening red spots were growing fewer and further between. That didn't slow us down much, though. If the dust was good for one thing, it was leaving tracks. As long as the wind didn't pick up, there was no way the Whitefinger girl could escape us.

We were out past the execution stakes now, well beyond the protection of the Stormsphere. We crested a hill and I looked back at the perfect circle around Angel City, where the destruction of the storms was suddenly blunted. Sand and wind had etched the broken and tumbled buildings. But ten feet further away, they had been scrubbed down to their foundations. Was that line closer than before? I wasn't sure.

Occasionally, the ruins of old Angel City rose up from the sand. A stretch of overpass supported by a few vast concrete pillars cast a multi-legged shadow across the ground like some vast tarantula.

Girders thrust up from cement centuries gone to dust, reminding me of the bones of a picked-over carcass. Before the Wrath, Angel City had stretched for miles and miles in every direction, but all that remained of the ancient city were a few dusty buildings and broken roads that the sandstorms hadn't gotten around to obliterating yet.

Blackthumbs were the only ones who regularly ventured outside the Whisperward, and even then it was rarely further than the execution stakes. Anyone who ran into the desert was generally considered just as dead as those chained up for the storms. I hoped that wouldn't include me and Zach, but I wasn't about to let another storm steal my answers. Still, hunting them down meant ranging out into wild, dangerous new territory.

There was a good reason smart people didn't range out beyond the city walls, even beside the storms. Basements and even entire buildings lurked beneath a thin crust of sand, weakened and buried by centuries of storms, waiting for the unwary traveler. Above, the crumbling remains of bridges were so storm-battered and ancient that any breeze might be the one that finally sent them crashing down to earth.

And then there were the mutants. Back in the Whisperward, scale and bug farmers culled the most deformed offspring from their herds, keeping the biggest, fattest and purest bloodlines. But out here, nature didn't seem to have quite the same selective sensibilities. Extra or fewer limbs, twisted skeletons, patches of oddly colored skin and tumors were just some of the weird deformities to be found in the wastes.

Only a dozen yards past the execution stakes, I saw a sunning alligator lizard so big that I could have ridden it back into Angel City. Insects couldn't get very big because they breathed through their skins and tended to strangle when those skins got too thick, but they had numbers to make up for it. Spiders and scorpions had rudimentary lungs, though, and could grow frighteningly large outside the Whisperwards. Most were slow and ponderous, but some had enough extra legs that they could outrun a human.

And then, of course, there were the Whitefingers. In the Whisperwards, we rooted out mutation to keep humanity pure. Nature didn't seem to care, so long as a creature could survive the deserts and storms. But the people who lived out here in the wastes not only didn't kill their mutants, but bred the most dangerous deformity of all: the psychic power of the dreameaters.

Zach left the tracking to me while he watched out for all the ugly things that could kill us. I stopped frequently to wipe the dust off my goggles. I didn't want to miss a single footprint. The Whitefinger girl wasn't as stupid as I would have liked and moved over stony ground where she could. But without the sweepers that kept Angel City relatively clean, a film of grit covered everything and even as light as she was, our suspect left plenty of clear tracks.

Zach could have nearly touched his fingers around the Whitefinger's waist, but for all her tiny size and short legs, she was making damned good time through the ruins. Her footprints were still evenly spaced, unfaltering and sure. Even wounded and after two hours of running, she wasn't slowing down much or stumbling. She must have been a tough little thing.

But you don't become a Greenguard by being weak or fragile. Zach and I were in good condition, too, and we weren't slowing down either. In fact, we were picking up speed. The wind rose and the fine layer of dust that was so receptive to tracks was swiftly churning into the air now. I guessed that we had half an hour before there wasn't anything left to follow.

"Are we close?" Zach asked. "We're running out of time."

The sky was turning green around the edges like old snake meat – there was a storm on the move. It could rear up over the horizon and be on us before we made it halfway back to the Whisperward. If we were fucked anyway, then I wanted to find the Whitefinger first and make her talk. I'm a stubborn bitch that way.

"We're rosy," I insisted. "We're getting closer."

I heard the sand crunch under my boots, but I was moving too fast, bent nearly double over the dwindling tracks. I had to find the girl before the wind whipped away any trace of her passage. Something in my brain registered the danger, but not loud enough.

Our Whitefinger murderer was five feet tall on her tiptoes and maybe a hundred pounds. I was seven inches taller and my weight is none of your business. But Zach topped six feet and was over two hundred pounds of solid muscle. The Whitefinger had passed over the thin layer of fused sand easily. It cracked under my weight and then shattered as Zach hurried after his stupid, impatient partner.

There was a loud crunching sound and I turned back just as the earth gave way beneath him. I watched Zach's eyes go wide behind his goggles. He threw his arms out and grabbed desperately for solid ground, but he was falling. Zach vanished up to his shoulders down the hole and scrabbled in the sand for purchase, but the dirt was cracking and falling in all around him.

I drew my knife, threw myself to the ground and slammed my blade into the sand as hard as I could. I had to hope that it was solid beneath me, or I had just killed us both. The knife went in deep, but held steady. I reached for Zach's hand and gingerly inched my fingers under his, trying to get a grip without dislodging the one he had.

"Hold on, Zee!" I grunted.

"Let go of me, Julia," he said in a strained voice. "Get the fuck off this sand."

"Bugshit. I'm not going anywhere."

Bits of fused sand broke free from the edge of the hole and rattled down into the darkness. I stared after them, down at the yellow-gray glass sloping away beneath Zach.

It was a fulgurite. That's what happens when lightning hits sand – it strikes through the ground, forking like the tongue of a mutant rattler and fuses the ground into jagged glass. Most of the time, they're only a few inches or feet long. Over time, the wind blows away the sand and leaves razor-edged bits of glass sticking up from the ground. Of course, the wind breaks them down, too, and the fragments of glass get swept up into the storm, just to make everything worse.

But the biggest storms punched yard-wide holes into the earth and dug fulgurite tubes that stretch twenty feet or more, spreading underground like the roots of an orchard tree.

"I... can't get a foothold," Zach said.

His boots thumped uselessly against the glass sides of the hole. I got my hand into Zach's and his strong fingers curled painfully around mine.

"Fuck, you're heavy!" I groaned.

"I told you to go, Julia!"

"Shut it and climb, dumb-ass!"

Zach pulled on my arm. The big bastard hardly budged and I slid a few inches closer to the hole. I desperately wanted to shift my grip on my knife, but didn't dare let go, even for a second. I leaned back away from the fulgurite with all my weight and wished for the first time that I was a hell of a lot fatter.

We were both groaning like tortoises in mating season. Every inch Zach managed to pull himself up seemed to stretch my arm an inch out of its socket. I kept an aching death-grip on my knife that I really hoped wouldn't become an *actual* death grip. But at last, we wrestled enough of Zach's bulk out of the hole that he could heave himself the rest of the way onto solid land.

"Careful," I said. "We might still be on top of the fulgurite."

Zach nodded and slid a few feet away from me so there wasn't so much of our weight concentrated in one spot. Sweat streamed down Zach's skin and his eyes were still wide enough that I could see white all around the dark irises. We crawled on our bellies for a few dozen yards. Who knew how many fulgurites might be below us? I was really going to have to nerve myself up just to stand after this. For now, I settled for rolling over and slowly sitting. I found a low chunk of stone that was reasonably flat on its leeward side and leaned back against it. Carefully, Zach joined me.

I unscrewed the cap of my canteen and took a long swallow. I swished the water around my mouth, savoring the relative coolness, then offered the canteen to Zach. He shook his head and grabbed his own. I was glad that he hadn't lost it down the fulgurite shaft. He still had his crossbow, too, though the quiver on his hip looked a few bolts light. When Zach turned to put his canteen back on his belt, I saw wet red.

"Shit, Zee. Hold still," I said.

I made my partner lace his fingers behind his head so I could take a closer look. The edge of the broken glass beneath the sand had sliced across Zach's ribs, just under his right arm. The cut was shaped like a horrible too-wide smile, but it wasn't terribly deep, only bloody.

I tore the hem off my undershirt and folded it up, then slipped it through the gash in Zach's carbon-microfiber fatigues to press it against the cut. It took a lot to slice through our uniforms, but I guess lightning-blasted glass was enough to do the job.

"Put your arm down and keep it tight to your body," I instructed.

Too tired to speak, Zach nodded and did what I asked without argument. He winced a little as the adrenalin faded and the pain set in. I settled back against the rock and looked around. We had crawled some distance away from where Zach fell through the sand. Maybe I could go back to where I last saw the Whitefinger's tracks, but there would be nothing to find now. The wind was churning and already erasing the signs of our awkward crawl. The light footprints of a girl less than half Zach's size were surely long gone.

The sky overhead had turned a nastier green, too, and the horizon was bruised black. Even from this distance, I could see the pale flashes of lightning as the storm built up energy. Probably making new fulgurites out there, damn it. I knew we had to get back to the safety of the Whisperward, but I didn't want to admit it. Zach saw it on my face, though, even through the bandana and goggles.

"We have to go back, Julia," he said.

I remained stubbornly silent, glaring out at the storm.

"We did our duty," Zach said. "She didn't get into the Storm-sphere and the Whisperward is safe. That's all that matters."

"What about Byron?" I asked. "What about Liam?"

"There's no shelter out here, Julia. She's wounded now and there's a storm coming. She'll be dead soon."

"That girl's a Whitefinger," I argued. "They *all* live outside the 'Wards."

But Zach was wounded with a storm on the way, too. Even if the Whitefingers somehow managed to weather the deadly storms of the wastelands, we didn't know their secret. I couldn't bring myself to agree with Zach aloud, but I did stand – carefully – and turned east, toward the Whisperward. My partner rose, giving the ground an even more distrustful look than I had, and we started picking our way gingerly back home.

At first, fear of another sand-covered fulgurite pit or mutant scorpion burrow slowed us down, but the sky was turning rapidly from green-gray to black and we began moving faster. Wind hissed in our ears and I found myself missing the unsettling rasp of the Whispers very, very much.

It wasn't long before we were running. The leading edge of the sandstorm tore at our bandanas and the skin beneath. Everything around us turned into a murky brown-black haze and I could no longer see where we were going. My whole world was reduced to swirling sand and stinging skin. The Whisperward had long since vanished and I had no idea if we were even moving in the right direction anymore. But we kept the wind to our backs and stag-gered on, hands clasped tightly together to keep from losing one another in the storm.

I desperately wanted to apologize to Zach for all of it, for dragging him out here and getting us both killed, but I had to keep my free hand on my bandana to hold it down over my mouth. I just had to hope that heaven or hell, we would end up in the same place so I could make my apologies there. Not a chance... After years of questions and disobedience to the Gardeners, there was no way I was going up with Zach.

"Zee–" I began, but then I squinted through my goggles and skidded to a halt.

Zach tugged at my hand as he stumbled forward a few more steps and I yanked him back until he saw them, too. Five dark figures spread out in front of us, heavy cloaks whipping in the sharp wind. Their layered clothes were dusted with salt and their white hands clutched long metal spears. One of the cloaked shapes was small and slender.

When things went stormy, they *really* went stormy. Crossbows would be useless in the wind and blowing sand, so I jerked my knife from its sheath and saw the dim shape of my partner doing the same. I angled myself to face the Whitefingers edge-on, putting my back to Zach's so they couldn't surround either of us.

The wastelanders moved forward, leaning into the wind. Their slow-motion advance didn't take away the advantage of their longer weapons, though. I *might* have been able to land a shot with my crossbow at this range, but by the time I got it off my back, I'd be bristling with spears like a barrel cactus.

I ducked the first spear jab and leapt away from another. Zach had to fling himself aside to avoid the darting spears, too, and I no longer felt his back against mine. It didn't take much to separate us and I wished I had the breath to swear. I managed to grab the haft of the next spear and slashed back. I was rewarded with a pained grunt and a retreating Whitefinger holding a hand over his wrist. This wasn't going to last long, though. They outnumbered us and had more than twice our reach.

The storm flashed yellow-green and less than a second later, thunder boomed. The heart of the storm was almost on us.

I'm sorry, Zach, I thought. *I really fucked this up, didn't I?*

"Rods!" someone shouted into the howling wind.

The Whitefingers jabbed their spears point-first into the sand and leapt away. What the hell? Were they surrendering? But they were winning. Why the hell would they give up now?

Then the short Whitefinger girl appeared in front of me. She stretched one gloved hand out toward Zach, who was standing in a ready combat crouch a few yards away. His eyes went wide and my partner slammed to the ground as though shoved by something even bigger than he was.

"Zee!" I shouted.

I started toward him and the girl tackled me. She wasn't big, but she caught me off guard and we went down to the earth in a tangle of cloth and flailing limbs. I squirmed and fought to get my arm clear enough to stick my knife into her, but a flash of light blinded me and the afterimage of jagged lightning blazed against the back of my eyelids. Sparks rained down around us and one of the spears glowed white-hot. Struck by the lightning, I realized.

I think Zach shouted something, but I couldn't hear him over the roar of thunder. The Whitefinger girl was still on top of me and her hipbone dug painfully into my stomach, but she didn't weigh much. Her body was small and soft against my chest. Her face was covered again, except for her slanted bronze eyes. I think I saw the Whitefinger girl's mouth move beneath the cloth, but I was still deafened by the thunder and couldn't hear anything despite our closeness.

Then something smashed into the side of my head. There was another blaze of light – red this time – and then nothing.

10

SOMEONE WAS TRYING to wake me. I told them to fuck off, or at least as close to those words as I could mumble. Who was in my room, anyway? Sometimes, when I had too much mezcal, Zach had to come and rouse me for work. My skull hurt like hell, but I didn't remember any drinking and even Zach wouldn't just sit there poking me in the head.

I opened my eyes as little as possible to find a pair of fuzzy shadows looming over me, and opened my eyes the rest of the way. Needed more information to figure this out.

I blinked a few times and the two shapes coalesced into a single man that I didn't recognize. He was daubing my aching head with a rag soaked in something. The man was in his thirties, with bronze skin and a head full of close-cropped brown hair. His clothes were made of some dark, stiff weave, but stippled with white where salt had been ground deep into the cloth.

Whitefinger!

I leapt into a fighting stance. At least, I tried to. My body actually gave a sort of limp jerk and I half sat up, but my hands were bound behind me with a rough rope.

"Get away from me!" I said out loud.

Control over my mouth had returned – at least as much control as I ever had over my mouth – and my body was starting to do *some* of the things I wanted it to. My brain was still lagging behind, though.

"Kiyu gave you a good bump on the head," the man told me. "I'm trying to take care of it. But if you'd prefer to die of dehydration or infection, I'll leave."

Smart-ass. I was the one who was supposed to say stuff like that. But I lay back down on what felt like a scratchy mat and after a moment, the Whitefinger took that as permission to continue tending to my pounding skull. He was using a salve made out of cactus pulp to coat the swollen gash on my head, but I recognized the small clay jar in his hand. I saw that same potter's mark every week when I went shopping – the medicine was from Angel City. I sure hadn't brought any with me, so the fuckers must have stole it.

Whitefinger thieves.

Apparently the man had almost been finished when I came to; it wasn't long before he moved away and squatted down next to Zach. He was bound, too, and still unconscious. My partner had a nasty purple tortoise-egg on his head that the Whitefinger was now smearing salve over. Zach groaned.

We were in some sort of basement. Storms had knocked down part of the floor above and its rubble filled half of the room, but the other side was dug out to expand the space. The corner where Zach and I were tied up contained several more woven mats and a small fire pit, currently cold and dark. A larger pit burned further down, where the basement had been enlarged and the smoke bent gently toward the slope of the fallen wall.

Good. That meant airflow, which meant that was our way out. If I could just get out of my ropes...

Four more Whitefingers sat gathered around the fire. Two of them held lizards speared on knives over the flames, but a pot hung above the fire, too. I smelled something cooking inside, but the scent wasn't familiar.

The girl was there. She had removed her hood and bandana to reveal her delicate, heart-shaped face, but she wasn't looking at me. Her attention was on one of the other Whitefingers. The guy *must* have been a mutant – he was even bigger than Zach. His skin was dark brown and his head shaved smooth. When he turned to look at the girl, I saw the scars. They were shiny and red and burned all over the side of his face, clear down his neck until they vanished under the collar of his cloak. The old burns turned the big guy's left eye into a permanently narrowed slit and his ear was gone, no more than a hole in the side of his head.

I strained to hear what the scarred man was saying. Zach made it hard to listen, groaning as the Whitefinger healer started rubbing stolen salve on the fulgurite cut under his arm, but I picked out some of the words.

"No," said One-Ear. "We should have turned back when Lekan died. We needed another yin. This is no job for a yang."

"Jacks, I can do this!" the girl protested. Kiyu, based on what my surly nurse had said. "Even I can hear the call. They *need* help!"

"We already knew that," Jacks said. I guess *One-Ear* wasn't actually his name. Pity. It was a good fit. "Did you help them?"

Jacks reached down beside him to stroke something. I craned my head as unobtrusively as I could and saw a brown and white animal lying at Jacks' side. A dog? As a... pet? I'd seen a couple in the wastes since joining the Greenguard, but they had a tendency to come up mutants and no one in their right mind kept an extra mouth to feed in a Whisperward.

"Well... no," Kiyu admitted. She had a soft, sweet voice that clashed with her indignation. "But I got the key, Jacks!"

"You killed three people retrieving that thing. And then got caught trying to use it."

"I got away," Kiyu said.

"And they followed you."

I'd been on the receiving end of enough chew-outs to know one when I heard it. Jacks was definitely in charge, and Kiyu was in trouble with her boss. I tried not to sympathize with the White-finger girl.

Jacks glanced pointedly past Kiyu to me and Zach. I almost looked away in time, but he saw I was awake and nodded, lowering his voice for whatever else he had to say to Kiyu. Not that I would have been able to hear much over Zach.

"Get away from me!" he growled.

Partners really do rub off on each other, I guess.

The Whitefinger man dropped his rag with a sigh, rolled his eyes and closed the lid of the clay jar. He walked back to the others, shaking his head. Jacks asked him a few questions, but the burn-scarred man kept watching us.

"Zee!" I whispered.

"What happened? Where are we?"

"We got our asses kicked, remember? We're in some kind of basement or buried building, I think. Exit's on the far side of that fire pit," I reported. I scanned the room as surreptitiously as I could manage – which wasn't very – but thankfully, what I was looking for was not hidden. "Our weapons and water are right by that fire."

Zach blinked bleary eyes and made his own inspection. His gaze paused on the fire, the exit, our gear and each Whitefinger. Cataloguing threats.

"Julia, we have to–" he started.

But Jacks had risen to his feet and was walking over to us. The dog stood and followed. It had two front legs on the right side, one right next to the other, but ambled along easily enough even with the extra limb, a long pink tongue lolling from its mouth. Jacks stopped a few yards back from us.

"You had better kill us now," Zach snarled. "Or I'm going to kill you."

The dog peeled its lips back from long, sharp white teeth and growled right back at Zach. Jacks made a downward motion with his hand and the dog silenced instantly, but kept its amber eyes glued to Zach.

"That girl is a dreameater and a murderer!" Zach said, glaring at Kiyu. "We're taking her back to the Whisperward to face justice for her crimes."

"She's inexperienced," Jacks answered. His voice was low and rumbling, almost like thunder. "What happened was an accident. Kiyu didn't mean to hurt anyone. You Greenguard are the ones who hunt *us*, not the other way around."

Zach wasn't buying it. "How can you harbor a damned dream-eater? Choose to keep those God has cursed? Or did she just gut your mind? Are you her puppet?"

Kiyu followed Jacks and stood a few feet behind him, to one side. She gave us a dark-eyed glare.

"Do I look like anyone's puppet?" Jacks asked.

"Then why do the Whitefingers tolerate psychics?" Zach's voice was still raw with anger, but he was sincere. "You don't have to live in the wastes like animals. You could have the safety and protection of the Whisperward. You could share in the grace of God."

Kiyu let out a short, sharp laugh. "We've seen how you live. Your Gardeners control a lot more than the greenhouses. And Green-guard like you kill anyone who doesn't fall in line. You would execute us just for taking what we need–"

"Thieves!" Zach snapped.

I remembered Gardener Matthew from the Whisperward in Bridge City, what he had said about the Whitefingers looting his fallen city. Zach was right.... But I had to agree with Kiyu's assess-ment of Whisperward life, too. Her take was a little over-simplified, but still more or less accurate. And not so different from my own judgment.

Damn it.

"Why were you trying to get into the Stormsphere?" I asked before Zach could make things worse. The irony of our sudden role reversal was not lost on me, but I wanted answers. "What did you do to the Tear in Bridge City?"

"We have harmed nothing and no one," Jacks said, then hesitated. "Except for that Gardener and his Greenguard in Angel City. We don't want to share your lives, but we don't want to destroy them."

"Can't you hear the voices in the sphere?" Kiyu asked. She was still angry, too, but seemed genuinely curious. "Can't anyone hear them calling?"

Liam. The boy told me that something had called to him, had wanted him to come to the Stormsphere. And I called him a liar. Was whatever summoned Liam the same as what Kiyu was talking about now?

Zach hadn't made the connection yet. "What?"

"You don't know?" asked Jacks. "You don't know what's inside the Stormspheres?"

Zach kept his face neutral, but I doubted that I was hiding anything. Poker's never been my game.

"No," I admitted. "No one knows what's inside the Stormspheres or how they work. Except maybe the Gardeners."

"Where do the Whispers come from?" asked Jacks.

"They're the voices of angels," Zach answered promptly.

"Only if angels can die," Jacks said.

"Die?" Zach and I echoed.

"We were too late in Bridge City," Kiyu told us. Now she actually sounded sad.

"There's... something in those things?" I asked. "And when it went silent, the Stormsphere stopped working. Then the storms came, right?"

Jacks and his dog watched us carefully, but Kiyu nodded. The Whitefingers' story made sense... If Jacks and Kiyu were telling us the truth. But it matched up with what I'd overheard of Thorn and Matthew's conversation, what Liam told us, and with what everyone knew and feared. The Whisperwards were failing.

I had always assumed that the Tears of God were pretty much solid. Just huge, glistening black all the way through, mysteriously constructed with the old science to repel the storms. But I'd already seen the Door and the passage inside. The Gardeners took offerings into the Stormspheres. Were there really angels in there? Or something else?

"They don't know," Jacks muttered, apparently to himself. He sounded frustrated. "They can't hear the distress call."

"They don't have yins," Kiyu said.

"Yins?" I asked. My curiosity was off and running again. It didn't give a shit about the ropes holding the rest of me back.

"Psychics with the power to listen and feel," Kiyu said. "Yangs can move things."

"Dreameaters," Zach simplified. "You can kill with your minds and you can steal thoughts. We kill creatures like you to protect the innocent."

"They don't steal anything," Kiyu snapped. "Yins just listen. And they don't even do that unless it's important."

"Our yins have heard a call for help coming from the Whisperwards," Jacks said, returning his attention to me and Zach. "It's been going on for a few years, but getting clearer and more urgent over the last few months. Whatever is inside your Tears of God, it's becoming desperate. The cry is now so loud and sharp that... Well, some of our yins can't stop listening and have lost their minds. Others have died."

"But the call is getting weaker, too," Kiyu went on. "Your Whispers may be desperate, but it hasn't been enough to save them. At least two of the Stormspheres have died and the remaining ones are failing."

"Sun and Bridge City," I said.

"And you fools hunt down the only people who could have told you what was happening," Jacks said.

The big wastelander stood abruptly and I couldn't help stiffening a little at his obvious anger. But Jacks just shook his head and the dog mirrored his gesture.

"We need to figure out what to do next. With Lekan dead, we don't have anyone who can commune with the Whispers. And we've got to figure out what to do with you two." The scarred man looked down at us for a moment and then turned away. "Diesel, watch them."

The five-legged dog gave a bark and sat back on his haunches to stare at us. Kiyu lingered a moment and then began to follow Jacks, but he held up his hand.

"You too, Kiyu," he said.

"What?" she protested. "Don't I get a say?"

"You've made enough mistakes already. Help Diesel watch the Greenguard."

Yeah, Kiyu was in the shithouse. The dog looked up at her with sad eyes. When Kiyu sighed and sat down, he laid his snout across her knee. I had a creeping suspicion about the animal.

"Is that dog a dreameater?" I asked.

"His name is Diesel. It's an ancient word that means *power*," Kiyu answered in clipped tones. "And he's not a *dreameater*. He's just a little psychic. Mostly a yin."

"That thing has the Mark of Caine," Zach said. "It's cursed."

"It's just another mutation," I argued. "Like rotting skin or tumors... or extra legs."

I glanced at Diesel's fifth leg. The dog had managed to fold it under himself along with the rest of his limbs without looking too awkward. Mutations cropped up every generation, even in humans, and they went out to the execution stakes, too. Their blood was contaminated, the Gardeners said. But most animals had a faster breeding cycle than humans, so they mutated much more rapidly.

Tenders in the scale and bug farms had to keep careful watch and cull their herds often.

"Don't listen to them, Diesel," Kiyu told the dog. "What do they know?"

She scratched the dog behind the ear, suddenly reminding me that my hands were bound and I had no ability to scratch. Naturally, a fierce itch promptly manifested on my nose. Kiyu remained silent, looking offended, and I realized too late that she was a dreameater... a *yang*... too, and that I'd pretty much called her a rotting mutant.

Jacks sat with the other three Whitefingers, in a tight circle around their fire. The roasting lizards were done and they passed around the food. I noticed that a few lizards had been set aside. Dinner for Kiyu and Diesel, probably. And maybe Zach and me... if they decided not to kill us.

Which didn't seem likely.

"Are you alright, Zee?" I asked. I pointed with my chin as best I could to the wound on his head and the gash under his arm.

"Yeah. Rosy, just..." His eyes flicked over to Kiyu.

I was unsettled, too. What the Whitefingers were saying about their yins and yangs was a little different than what the Gardeners told us in Sunday school, but I kept thinking back to Byron's body, riddled with glass shards. Kiyu did that. There was no doubt that psychics were dangerous.

We sat there in silence. I tried to listen in on Jacks' conversation, but our captors were speaking too quietly. Kiyu busied herself petting Diesel. Zach tensed once, flexing his powerful arms against the rope around his wrists. The dog's ears pricked forward and he gave a single sharp, warning bark. Jacks looked up from his council, then turned away again when Zach relaxed and Diesel settled down.

I couldn't take the silence anymore. "Why did you kill Byron?"

"Byron?" Kiyu asked.

"The Gardener. That was his name."

"I... was only trying to get the key," Kiyu said. She scratched Diesel behind one furry ear. "Lekan listened into the Gardeners' minds until he learned about the keys. There were only three men who carried them. We picked out your guy. Byron. He spent a lot of time alone in the greenhouses. Working on the flowers, Lekan told me. We just had to take his key and then we could get into the Stormsphere and see what was making the psychic cry."

"What happened?" I asked. "Something went wrong, didn't it?"

"We were coming back here to report in with Jacks and figure out how to get the key when Lekan got bit by a snake. It was a bad one and Lekan... he died. We're a week out from the warren here and I convinced Jacks that we didn't have to go home. I told him that I could get the key and use it."

Kiyu's voice cracked as she spoke and her dark eyes glistened with tears that she refused to shed. I believed Kiyu that she hadn't meant to kill Byron and the Blackthumbs. It didn't change the fact that she *had* killed them, but it was a different story than the evil Whitefinger monster coming to murder good people in their sleep. I thought about the Whitefingers that Zach and I had hunted and killed over the years. What if they hadn't been there in our city to hurt anyone? Just to get things like medicine and information? And what about the dreameaters? What if they were all like Liam?

"So I went back in to finish the job," Kiyu said. "But someone outside saw me. He shouted and I panicked. I shattered the greenhouse. It was an accident. I really didn't mean to do... that."

"Why don't the Whitefingers kill dreameaters?" Zach asked, speaking to Kiyu for the first time since Jacks walked away. "Your powers are clearly dangerous. Look what happens when you're scared."

"The warren needs all of us," Kiyu answered. "Yins and yangs and everyone else. I protect the warren from the mutants. A lot like you, actually. Except I don't kill babies."

"Hey," I protested, but I didn't have any other arguments to follow up with. She wasn't wrong.

"You have your weapons. So do I," Kiyu said.

Zach grunted, grumpy about being compared to a dreameater. Diesel cocked one ear toward my partner, but apparently decided that he wasn't going to do anything violent. How much of that was animal instinct and how much was the dreameater dog's psionic ability? I wished that I still had the Halo, but Zach delivered it back to Gregory days ago.

Oh well... The polished polymer probably wouldn't have survived hauling Zach up from his fall into the fulgurite tube, much less the sandstorm.

Kiyu was still watching me. "Can I ask you a question?"

"Can't you just read my mind?" I asked.

"No, I'm mostly a yang. My yin powers aren't very strong. You would have to be feeling something pretty intensely for me to sense it and I can't really read individual thoughts. But I can pick up a grown man and throw him like a ball." Kiyu smirked at Zach, who shifted uncomfortably. "So, can I ask my question?"

I nodded.

"Why do you call us *Whitefingers*?" Kiyu asked.

"Seriously?" I asked. "*That's* what you want to know?"

"I've been to Bridge City and Sun City, but both of them were abandoned. Angel City is the first Whisperward I've ever seen that was still inhabited. The people there talk a lot about the White-fingers. Why do you call us that?"

"Uh... Because of your white fingers," I said.

Kiyu lifted her small hands, looking at them. Her skin was a light gold color and she had surprisingly nice nails.

"Your gloves," I clarified.

Kiyu took them from her belt and examined the salt ground into the cloth. She smiled a little. "Okay, fair enough. But why are you called *Blackthumbs*? Your gloves aren't black."

"That's not our official name. We're really called Greenguard," I explained. "Blackthumb is just a nickname because we're soldiers. It's what we say when someone's good at fighting and killing. You've got a fairly black thumb, too."

Kiyu's high cheeks colored and I couldn't tell if she was flattered or insulted.

"Whitefingers. Blackthumbs. Greenguard," she said. "Don't you get confused with all those names?"

"Stop talking to her, Julia," Zach warned me. "She'll get into your head."

"She said she can't do that, Zee." I wasn't really sure I believed the Whitefinger girl, but I said it anyway. "Hey... Kiyu, right?"

The Whitefinger nodded, regarding me warily. So far, Kiyu had been speaking fairly freely, probably more freely than she should have with a pair of prisoners. She was actually answering my questions and I didn't want to waste this opportunity. I struggled to get my bound hands down to my hip pocket. No luck. Diesel lifted his head and sniffed, but the dog must have sensed that I wasn't trying to escape.

"I have something. It's in my pocket and I can't reach," I said.

Kiyu's expression darkened. "I'm not untying you."

"I know. Can you grab it for me?"

Kiyu stared at me. Hard. Her dark brown eyes were flecked with gold and amber. I braced myself, wondering if all the stories about dreameaters were true after all and if I had just set myself up for a terminal brain scramble.

Rosy. Good one, Julia.

But I didn't feel anything and Kiyu didn't seem able to read my thoughts – she looked to Diesel for confirmation. The dog sniffed at me again and his furry tail thumped against the basement floor.

"Fine," Kiyu said. I wasn't sure if she was talking to me or to the dog.

Kiyu approached cautiously and knelt down. I stretched my hands away in what I hoped was a reassuring gesture and rolled my hip up toward her. The Whitefinger girl slipped her hand into the front pocket of my fatigues. Her slender, delicate fingers slid down my thigh. I bit my lip as a hot shiver shot along my spine and tightened my throat. I really hoped that she wasn't yin or whatever enough to sense that.

Kiyu felt around for a moment, then touched on the scrap of lace I had found at the shattered greenhouse. Her fingers curled around it and pulled the lace slowly out of my pocket. Kiyu's eyes lit up and she smiled.

"Is it yours?" I asked.

"Yes," Kiyu said. She ran her thumb gently over the intricately coiled and knotted thread. "It's mine."

"What's it for? Does it help you control your powers? Or enhance them? Did it belong to someone important?"

Kiyu looked uncomfortable and wouldn't meet my eye. Maybe it was some sort of Whitefinger secret. God knew the Gardeners had theirs, and we had our own secrets in the Greenguard, too. I wasn't about to explain Halos to Kiyu, regardless of how hot I was feeling between the legs with her this close.

"I found it in Bridge City," she said so quietly I had to lean in closer than was entirely comfortable or wise to catch the words. "It's... pretty."

Kiyu pulled open a pouch hanging from her belt and carefully slipped the lace inside. I heard other things clinking together and craned my head to see a marble, a ribbon, maybe a colorful piece of broken glass and a folded piece of paper that looked like it had been drawn on.

Kiyu pulled away, blushing again. I couldn't help noticing how pretty the pink flush looked on her. I was still trying to phrase my next question while ignoring dirty looks from Zach when Jacks returned. Firelight threw the Whitefinger's long shadow over us.

Hastily, Kiyu closed her belt pouch and stood. Diesel padded to Jacks' side.

"When the storm is over–" Jacks said.

Here it comes. We're dead. Sorry, Zee.

"–We'll take you within sight of the Angel City walls and release you."

Unless that was some very strange euphemism for killing us, it wasn't the decision I had expected. I risked a sidelong peek at Zach, who wore a confused look that probably matched my own.

"Release us...?" Zach asked. I wondered if he remembered his own threat about killing Jacks if the big guy didn't do it first. "Why?"

"This isn't personal. That Gardener's death was an accident. We just came to find out what's going on and help. The Whispers' call is hurting our yins and their failure is turning your people into homeless refugees."

Jacks crouched down to look me in the eye. I wondered where that scar had come from, but now didn't seem like the time to ask.

"I need you to carry a message back to the Gardeners," Jacks said. "Tell them we had nothing to do with Bridge City. Tell them what I told you, and that whatever lives inside their Stormsphere is dying."

THE WHITEFINGERS FED US. Literally, since our hands remained tied awkwardly behind us. The roasted fence lizards were familiar, but their soup was strange – salty and tangy and full of green strips of a plant I didn't recognize. It left an odd taste in my mouth long after I had swallowed.

"What is it?" Zach asked skeptically.

"Fish broth and seaweed," said the Whitefinger crouched in front of us.

"What and what?" I asked.

The man just shook his head and offered me another spoonful of soup. I glanced over at Kiyu. She was next to the fire again, talking to Jacks. Probably getting filled in on the discussion she had missed. I got the feeling that Jacks and his group were a bit like Zach and me right now, operating alone for the moment and making their own decisions. They would eventually report back to someone important, though. That was always how it worked… The important people didn't do field work. They stayed safe in their offices and sent other people to die.

I considered asking our Whitefinger server to switch out for Kiyu. Being spoon-fed by a beautiful girl sounded like a lot more fun, but even I knew how stupid an idea that was. The soup wasn't so bad that I wanted to eat someone's boot instead. I try to save my stupid remarks for the really important stuff, thanks.

The Whitefingers arranged their mats near us and the smaller fire pit, but far enough away to remain outside our striking range. They lit the second fire and then smothered it down to coals to keep the basement warm without choking us all with smoke. Zach eyed the wastelanders cautiously, but Jacks ordered a rotation of watches and even with his eyes closed, Diesel kept one ear cocked toward us throughout the night.

Having already been unconscious for several hours – to say nothing of being bound in the semi-darkness and surrounded by people that my mother repeatedly warned me ate children – I didn't exactly fall right asleep. I lay uncomfortably on my side, listening to the hiss of breath all around me. Zach was still awake too, I was certain.

I tried not to wonder if Kiyu was asleep yet or when it would be her turn at watch. The short, dark-eyed wastelander girl was beautiful. I could admit that. But she did kill three people, even if it was an accident. And she was a thief. She stole Gardener Byron's key and tried to break into a place that even eternally questioning and back-talking Julia Reed felt was sacrosanct. And Kiyu had stolen all those baubles in her little pouch, too. I wondered why she kept them. Because they were pretty? It was stupid, childish.

Kiyu really had an amazing smile... But she also hit me on the head. No pretty smile or lovely eyes could make up for the huge welt on my temple, right?

Right.

Best to start thinking about what the hell we were going to tell Gregory. He wouldn't believe any of this. At least Zach would back me up. He would never lie and was too smart to totally ignore what Jacks had told us. Zach might not like it – and I doubted that he had noticed how beautiful Kiyu was – but the Whitefingers' story lined up with the one Liam told and everything Gardener Matthew said about Bridge City.

I tried to imagine a way to recount this story without sounding crazy, but by the time I fell asleep, it still sounded like a dream.

———

I WAS WOKEN BY A WARM, wet tongue stroking my ear. I groaned and reached out, but my hand lurched to a sudden and painful stop behind me, finally jerking me fully awake. Diesel looked down at me, then gave my ear a sniff and another quick lick. My face burned and it wasn't because of the mutant dog's drool.

"Diesel, stop that," Jacks said. The dog barked once and then did his strange five-legged scamper back to his master.

The Whitefingers were all awake and getting ready to leave. The fire pits were extinguished, their mats rolled up and laid against the wall. Our captors wound their faces in long cloths and cinched cloaks around their shoulders. One of them gave his metal spear a sharp twist and it came apart in the middle. Carefully, he blew sand out of the threads and then screwed the pieces back together. So that was how Kiyu had concealed her spear in Angel City.

The tall Whitefinger who had tended our injuries yesterday walked over to me and Zach. "Time to go. Get up."

He had to help me stand. Being upright sent the blood draining suddenly from my head and I grew dizzy. When it came surging back to my brain, the knot on my temple throbbed. I took a few deep breaths until I felt slightly steadier on my feet.

Zach was doing better and showed no sign of my wobbliness. He tensed, shifting his feet a little wider. I knew he was contemplating jumping the Whitefinger. Even with his hands tied, Zach was a good fighter and I had no doubts that he could kill a man with his feet alone. But there were five of them and a dog. They were armed and one of them was still a dreameater. A yang, which

Kiyu said meant she could scoop up the rubble and stone us to death without getting her nice nails dirty.

I widened my stance, too, just in case Zach went for it. I thought it was a bad idea, but he was my partner and you *always* back your partner's play. Thankfully, Zach seemed to decide that since they were returning us to the Whisperward anyway, escape wasn't necessary. Instead, he only cleared his throat and coughed. The Whitefinger gave us some water from our own canteens and then circled around behind us.

"We can't let you know where our hiding holes are," he said almost apologetically.

With that, he pulled a bag over my head and I heard Zach grunt as the same happened to him. A hand took my arm in a firm grasp. It felt small enough to belong to Kiyu... or was that just wishful thinking? Whoever it was, I let them lead me out of the buried building.

The Whitefingers didn't remove the bags from our heads after climbing up the sloping tunnel of their basement outpost. Zach and I stumbled over invisible stones and our feet dragged through the sand. I felt hot sunlight against the back of my neck, but could see nothing. We had to trust that the Whitefingers knew what they were doing and wouldn't accidentally drop us down any holes not of their own making. Someone always held on to us, but we made slow, painstaking progress.

There wasn't much conversation. I didn't know if the Whitefingers were usually silent when they roamed the Pacific Desert or if it was just because of us. The only time anyone spoke was a few hours out, when Diesel barked out a harsh warning. It was followed by a noise like pebbles skittering down a hole, the unmistakable rattle of a snake. It sounded big.

"Quiet," Jacks ordered. Diesel stopped barking, but I could still hear the mutant dog growling deep in his throat.

"Don't run," whispered someone in front of me.

"Slowly," Jacks said.

Kiyu tugged my arm, moving me backward. I took cautious steps in the direction she pulled, but with the sack over my head, I was blind. My heel hit a rock and I stumbled. The snake hissed and rattled again, sounding more like tumbling stones than pebbles this time. Yeah, that was definitely a big one.

"Kiyu?" Jacks asked.

"I've got it," she said. "Back me up."

She released my arm and another hand quickly replaced hers. My new escort held me tightly, but I didn't complain. They would be my only defense if the snake struck.

I strained to listen, trying to see with my ears, and heard Kiyu's light footsteps move forward, closer to the snake. Sand ground beneath its scales as the huge beast shifted. Then there was a loud, heavy-sounding thump that I could make little sense of. I heard running feet and the snake hissed savagely, then its tail rattled as it thrashed.

The air tasted of dust and my own sweat. I heard grunting and heavy breathing, and then the unmistakable sound of sharp things piercing softer ones.

"Hold it," someone grunted, the only words spoken during the entire battle.

My captor's hand tensed on my arm, but didn't jerk me away or release his grip, so I guessed that Kiyu and the others had killed the snake.

"Peter, Ahmet," Jacks said. "Once that beast finishes squirming, check it over. If it's tainted, catch up with us. If there's anything good, take it back down the hole."

"Come on," Kiyu told me.

Her small hand replaced the larger one on my arm once more. I wanted to ask her what had happened, but then we were moving again and I was too busy concentrating on my footing to talk.

––––––

"THIS IS CLOSE ENOUGH," Jacks said.

As best I could guess, about five hours had passed since we set out. Someone yanked the bag off my head and I had to blink a lot to adjust to the sudden light. Where the hell were my goggles?

Kiyu picked at the knotted rope around my wrists for a moment and then my hands were free. I gasped as my arms finally came under my own power once more and rolled my aching shoulders in slow circles. The joints burned. Zach rubbed his wrists and glared at the Whitefingers. The one who untied his bonds was backing swiftly toward Jacks with one hand on the spear jutting from under his cloak.

The burn-scarred Whitefinger leader held a tangle of straps and gear in each hand. He threw it all toward us and our belts, canteens, goggles and bandanas thumped into the sand at our feet, but Jacks had gotten the two jumbles of equipment mixed up. I handed Zach's stuff over to him and took mine. But our knives and cross-bows were gone.

"What about our weapons?" Zach asked.

"Sorry," Jacks answered curtly. "We can't trust you. You're still dangerous."

But the Whitefinger did toss back Zach's hat. My partner caught it out of the air and frowned suspiciously before brushing the dust off the wide black brim and settling it down over his head again.

"There's your Whisperward," Jacks said. "And take a look at the storm line."

He pointed over our shoulders and I turned to find myself at the edge of the ancient city. I squinted. Was Jacks right? The border between the ruins and the Whisperward's protection looked blurred, like the storm damage was closer to the walls than before. Beyond them were the tall, lumpy city walls and then the more orderly buildings of my home.

The Stormsphere rose up over it all, still utterly smooth and polished black. It was hard to believe that *anything* could harm that obsidian immensity, but...

When I turned back, the Whitefingers were already fading away into the dusty haze once more. One of them – the smallest one, if my imagination wasn't just trying to give me fodder for fantasy – stopped and looked back over her shoulder at us for a moment. But then they were gone. Within hours, even their tracks would be only memories.

"I don't trust them, Julia," Zach said.

We watched the ruins where the Whitefingers had disappeared and then turned toward Angel City. I took a long drink from my canteen. My mouth still tasted like dust.

"Specifically or on general principle?" I asked.

"Both," Zach said. "Specifically, why not talk to the Gardeners themselves?"

"Zee, our job is to kill them. On sight. We don't exactly give Whitefingers the chance to talk."

I didn't really want to think about that too much. It made even the heroic parts of being a Blackthumb feel like birth control duty.

"I suppose not," Zach admitted. "But there's something else going on here."

"Yeah," I agreed. But what I didn't say was that I was starting to think it was happening on our side of the wall. "That storm last night looks like it came closer to the city than before."

"Let's get moving," Zach said.

We did, breaking into a trot as we neared the city gates. I waved up to the Blackthumbs on the wall with actual enthusiasm. After a day away from the Whisperward, I would even have hugged Woods if he would open the gates for us.

"Who's there?" someone shouted from on top of the wall.

"It's us, damn it!" I shouted back.

"Zachary Dias and Julia Reed," Zach supplied more helpfully.

"We thought you were dead!" called out the man on the wall. "There was a storm."

"Then let us in and plant us in the orchard already," I shouted. "I'm about ready to start pissing sand out here!"

The city gates ground slowly open. I didn't recognize the Blackthumb who greeted us, but as I may have mentioned, I wasn't very popular among the Greenguard. I didn't have a lot of friends, but I was about ready to kiss the ground when we hurried through into the city.

"It's the middle of the day," Zach said as the gates began to swing closed behind us. "Why were the gates closed?"

"No new refugees today," answered a tall woman in olive drab.

The urge to make out with Angel City passed. We had chased Kiyu through dozens of refugees coming in the day before. Zach and I traded an unhappy look. There should have been more of them today. But the storm...

There would be other refugees, I reminded myself. Yesterday's storm couldn't have killed them all. Before long, even more new people would be piling into the Whisperward.

The other Greenguard didn't linger to talk to us. There may not have been any refugees outside the gate that morning, but there were still plenty inside, piling up in the streets of Angel City. I saw one Blackthumb with his hand on someone's head, the Halo image turning green as the scan came up clear. The woman who had let us in grabbed a young man and inspected his hands closely for salt.

Zach and I made directly for the base, still wearing our blood- and sand-stained fatigues. There were stares and questions and regulation concerns, but we waved them off and headed straight for Gregory's office.

"Dias! Reed! I can't believe you're back," Gregory said when we came through his door. He came around his desk and actually shook our hands. "When you went after that dreameater, I figured the heat had driven you both mad!"

Zach shot me a look with a lot of raised eyebrow in it, but didn't actually agree with Gregory.

"No, sir," he said.

I stood at a tired mutant version of attention and let Zach lay out the details of our chase, tracking Kiyu and then our strange captivity. Gregory asked some questions, but surprisingly few. Mostly, he just listened and drummed his fingers against the wood of his desk.

"That's... quite a story," he said in an even voice when Zach finished. Without Thorn here to give his strings a tug, I suspected that the Greenguard chief had no idea what to make of our tale. "You've both been through a lot."

"You'll tell Thorn, though?" I asked. Maybe a touch more intensely than was strictly necessary, but it was important. "He needs to know about what the Whitefingers said."

"Yes." Gregory nodded his answer just as emphatically as I had asked the question. "I will tell the High Gardener. I'll go see him at once."

"Thank you, sir," Zach said.

"You two go get some rest. Tomorrow, we'll issue both of you new weapons. And try not to lose them this time." Gregory flashed us the ghost of a real smile. "Dismissed."

———

ZACH BADE me a weary farewell in the hallway of our building, but I didn't let him leave until he promised to get that slice under his arm looked at. Zach assured me that he was fine, of course, but agreed to have it checked out.

"Just to shut you up, Julia," he told me firmly. "Not because I'm worried."

"Get your ass moving. I'm too tired to stand here arguing with you, Zee."

Zach smiled and nodded, then turned away down his hallway. I practically crawled past Silva leaning out her door to ask me what had happened, grunted wordlessly at her and went into my apartment. I was hungry, but before I could even think about digging up something to eat, I had to get clean. Dry cactus pulp was clumped in my hair and my clothes were saturated with dust and sweat.

I checked the water in my bath jug. It was about half full. Good enough to get the job done. I stripped out of my boots and crumpled fatigues, throwing my sweat-soaked underwear on top of the pile and promising myself that I would take care of the laundry later. I untied my tangled auburn braid and stepped into the washtub, then poured cool water over my head. I worked my fingers through the knots of my hair and pried loose bits of dried salve the Whitefingers had applied. My scalp stung around the bump, but it felt good to wash the grit out of it. I poured another stream of water over myself and watched it turn brown as it ran down my legs, but leaving my skin cleaner beneath.

I finished off the jug and then dripped my way across the apartment to my water barrel and refilled it. I was going to spend most of my barter this month – vegetables and fruit from the Houses that were the Greenguard's pay – to get more water, but I'd grown up on cheap crickmeal and saguaro. I would manage.

I returned to the washtub and inspected my nails. They were filthy, with what seemed like an entire storm's worth of dust crusted beneath them. I scrubbed my nails and then the rest of my body until I glowed pink all over. The brush stung my storm-abraded skin and the rope burns around my wrists, but it felt good. Purifying, somehow.

But thinking of the Whitefinger's ropes reminded me of Kiyu, too. The slender girl was certainly not what I had expected from a Whitefinger or a dreameater. She was young, for one thing. I had always imagined Whitefingers as storm-weathered old men with skins burnt snakeskin-rough by a lifetime in the desert. It made sense that there were women among the Whitefingers, too, and that they would have children, or else the wastelanders would have disappeared generations ago.

Kiyu was a far cry from my craggy and dangerous image of a Whitefinger. If my mother ever said that a dreameater like *her* might eat me, I wouldn't have been nearly so frightened. I couldn't help laughing a little at myself, but I felt my nipples stiffen, too. I looked down and found my hand cupping my right breast. I didn't remember telling it to do that. But as the water beaded on my skin and thoughts of Kiyu refused to leave me alone, I let the scrub brush fall into the muddy bottom of the washtub and pressed both hands to my chest. I let my hands trace the curves of my chest and linger on the hardened peaks.

Kiyu's sleek hair and dark, angled eyes were as clear in my thoughts as if she had been standing right there in front of me. I remembered her throwing herself on top of me when the storm hit, tackling me away from her spear-turned-lightning rod. Kiyu was small, but I had felt her muscular and lithe body against me as we fought for my knife. She was determined and energetic, beautiful and deadly, all crammed into one tight, tiny body.

I picked up the jug and poured the last of the water over my body. My hand followed the flow down the slopes of my breasts, over my stomach, and to the soft, heated juncture of my legs. My cunny was slick, the lips parted like those of a blooming orchid.

Kiyu was beautiful, so much like the baubles she collected. Why did she do that? I truly wanted to believe that it was some childish habit or, even better, a thieving compulsion that proved true everything that the Gardeners told us about the Whitefingers.

But no, the horror stories I had always heard didn't seem to fit Kiyu. Not many people bothered to look for beauty in this dusty, sand-blasted world. They went about life with their heads down, just praying to get through the next day, the next storm. The Gardeners had their bright, beautiful flowers... But they kept all those blossoms locked away, drinking up half the city's water for our great leaders' mysterious rituals.

My hand didn't care about my self-righteous rambling or confused thoughts, though. It knew exactly what it wanted and traced the petals of my sex without indecision. My finger slipped inside and my brain just gave up trying to talk sense. Helplessly, I let the moment take me, let myself picture Kiyu's heart-shaped face. I moved to the small bud at the apex of my cunny and caressed it in swift strokes, biting my lip against moans that threatened to become cries. My other hand squeezed my breast and pinched at my nipple, reaching for the peak.

And found it. My climax seared through me and hot, tight shudders shot through my body. I cried out once, hard and loud.

I came down slowly, panting and feeling even more confused than before. I distracted myself by scraping the last of the water from my skin, trying to avoid lingering on my breasts or between my legs, lest I go back for seconds. When I was done I dressed quickly and went in search of food. Yes, that was what I needed. Dinner.

I REMEMBERED to close the curtains this time, but it wasn't long after dawn that the heavy drumbeat of bootsteps woke me. It was incredibly rude to just barge into someone's home without announcing yourself, but Greenguard claimed the sole exception to this social rule, so I wasn't surprised to find several of my fellow Blackthumbs storming into my apartment.

Well, actually... I was surprised. Very. What the hell were they doing here?

Five crossbows were cocked and loaded, braced against tensed shoulders, and steel arrowheads flashed in the narrow beam of morning light that knifed between the curtains. I kicked my way out from beneath my sheets with my gut knotted and blood rushing in my ears. I jumped to my feet, still in my underwear.

"What the hell is going on?" I asked.

Woods led the Greenguard pack, his fingers so tight on his crossbow that his knuckles had turned white. He looked me slowly up and down, but I wouldn't give him the satisfaction of blushing under his inspection.

"We have to take you to the High Gardener," Woods announced. He actually seemed a little sorry about it.

"All he had to do was ask Gregory. He would have sent me out to Thorn before breakfast," I said. I *really* didn't like all of the crossbows pointing at me. "Must be important. Do you mind waiting outside while I get dressed?"

"Sorry, Reed," Woods answered. He sounded less apologetic this time.

The other Blackthumbs stood over me with crossbows cocked and ready while I changed. I felt Woods' eyes crawling over my skin like ants, but the other Greenguard watched me more warily – like Zach or I watched parents during birth control, to see if they would do something stupid.

Absently, I wondered how the Garzas were doing. Where was their baby girl now? Zach and I never actually went back to count their kids again.

I had no intentions of giving Woods a show, so I dressed as quickly as I could. I tied my hair into a quick ponytail and reached for my belt. My knife was sheathed there and I moved toward it slowly, just in case someone was feeling jumpy. Which turned out to be a good idea.

"Leave it!" barked one of the other Greenguard.

"No belt? Really?" I asked.

I wished that I'd learned the guy's name, but I had always preferred to keep my own company or Zach's. I guess I could have made a better effort to be popular among my fellow Blackthumbs, or at least talk to them once in a while. But it seemed a little late for that now.

"Fine," I said. "But it's on your head if my pants fall down in front of Thorn."

They hurried me from my apartment without even letting me grab my goggles and bandana. Woods led the way and three more Blackthumbs walked just behind me. I swore I could feel the tension in their bowstrings. I threw them a smile over my shoulder, but my heart was pounding. What the hell was going on? I applied my considerable intellect to the situation, but couldn't manage to come up with anything reasonable that wasn't totally stormy. Thorn had to be *really* angry with me. Had I said something? Something worse than usual?

I slit my eyes half shut against the bright white daylight as my escort propelled me along the street toward the Greenguard base and the Houses. Ranks of Blackthumbs were training in the base yard, but they stopped to stare as I passed. I tried waving once, but the other Blackthumbs glared suspiciously, some making the sign of the teardrop over their chests or turning quickly away, unable to meet my eye.

My heart sank another inch. Even I wasn't *that* unpopular.

The Whispers rose up around me, flitting through my thoughts as we marched past the Greenguard base and then into the Houses. Were they really calling for help? If so, I couldn't hear them. But I was growing increasingly certain that I was the one who needed help right now.

My oppressively silent escort led me up the smooth white steps and through the columns of the Gardeners' building. Their boots rang off the polished stone floor and then the stairs as we began to climb. No Gardener meant no elevator, I guessed. I tried to reassure myself that whatever Thorn wanted, he clearly wasn't in that much of a hurry. But another part of me pointed out that maybe the High Gardener just wanted me tired by the time we arrived.

My legs ached as we climbed the last flight of stairs to Thorn's office and I took some small satisfaction that Woods was breathing a hell of a lot harder than I was. He didn't spend much time actually running down Whitefingers or hunting mutants through the dangerous ruins between the city walls and the edge of the Stormsphere's protection.

But my heart plunged right through the floor when Woods finally prodded me into Thorn's office. Zach was already there, down on his knees with his head bowed. When he looked up at me, his dusky skin was sallow and there was a bright red mark on his cheek that was darkening into a nasty-looking bruise. Five more Blackthumbs stood surrounding him, crossbows pointed down at my partner.

The flowers potted all around Thorn's office, even the colorful paintings on the walls – none of it seemed beautiful anymore. The air in here was too damp, too close and the plants felt alien. The floral scent was too thick and too sweet.

Woods shoved me down to my knees beside Zach. I understood *me* getting into trouble, even if I wasn't really clear on what sort of trouble it was yet. But Zach? He was the perfect Blackthumb. What could he possibly have done wrong?

The door opened behind us and Thorn swept into the lush office. His robes swirled around his tall, gaunt body like black storm sands closing in around an execution post. Gregory hurried in after him, brushing at the front of his own robes with shaking fingers. His hands left sweat stains on the dark cloth.

"Tell me about your meeting with the Whitefingers," Thorn commanded as he seated himself behind the flower-strewn desk.

"Damn it, I would have come if you just asked," I said. "No need to march us here under guard, Thorn."

"Tell me about your meeting with the Whitefingers," the High Gardener repeated.

"We didn't meet them, sir," Zach answered. "They captured us."

"And how exactly were you captured?"

"We were outnumbered," Zach said. "A storm was coming down on us."

His voice was unsteady. Weariness and anger were all jumbled up with embarrassment and something else I couldn't quite read. Was Zach actually frightened?

"And what did the Whitefingers say when they took you in?" Thorn asked.

"They didn't take us in. We were *captured*," Zach growled again.

"They knocked us out," I said. "One of Whitefingers admitted to the murders of Byron and the two Greenguard. She said she was sorry and they sent us back with a warning."

"Ah," Thorn murmured. He sounded satisfied, like we were just getting to his favorite part. "A warning. The Whitefingers sent you to deliver their threat."

"No!" I barely managed to keep myself from adding *you idiot.* Our situation was bad enough and I hadn't been exactly polite so far. "The Whitefingers only wanted to help. Their yin dreameaters heard a call from something inside the Stormsphere. They don't know what's in there. But whatever it is, it's dying. And you know what happens when the Whispers go silent, Thorn!"

Around us, the Greenguard shuffled their feet and muttered. Bridge and Sun City had already met that fate. If the Tear failed in Angel City, the closest Whisperward was Boulder City and that was a very long journey through some of the worst storm-torn lands.

"No doubt that was why those Whitefingers were trying to gain access to our Tear of God," Thorn said, nodding. "To silence the angelic voices inside."

"Weren't you listening, asshole?" I asked. I half rose to my feet, but Woods shoved me down again and I felt the cold steel of his crossbow against the back of my neck. "The Whitefingers didn't do anything to the Bridge City sphere! The Whispers were begging for help and they were only trying to find out why!"

"And who told you that?" asked Thorn.

"The Whitefingers," I admitted.

Thorn smiled indulgently. I knew that smile. It was the one I had gotten all my life in Sunday school, when I gave the Gardeners my best but still wrong answer. At least, the answer that they *said* was wrong...

"Of course the Whitefingers told you that," Thorn said. "A lie which, if we were foolish enough to believe, would let them right into the heart of our Whisperward."

"I don't think they were lying," I argued. "We kill all of our dreameaters... our psychics and there's no one left to hear the call. Liam did, and he was trying to tell us that before we gave him to the storm. That's why he was in the Houses the night Byron was killed. Something is dying inside the Stormsphere and we have to help it!"

I looked to Zach, silently begging him to back me up. Thorn watched my partner, too.

"Sir, we've been to the edge of the 'Ward. We've seen the storm line," Zach said. His big shoulders were as taut as a bowstring. "It's moving. Not quickly, but the perimeter *is* shrinking. The Stormsphere is losing its power, High Gardener. The Whitefingers are right about that."

Zach drew a deep breath to finish.

"I think they were telling us the truth."

I let out a sigh of relief. Zach wasn't a mouthy little problem like me. Thorn knew that and so did Gregory. Zach would always do what was best for Angel City. He was a faithful man and just about worshiped the Gardeners, but the safety of our people was the one thing he cared about more than their approval. I looked up at Thorn. That *had* to be enough to satisfy the High Gardener.

Thorn stood. He hung his head and shook it slowly, sadly. He put some real pain into his resonant voice.

"The Whitefingers have compromised two of our best," he told Gregory and his office full of Blackthumbs. "The dreameaters have devoured their minds and very souls, filling them with lies and turned them against us."

"What?" I cried. "What the hell are you saying?"

"No!" Zach tried to rise, but four Blackthumbs held him down. "No one is controlling us, sir! We're only telling you the truth!"

"Is that not exactly what your Whitefinger masters would have you say?" Thorn said gravely. "Until all of the Whitefingers are dead and gone to dust, we can never be certain that anyone is cleansed of their ungodly influence."

Gregory nodded along with Thorn. "I'm real sorry about this, Dias, but it must be done. The High Gardener is right. You're compromised."

"This is bugshit!" I shouted. "We're not under anyone's control!"

I jumped to my feet. Fuck it. Nothing I said mattered anymore. Thorn would only twist every word and claim that some Whitefinger dreameater made me say it. I had no proof. Neither did Thorn, but he was the High Gardener. I was just an annoying problem that finally had a permanent solution. The other Blackthumbs descended on me and seized my arms before I could hurl myself at Thorn. They grabbed Zach and hauled him to his feet, too.

"You're lying, Thorn!" I shouted.

"High Gardener," Zach said only a little more calmly. "Please! We're telling you the truth. We're innocent! I swear it to God on His Tears."

"Yes," Thorn told him. "You are innocent, my child. And the greatest evil of the dreameaters and their Whitefinger masters is how they use the innocent as their tools," Thorn said. He turned to the Greenguard. "Take them out of the city. Let the storms cleanse them and return them to God."

"The Whispers are dying, you idiot," I screamed. "You're killing everyone, Thorn! Everyone in Angel City is going to die if you don't listen to us!"

Thorn's face reddened. "Enough!" he shouted right back at me. "*We* are the chosen of God, charged with tending His garden. *No one* will drive us back into the waste to wander like beasts, homeless and at the mercy of mutant abominations!"

"Sir, please!" Zach begged. "Don't do this!"

"Take them," Thorn ordered.

The Greenguard hauled us toward the door, but I stomped down on the nearest foot. The Blackthumb it belonged to probably didn't feel much through his boot, but it made him stumble and I twisted in his grasp. I drove my knee up between another man's legs and felt the satisfying double impact of my knee in his balls and then smashing into bone. His hands went slack on my arm and I ripped free.

"You're a fucking prick, Thorn," I said.

It seemed important the High Gardener know that before I ran, but then something cracked painfully across the back of my head and darkness swallowed the world. Not again...

———

WHEN THE DARKNESS RECEDED, I was watching my own feet hover a few inches off the ground. It took me several moments to understand that I was being held up and dragged through the dusty streets of Angel City by two other Blackthumbs. Collecting my scattered thoughts was like trying to clutch at sand that kept crumbling away. My head throbbed back and forth between the new lump and the older welt Kiyu had put there.

I finally got my neck working well enough to raise my head and look around. The western city gates loomed up ahead of us like an open maw and people were crowded all along the street. Most of them wore the travel-tattered clothes of the refugees, but there were more than a few local faces. Familiar faces: Harrison, who sold me snakes and lizards for dinner; Jin, the man who bartered candied ants; Greta, the mother of the girl who died in the elevator all those years ago.

There were some others with whom I had traded some words or goods over the years. Did they recognize me? Remember me? Probably not, but they all turned out to see a pair of Blackthumbs executed. All my neighbors would ever remember of me was my death. I guessed it was a little late to start worrying about my legacy, but I would have been lying if I said it didn't sting.

I tried to move and found my hands cuffed behind my back. Zach was bound the same way, though he still walked under his own power. There was blood running from his nose, but the Black-thumb gripping his arm had a swollen lip, too, and paused to spit blood into the dirt. Craning my head over my shoulder, I saw Woods and another man following us, crossbows aimed at our backs and fingers ready on their triggers. At least we had made an impression.

They must have been in a hurry to see us dead... We were still wearing our uniforms. Those things weren't replaceable and even the resilient carbon microfiber couldn't stand up against the power of a storm.

"Zee?" I mumbled.

"Don't worry, Julia," Zach said. "We're loyal Greenguard. Thorn knows that."

Sure, Thorn knew that. But he didn't care. He just wanted us gone and I couldn't bring myself to be surprised. I never believed in the Gardeners like Zach did. They were always the ones who refused to answer my questions in school, who always told me that I was going to come to a bad end. But then they recruited me to the Greenguard, even though I never wanted it. They kept me close, kept an eye on me. It was Thorn and Gregory who had controlled me my whole life, not the Whitefingers. And now that a privileged position and nice green uniform had finally failed to keep me in line, the Gardeners were cutting me loose.

The Greenguard dragged us through the crowd of onlookers, moving in a circle of empty space carved out by loaded crossbows and superstitious fear. One of our escorts spoke briefly to the Black-thumbs at the city gate. They darted angry, terrified looks back at Zach and me. They really believed it, didn't they? Thorn's bugshit about dreameaters taking over our minds, about us joining the Whitefingers...

I could use my legs a bit now as we were marched out of Angel City. I considered making the other two carry me every inch of the way, but decided that a modicum of dignity probably outweighed that petty revenge. I sneezed as dust rolled over us, but the winds were mild today. The high, white sky was blank, the horizon clear. I wasn't sure if we were lucky or not. Death by storm was second only to having your brain melted by a dreameater for horrible ends, but at least it didn't take long. No storms meant that Zach and I would hang from the posts until we died of thirst or some mutant got hungry enough to come take a nibble. Despite our duty to keep the area around the city empty of dangerous monsters, Blackthumbs seldom interfered when they were just sampling prisoner kebabs.

The metal rods thrust up from the sand ahead, tall and pitted and hung with well-worn chains. It was still early in the day and their shadows were long, dark stripes pointing imperiously to the west. The other Blackthumbs spread out, keeping their crossbows directed at us while Woods exchanged our cuffs for the manacles dangling from the posts. It was slightly less uncomfortable having my arms held over my head and there was some slack in the chain, but not enough to do anything useful. Not with my arms, at least.

Woods inspected his work with a frown twisting his lips. The slick little rattler probably thought he would have won me over in the end. Woods and his fucking apples. He lingered after the other Blackthumbs secured us and began pulling back toward Angel City.

"Come on, Woods!" one of them shouted over his shoulder. "We're done here!"

Woods nodded once and slowly turned his back on us. I glanced at Zach, who leaned against the post with his eyes closed and lips moving in prayer. Woods was only a dozen yards away. The others were halfway back to the city.

"Hey, Woods!" I called out.

Zach cracked his eyes open and Woods looked back at me.

"Come here," I told him.

Woods paused. He glanced at the retreating Greenguard, then made his way cautiously back in my direction and stopped about ten feet away. His crossbow was still slung over one shoulder, but he fiddled nervously with the strap. I wasn't too worried about him shooting and being able to hit me, even at this distance and with me chained up.

"Do I get to make a final request?" I asked.

Woods considered for a moment and then nodded. "What is it, Reed?"

"Can I get one last fuck before I die?"

"Uh... what?"

"I want it to be you."

It was a lie big enough to eclipse a Stormsphere, but it was just what Woods wanted to hear. He tried to glare suspiciously at me, but his eyes dropped hungrily down to my chest and then along my long legs. Chained up, I couldn't pose very well, but I did my best to arch my back and bat my eyelashes enticingly.

"Julia?" Zach hissed at me. "What the hell are you doing?"

"You had your chance, Zee," I said.

I made awkward little shooing motions at Zach with my cuffed hands that I hoped that Woods couldn't see. I kept my eyes on the eager young Greenguard.

"I'm going to die here." I said it softly so that Woods had to come closer to hear me. "Is it too much to ask to get laid one last time? You can even come inside, if you want. Not like it's going to matter anymore."

Woods closed the distance between us, still wary, but not even trying to disguise his naked lust anymore. I looked him straight in the eye and licked my lips, hoping that it wasn't too much. I was never any good at the seduction game. What, did you think my bed was always empty by choice?

But apparently I was good enough for Woods. He yanked the bandana down off his face and put his hands around my waist. He leaned forward and kissed me. I tried to pretend that his lips were softer, his chin more delicate and not prickly with stubble... That he knew what the fuck he was doing. I kissed him back, teasing his lips with my tongue and teeth. Woods eagerly opened his mouth and mashed his tongue artlessly against mine.

Woods slid his hands up my sides to grab my tits. I pulled my mouth away, but lifted my chin and encouraged him to suck on my neck. Woods yanked at my pants until he could get one hand down my underwear. I tried to make convincing *oohing* and *aahing* noises as he fumbled around my cunny and hoped he wouldn't notice how dry it was.

Zach stared as if I had gone crazy. He knew me better than this. Over Woods' shoulder, I watched the other Greenguard. They had almost reached the gate. I probably should have waited until they vanished into the city once more, but Woods wriggled his fingers like thrashing worms, trying to get them inside me. I wasn't going to be able to fake interest for much longer.

"Come on. Just fuck me, Woods," I breathed in his ear and gave it a nip for good measure. I shuddered.

He took a step back and started unbuckling his belt with hands that shook in excitement. I reached up and gripped the chains holding me. While Woods' attention was fixed on fishing out his cock, I lifted my legs off the ground. He looked up just as I wrapped my legs around his neck.

I swear he smiled at first. Maybe the poor idiot thought I was up to something kinky. But I locked my ankles together behind Woods' neck and squeezed his throat with my calves. His smile vanished and his eyes bulged.

I twisted my hips as hard as I could, but his damned neck didn't break. It's a lot harder to snap a human spine than anyone will tell you. There are bones and muscles and people tense up impressively when they're frightened or angry. I jerked my hips again and again, hoping to hear that fateful snap. Woods grabbed my calves and tried to yank them apart as he stumbled.

Zach was shouting... something. I knew it wouldn't be long before the Greenguard on the wall saw what was happening and our execution detail came running back. I squeezed harder, but my legs were locked around the sides of Woods' neck, not really on his airway. His face was darkening, but the Blackthumb wasn't going to pass out any time soon. Not before help arrived or my arms got too tired to hold me up.

Woods stopped trying to pry my legs open and pulled his knife. He slashed at my stomach, but I yanked him by the neck, grunting with the effort. His fucking spine still wouldn't break, but Woods staggered and his blade sliced along the back of my leg instead of through my guts. I felt a hot line of pain down my thigh and gritted my teeth against a cry.

Woods slashed again. I jerked and his knife left another painful cut along my hip, but I pulled as hard as I could and Woods' ankle turned. He toppled down at the base of the stake and my legs fell from around his neck. Woods coughed loudly once, but I couldn't let him stand again.

I heaved myself up by the chains and then smashed both my feet down on his head. Woods hit the ground hard. I stomped on his neck and he gurgled. The Blackthumb grabbed his throat, so I kicked his head and blood pooled in the dust, garish and bright red. Woods went limp on the third blow, but I gave him one more kick, just to be sure.

"Julia, what the hell did you do?" Zach shouted.

I looked up. Our Greenguard escort – plus several more from the wall – were sprinting toward us. They would cover the few hundred yards between us in short order. I toed Woods' body over and searched for his keys. He had fallen on top of them and I had to work my toes underneath to get them out. I trapped the key ring between my boots and tried to pull it off his belt. My arms ached and my legs burned, but I worked desperately.

At last, the keys came free. Carefully, I nudged them onto the top of my boot. A crossbow bolt whizzed past me, but I did my best to ignore it.

"Get ready, Zee!" I warned.

I kicked my foot up and sent the keys flying out toward him. Zach lunged and his chains rattled, but my aim was good and he caught the keys on one fingertip. He swore and fumbled for a better grip as another bolt slammed into the ground a few feet away. Two of the Blackthumbs had stopped to reload their crossbows, but the others were charging full speed toward us. We were out of time.

But then Zach was there next to me, jamming Woods' key into my manacles. My hands fell out of the chains and my limp arms burned like I had sleeves full of fire ants. I squatted down over Woods' body and grabbed his crossbow in shaking hands. I shoved it at Zach, then tossed him the quiver.

"Are you okay?" Zach asked, staring at the blood sheeting down my leg.

"No," I said. "Of course I'm not okay!"

"You... you killed a Greenguard, Julia. Woods was one of us!"

"They tried to kill us, Zee. Do you want to die for Thorn's lie? I sure as fuck don't!"

I seized Woods' knife from the sand where he had dropped it and snatched up his belt. Luckily, he had already unbuckled it. His cock was still horribly hard in his half-open fatigues.

"God forgive us," Zach said.

But he checked the bolt in Woods' crossbow, spun and fired back at the swiftly closing Greenguard. Zach's bolt hit one of them in the thigh and the Blackthumb fell to the sand, clutching his leg.

Seven more Greenguard were still charging toward us. Too many... We turned the opposite direction and ran. A bolt thudded into the ground behind us; hitting a moving target is hard unless you're really good. Zach could do it, but not very many others. We ran in a sidewinder pattern – anyone could score a lucky shot, after all, and I *was* limping – until we could dive behind the husk of a long-dead train sprawling through the sand like a discarded snake-skin.

Zach and I put our backs to the pitted and peeling train hull. Blood ran down my leg to leave dark stains in the sand. Zach worked the lever on his stolen crossbow, dropping a new bolt into place, and there was a metallic thunk as another one punched into the far side of our cover.

"We have to split up," I said. "Make them divide their numbers."

Zach considered, then nodded reluctantly. "Make them chase and search for us."

"We'll meet out there," I said. I pointed west, toward the pale expanse of Pacific Desert.

"In the wastes? Julia, we can't," Zach protested. He paused to lean through a window and fire. There was a shout and then a thump. Another bolt shot past our cover as Zach ducked back down next to me. "We'll die out there."

"We'll die here," I pointed out. "We can't go back to the city, can we?"

"Fair point," Zach said. "Alright, we'll meet where we lost the Whitefinger's trail."

"Good luck, Zee."

"Stay alive, Julia. I'll find you."

He leaned out and fired again. When the pursuing Greenguard recoiled from his shot, Zach broke cover and ran for it. The pack shifted aim and loosed a storm of bolts at my partner. Way too many of them. I picked up a broken piece of concrete and heaved it as hard as I could. I didn't hit any of the Blackthumbs, but it did get their attention.

I ran back down the length of the ancient train and slipped into the space between two cars, pressing myself against the corroded metal. My thigh and ass screamed in pain where Woods had cut me and my fatigues were sticky with blood. It was seeping down into my boot and my leg was shaking hard. Running was a losing game.

I fought to silence my rasping breath. The other Blackthumbs rounded the end of the train and began creeping carefully down its length. Their heavy boots crunched loud in the sand, but my hiding place wasn't very good and they would see me soon. I gripped Wood's belt in my mouth, then inched down into a painful squat. The pitted metal of the train was rough through my shirt and my injured leg threatened to drop me unceremoniously onto my ass.

I forced out the quietest hiss of labored breath I could and then rooted around the ground for another stone. The one I found wasn't terribly large, but it was large enough. I leaned against the ruined train and pushed myself back up, using my good leg as much as possible. The footsteps were getting closer. I threw my rock over the roof of the train car and it rattled off the ancient metal, then thumped down into the sand.

The other Blackthumbs froze for a second and then started off toward the sound. If they had only looked to their right, they would have seen me, but their goggles were pointed straight in the direction of my rock. I leapt onto the closest one, half to surprise him, half just to make him bear my weight for a moment. I clung to him with one hand and jabbed my knife into his side with the other. I twisted the blade so the suction wouldn't trap it in his body, ripped it out and stuck him again. The Blackthumb slumped and I let go to keep him from pulling me down to the ground.

The remaining Greenguard turned toward me. Her crossbow came up. At this range, even Woods couldn't have missed. I grabbed the belt from my mouth and swung it at her. It was damned awkward with the added weight of Woods' canteen, but the belt's free end tangled around the crossbow and knocked it down. It made a muted twang and the bolt fell out into the sand.

The Blackthumb dropped her weapon and backed away. She drew her knife in a swift motion and held it out point-first. Her grip was disappointingly experienced. She circled me slowly, moving toward my wounded side. I pivoted on my good foot to keep her in front of me.

"I'm not a traitor," I said.

"You just killed two Greenguard," she answered.

"Well... yeah," I admitted. "But they were trying to kill me. I'm not a Whitefinger and I'm not being controlled by their dream-eaters. Thorn is lying!"

The Blackthumb's only response was a low lunge with her knife. I jumped back, slapping at her wrist with my free hand. Her blade flicked past and only barely avoided slicing a chunk out of me. I slashed at her arm, but the other Greenguard leapt away much faster than I could limp after her.

I would have kicked sand up into her eyes, but she was wearing goggles. Good idea out here... Well, I would just have to be better than her. I feinted to one side and cried out as I put weight on my injured leg, faking a stumble that came way too close to being real. The other Blackthumb aimed a stab at my stomach and I let her arm pass under mine, then trapped it against my ribs. I switched my blade into my other hand and thrust it over her shoulder, into her neck.

The Blackthumb jerked back and pulled herself off the blade, but as soon as the obstruction was gone, bright blood spurted freely from the wound. She sank to her knees, but I didn't approach until she dropped her knife. I reversed my grip and stabbed over her collarbone, down into her heart to finish the job.

I felt sick, but I buckled Woods' belt around my waist and quickly searched the two new bodies. There would be more Blackthumbs hunting for me soon. I picked up one of the crossbows and collected all of the bolts. They had fired their quivers nearly empty during the chase, but each of the Greenguard carried a canteen of water.

I unhooked them from the other Blackthumbs' belts and hung them on my own. The extra weight made me waddle and one of the canteens bumped agonizingly against my injured leg, but the water was too precious to leave behind. I took the fallen woman's goggles and untied her bandana, too.

I crept back along the train and looked around. The shadows had grown shorter under the execution stakes, but not by much. Maybe twenty minutes had passed since Woods tried to grant my final wish, thinking to score with a dead woman. I spotted a knot of Greenguard moving back toward the city, dragging another green-clad shape between them. One of the Blackthumbs that Zach had wounded? I saw no sign of my partner, though. Time to go find him.

I turned my back on Angel City. I wasn't welcome there anymore. To the west, the land stretched off into the vast white Pacific Desert. There wasn't anything left for me in the Whisperward, but what else could possibly wait for me out there in the wastes? I didn't know, but I began walking.

I PUT a few miles between me and Angel City before I stopped. At hobbling speed, it took me hours to get even that far and the dark shadows had tipped back toward the east. I paused to lean against a storm-battered stone and catch my breath. My left leg was burning agony and my skull still throbbed from being hit in the head. It wasn't as bad as the knock that Kiyu had given me, though, so I figured that had been Woods. He had gone easy on me.

It struck me then just how often I'd thought of killing Woods, or at least kicking his ass. But creepy and spoiled though the kid was, I never wanted him dead… not really. But Woods chained me up to die. He stabbed me, and I refused to feel guilty for killing him or the other two Blackthumbs. I didn't owe them bugsquat. I only wanted to live and I was not sorry for that. I wasn't.

I had more to worry about than my conscience, anyway. There were two slashes down my left leg, and the worst of the pair was on the back where I couldn't see very well. How bad was it? I dropped my pants and used some of my water to wash out the long cut. It was a dangerous waste of resources, but all the water in the world wouldn't do me much good if I died of infection. I sliced my undershirt into strips that I bound tightly around my thigh. There wasn't a whole lot more I could do.

My next survival hurdle was shelter. I took a long drink of water that finished off the canteen I had used to wash. I debated keeping the container and decided against it. Right now, it was just extra weight. A hindrance, not a help. I dug down into the sand and buried it in the lee of the stone so the wind wouldn't uncover it for a while. No sense in making it easy for the Greenguard to track me.

I scanned my surroundings and found the largest pile of rocks. Something big would be my best bet at shelter. The sky remained clear and it was always warm, even at night, but the dry winds would dehydrate me faster out in the open. And I needed a place to hide.

The landscape didn't look familiar. I searched for landmarks as I trudged toward the rocks, but I recognized nothing from the day Zach and I spent tracking Kiyu. Had I gone in the wrong direction or had the storm just erased anything remotely familiar? It was certainly possible. Most of the ancient buildings were long gone and it wasn't as if I would have recognized one patch of sand over another. Maybe I could spot the hole where Zach fell through the fulgurite glass.

I tried not to think about the possibility that Zach and I would lose each other out here. I looked back east. Angel City was only a haze of heat shimmer on the horizon. Even the huge Tear of God was just a tiny black shadow that seemed to float above the ground. If I went much further out, I would lose track of that last landmark. And if a storm came – and I somehow survived it – I would lose my own tracks.

I limped on toward a jumble of rocks in what seemed to be the right direction, though it turned out to be the stump of a building. Broken slabs of concrete lay in heaps around the foundation and half a ceiling. There was always the danger that the whole thing would fall down on top of me, but lying exposed in the open wasn't a much better option. I resolved to just sit my ass close to the collapsed wall so I could get the hell out of there if the place shifted suspiciously.

The crumbling building had created a sort of square-shaped cave. I had to crawl on my hands and knees between two fallen chunks of masonry into the dim brown space inside. The opening faced northwest and the bright smear of the sun was slinking wearily down over the horizon, illuminating a patch of dusty floor about as long as I was tall. I stopped and unslung the crossbow so I could lean against the wall. I sat crookedly, tipped up on one hip to avoid putting weight on my wounds. My belt was heavy and ungainly with the knife and two canteens, so I was unbuckling it to make myself more comfortable when I heard the hiss.

I should have been more careful. The deserts weren't exactly teeming with life, but there were enough mutant bugs and reptiles – even some mammals – that not much in the way of shelter went unused. In the shadows beyond the failing sunlight, a jumble of coils slipped and slithered over each other. It was too dark to see how many there might be, but each loop of scaly body was as big around as my thigh. There had to be forty or fifty feet of snake back there. I wasn't sure if that was one snake or a nest of them. But either way, it wasn't good news for me.

I inched back through the sand. I could only feel for the exit; I wasn't about to take my eyes off of the monstrous mass in front of me. The coils loosened and the snake – it seemed to be just one, though I saw several tails in the darkness – slithered toward me. A crooked, forked black tongue tasted the air... which probably tasted like dinner. I cursed and flicked my eyes back to where I had been sitting. My crossbow and belt were both lying on the floor, now only a few yards from the snake.

Without that water, I was dead. Snakebite was a marginally quicker death, at least, so I leaned into the hole and grabbed the end of my belt, dragging it across the dusty floor. The snake wove through the sand and broken concrete, pulling its tails beneath it once again. The scaled coils were only a yard from the crossbow now. I would have to manage without it. I backed away until I was outside the building. The snake's tongue darted out once more. It was purple, I could see now, and forked into three points.

I rose slowly and slipped sideways until I was out of sight. I had to hope that the monster snake wasn't *that* hungry or didn't like how I smelled, otherwise I was going to find out just how fast that huge, twisted body could move. Fortunately, the snake didn't feel like leaving its den and venturing out into the cooling night.

My crossbow was still in there. I contemplated waiting until the snake fell asleep and then creeping back inside. Maybe I could even kill the mutant. But it was one hell of a risk. If the snake wasn't sleeping or if it woke up before I got to the crossbow, then I was in trouble. And a dying snake that size thrashing in a small space would be almost as dangerous as a live and angry one.

I crept away until I could barely make out the ruined building before I felt safe from its huge, scaly inhabitant. The night wasn't cold, but my drying sweat gave me chills and it wasn't long before I was shivering. There wasn't much else in the way of shelter and the light was nearly gone. The pearly pale moonglow lay low on the horizon, turning the sandy ruins as white as the Pacific Desert. I limped to a much smaller stand of concrete boulders, searched them thoroughly – finding only some small brown spiders that scurried back into the cracks at my approach – and picked a spot in the lee to settle down.

I removed my belt, but buckled it closed again and looped it over one arm, just in case. I laid down on my right side and found myself really missing my Greenguard apartment. Even my mother's little eighteenth-story home seemed like a palace right then.

———

When I woke up, the bright glow of the sun had crawled halfway over the horizon. The ground was still cool, but the air was already warming. I took a drink and shook the canteen. It was less than half full. One of those Blackthumbs hadn't been very careful with their water, but I guessed I couldn't blame them for not having my survival in mind.

I had a knife and a quiver with four bolts, but no crossbow to use them with. I could use the bolts as stabbing weapons, I supposed, and that might save some wear on the edge of my knife. I just hoped that I wouldn't be out here long enough for it to be important. I had to find Zach. After that... I had no idea, really, but we could figure it out together.

A lizard had crawled out into the early morning sun to bask. It had a short tail, but its body was fat and made the scaly little beast waddle. It was as long as my hand and almost as wide. I didn't have anything to cook it with, but a promising amount of meat sat there on the stone and I hadn't eaten since... when? Thorn had us hauled into his office before breakfast and then chained to the execution stakes without a last meal. Maybe that should have been my final request.

The fat lizard didn't move nearly fast enough and I stabbed it easily with one of my bolts. It squirmed for a moment, but died with satisfactory speed. I slit its belly open with my knife and began peeling back the scaly skin, then dropped the lizard and felt acid rising in the back of my throat.

It was full of shiny black lumps that oozed dark blood where my knife had grazed them. Tumors. There had to be a hundred of the cancerous nodes.

I kicked the lizard away, but after a minute of listening to my stomach growl, I picked it up out of the sand and gingerly poked around inside it more thoroughly. No, the little animal was literally bursting with cancer and probably dying before I hastened things along. Even its stumpy tail was riddled with black tumors.

I considered the blood. I knew it was used in some soups and puddings. We die pretty swiftly without blood, too, so there must have been something nutritious in it, but I wasn't ready to take the chance. I dropped the lizard's body between some rocks and then scrubbed my hands clean with sand.

————

I WALKED a crooked spiral out from my sleeping spot, hoping to find a trace of Zach or something else that I recognized. I didn't manage either one, but my limping progress was slow and I didn't cover much ground. With my bum leg, at least it was easy to walk in circles. I encountered a few insects and more lizards, but without bodies bloated by cancer, they slipped effortlessly away from my faltering attempts at hunting.

I drank more water than I should have, trying to keep my stomach full and quiet. From a conservation standpoint, it wasn't my best idea, but between the blood I had lost yesterday and the lack of food, I was low on energy and not thinking very clearly.

By the following day, I was out of water entirely and still found no sign of Zach. I had long since lost the center of my spiral and any idea where I was anymore. Still in the desert – I figured out that much – but after God's Wrath, that wasn't saying a whole lot. Most of the world was desert. This was already further than I had ever been from Angel City.

With the aid of some helpful shadows, I could tell west from east, but there was no sign of Angel City. I thought that I spotted the remains of some buildings preserved by the Stormsphere's protection, but the distant images remained stubbornly distant no matter how much I walked toward them. Maybe they were mirages or maybe I was even slower on my injured leg than I gave myself credit for, but I was getting nowhere fast.

My thoughts swirled around like dust devils. Where was Zach?

Did he even get away from the Blackthumbs? They were carrying someone, weren't they? I had assumed it was one of our pursuers or even Woods' body.

But what if it had been Zach?

It was my fault he was out here. Me and my big fucking mouth. I was the one thick-headed enough to insist on chasing Kiyu into the wastes. If Zach was dead – either in the desert or back in iron chains outside Angel City – it was all my fault.

Wasn't it? Or was this something bigger than just killing off pain-in-the-ass Julia Reed? The Gardeners didn't need an excuse to do whatever they wanted. Thorn could have sent me off on some suicide mission years ago if that was all he wanted. So did the High Gardener truly think that the Whitefingers had corrupted us? Maybe, but it didn't seem likely.

What the hell was happening in Angel City? Thorn refused to listen to the Whitefingers' warning. Why? I struggled to recall exactly what Thorn had said in his office before I started calling him a liar and Woods tried to brain me. But all I could remember was my indignant rage and then pain and darkness.

Was there something behind all of this? Or was my addled brain just trying to absolve itself of guilt over Zach's death? No, I told myself firmly. He wasn't dead. I would find Zach and then... and then...

———

I SLEPT a lot and it became hard to tell the difference between my own panicked, heat-scrambled thoughts and dreams. I saw Zach... And I saw Liam, too. The boy was chained to the stakes outside Angel City, trying to tell me something important, but he could only whisper. But no matter how close I leaned in, I could never hear the words.

I dreamed of Kiyu, as well. We were naked and lying in my bed.

I pressed my body urgently against hers, but the dream-Kiyu didn't seem to notice.

"I want to show you something pretty," she said.

Kiyu opened up her little leather pouch and held it out to me. I recoiled at first – it was full of shiny black orbs, just like the lizard. But the things inside weren't tumors. They were hard and clean and smooth, like a hundred Tears of God in miniature. Kiyu poured them out into my hands. I tried to catch them all, but they overfilled my palms and fell through my fingers. They made soft sounds as they fell.

"You stole them," I accused.

"No," Kiyu whispered into my ear. "I set them free."

I woke up grasping for something that wasn't there.

————

THE NEXT DAY, I managed to catch another lizard. I killed it with my bolt again, though I think I might have dropped the arrow and forgotten it there. The lizard had two tails and too many toes, but I was hungry and my mouth felt as dry and cracked as the earth around me. The tails fell off in my hand and I ate them raw. The scales were slightly crunchy, the meat sour and chewy. I choked it all down, though, then slit open the lizard's belly. I closed my eyes and sucked without looking. The blood was salty and thick, but it was wet.

The headache that had been my only companion for the last two days abated a little, but if I improved conditions for my head, it was at the expense of my stomach. An hour after my first meal in days, I was on my hands and knees, vomiting up everything I had eaten. It only took two or three good convulsions to empty my stomach, but the heaving went on long afterward.

When it was over, I pushed sand on top of the puddle of red-tinted bile and pulpy lizard meat before the smell of it made me throw up all over again. I vaguely recalled that I was supposed to be hiding. I sat down and wrapped my arms around my knees. My left leg hurt where the hot sand seared my sliced flesh... but it all seemed far away, too distant to care much about.

I began considering the idea that I was really going to die. I rolled the thought around in my pounding head for a while and wasn't sure if I liked the sound of it. Was dying a good idea or not? I wondered if I should ask the shadow stalking closer across the sand, but I doubted he had much of an opinion. Death is a very personal thing, you know.

I fell over and got to it.

SOMEONE WAS SHAKING ME. It was gentle and didn't seem very important, so I kept sleeping and hoped that whoever it was would just go away. Awake was a place full of hunger and thirst and guilt and fear. Sleep was a soft, dark place. Sometimes the dreams were confusing, but it was safe.

The shaking didn't stop, though. It was getting rougher, more urgent, so I decided to get it over with and wake up before whoever it was shook me into little pieces. I cracked open my eyes and squinted against the bright white sky. I moved my too-heavy head until it was protected from the sun by the silhouette leaning over me. My eyes adjusted reluctantly, but I recognized Zach's square jaw and flat-brimmed hat before he even spoke.

"Julia, are you awake?" he asked.

"Yes," I groaned. "And it's your fault."

"Are you okay? You look like shit."

"Fuck you. I'm rosy."

I sat up gingerly and only managed it with a great deal of help from Zach. I vaguely recalled keeling over in the middle of open sands, but the sky here wasn't as bright as I first thought and we were in the shade. Zach must have moved me. We were sitting near a section of old overpass that had collapsed long ago, but he had chosen carefully and the ancient structure didn't seem like it could fall down much more.

I looked Zach over. The bruises on his face had darkened to purple, but they were already healing to an unpleasant yellow color around the edges. He had a crossbow with a full quiver and his belt was hung with a pair of canteens. He took one and handed it to me, then helped me raise it to my lips when my hands proved too unsteady to do it on their own.

Zach pulled the canteen away before I could drink too much and make myself sick, but my stomach cramped anyway. I clenched my teeth as hard as I could and kept the water down. Zach waited before he gave me another drink.

"Slowly," he said.

I took small sips and swished the water around my parched mouth until it lost all coolness before swallowing. I felt life seeping back into my body. But with life came pain – the ache in my head was deep and my left leg was stiff, pulsing with agony. I sagged into the sand and rolled over onto my good side.

Other than the bruises, Zach looked like he'd come out of his escape much better than me. He opened a pouch on his belt and unwrapped a slice of prickly pear cactus. I'd have preferred the pear itself, but the paddle-shaped leaf was a lot tastier than my last meal.

"Where did you get this?" I asked. My voice still cracked, but came out a bit stronger with use. "Did you find it out here, or get it off one of the Blackthumbs?"

"I..." Zach trailed off and looked away.

The expression across his broad face was unhappy. He must have gotten his supplies the same way as I had – by killing other Greenguard. I guess we were lucky that one of them had been carrying lunch when he escorted us out to our deaths.

I ate the green cactus slowly. Zach had grown up poor like me and had fought his way into the Greenguard, but the difference between us was that he *wanted* to be there. Some of the other Black-thumbs gave Zach a hard time because of his background, but I think they were afraid he would kick their collective asses if they pushed their luck. And he could have.

But what they never understood was that Zach wouldn't do that. He *believed* in the Greenguard. He wanted to protect the people of the Whisperward.

I could only imagine how much it hurt Zach to fight other Blackthumbs, people that he thought of as brothers and sisters. I put my hand on his arm and squeezed gently. The thick muscles were as taut as a drawn crossbow.

"You don't have to talk about it," I told him. "I'm just glad you're alive, Zee."

"Julia... I..."

Zach looked down at me with dark, wet eyes. I didn't know if that wound would ever heal. I gave his thick arm one last reassuring squeeze and did the only thing I could to help – I changed the subject.

"What now, Zee?" I gestured around us. "I have no idea where the hell we are. A long way out from Angel City, I guess."

Zach adjusted his hat. The leather was looking more dusty and sun-faded than I'd ever seen it. He squinted out at the broken ruins.

"We're about two days from the Whisperward," Zach said.

"I've been wandering around out here for three days, at least," I protested.

"More like four, Julia. But mostly in circles."

I flipped Zach off, but I did it with a smile. It was good not to be alone out here anymore and I was happier to see Zach than I could ever have put into words.

"So we're close enough to get back to Angel City. But they'll kill us as soon as we get through the gates," I said.

Zach nodded. I sighed and finished off the cactus, wondering if Zach had any more.

"Do you think we could make it up to Boulder City?" I asked. "If their Stormsphere is still working and anyone's even there. What's the next 'Ward after that? Wind City?"

Zach shook his head. "Too far. We don't have the supplies to make it halfway to Boulder, much less Wind City."

"There has to be a way to live out here. The Whitefingers do it all the time. I know there are animals to catch. There might be wild cactus, too."

"What about the Whitefingers?" asked Zach.

"Um... what about them?" I didn't understand Zach's question. "I don't really know *how* they survive outside the Whisperwards, but–"

"No, that's not what I..." Zach hesitated. "Do you think we could find them?"

My first thought was that it wouldn't be at all bad to see Kiyu again. It wasn't often that I met a woman who caught my interest. And even when I was done admonishing myself for thinking with my cunny, Zach's idea still made some sense. The Whitefingers had been fair to us as captives. Jacks and his people hadn't tortured us. They even fed us and tended our wounds. But I doubted the waste-landers would be very happy to see us, even if we knew where to find them.

"We're Greenguard, Zach. We hunt them. I'm not sure they would help us."

"Julia, you know we're not Greenguard anymore."

I flinched at the bitterness in Zach's tone. Did he feel as betrayed as I did? Even more, I suspected. He had been loyal to the Gardeners and the Greenguard from the beginning, right up to the point where they chained him to a stake to die. Zach had even been yelling at me about killing Woods, I seemed to recall.

"Aren't you afraid of the Whitefingers?" I asked.

"Yes," he admitted. "And you should be, too. But I have no other choice."

I felt like shit. He was right. Zach had dedicated his life to the Greenguard and the Gardeners, but lost it all because of me.

"Alright, Zee," I said. "Let's see if the Whitefingers will take us in. Any idea where the hell to find them?"

———

ZACH HELPED me to my feet – noting that at least I had lost some weight – but I had to hop around for a bit until my legs worked properly again. When he asked how bad it was, I had to confess that I didn't really know. I bit my lip and dropped my pants so he could take a look. I blushed hard, but it was Zach.

He peeled away the bandages I had made and cleaned the wounds free of crusted blood and sand. Fortunately, Woods hadn't cut me too deeply. It was a jagged slash from the bottom of my left ass cheek to a point an inch or two above the back of my knee. The cut was long, but shallow. The one on my hip was about the length of my finger and only a little deeper. The muscles weren't damaged, as far as Zach could tell, so when my leg stopped hurting, I probably wouldn't keep the limp.

Zach couldn't find any signs of infection, either. He cut some clean new bandages from his own undershirt and then re-wrapped my leg.

"You've been lucky so far, Julia," Zach told me. "But you're going to need medicine to stay that way."

I couldn't face my partner as I pulled my pants back up, but I watched him out of the corner of my eye. Zach's expression was perfectly neutral. I should have known that I could trust him not to be a pervert even with me sticking my ass in his face. Zach scanned the horizon in a slow circle.

"I think I can at least get us back to where we lost the girl last time," he said. "You know, where you were supposed to meet me. We can start there."

Zach set out, walking slowly so I could keep up. It was already midday and I wondered how much ground we would be able to cover. I felt bad for dragging Zach down yet again.

"Well, at least we can tell the Whitefingers we delivered their message," I said. "They might even be hoping for a response. Maybe we can use that to get their help."

"And hope they don't throw us out into a sandstorm when we tell them Thorn ignored us."

"Yeah," I chuckled. It faded quickly.

Thorn hadn't simply ignored us. Woods and the other Blackthumbs, even Gregory, seemed nervous and afraid at the warning, to think that Angel City might be the next Whisperward to fall. But Thorn hadn't looked surprised at all. Like he already knew exactly what was going on.

"Zee?" I asked.

Zach grunted in response.

"Did Thorn seem surprised to you when we told him what the Whitefingers said?" I asked. "That the Whispers were dying?"

Zach thought for a moment. "No, not really. I suppose the Gardeners would be the first to know if there was something wrong with the Tear."

"And not tell anyone about it?"

"Tell anyone? What could he say? Everyone in Angel City is frightened enough with the stories of other Whisperwards failing. What do you want Thorn to do? Start a panic? Send everyone away, out into the desert and storms?"

"No..." I agreed reluctantly. "I guess not. But Thorn knew that the Whitefingers were right. He lied to the Greenguard when he said we were tainted."

Zach winced, but nodded grimly. "Yeah, he did."

"He's hiding something."

"Yes."

"Do you know what?"

"No, Julia. I don't know what's going on. I just want to find the Whitefingers and get this done."

I limped on in silence for several minutes, replaying Thorn's interrogation over and over again in my head. My thoughts were a little less sandy now and a bit more of the scene in the High Gardener's office was coming back to me. He hadn't seemed surprised at the Whitefinger's warning, so why did Thorn ask us questions about it? Because he wanted to find out how much the Whitefingers knew. Once we told him that, Thorn stopped questioning us and pronounced sentence.

Something else was nagging at me.

"Zee, do you remember what Thorn said at the end? Something about wandering the wastes?"

"The High Gardener said that he refused to see his people wandering the desert like animals. He thinks they deserve better than being prey to storms and mutant creatures," Zach answered.

"No! That's close, though," I said, and then I remembered. "He said he refused to see our people go *back* to the desert."

I smiled. I had found it. And I had no idea what it meant.

"Go... back?" asked Zach.

"After God's Wrath, He was supposed to have wept the Tears, right? According to the Gardeners, that's the only reason anyone is still alive."

"His compassion saved us," Zach said.

"That's what the Gardeners tell us. So when exactly did people wander the Earth?"

"The Whitefingers do," Zach pointed out.

I could tell he didn't like that thought very much. The Whitefingers lived outside the Whisperwards and if I remembered what Thorn had said correctly, did that mean we had *all* been Whitefingers once?

I limped a little faster. Maybe Kiyu and her people knew even more than we thought.

WHEN I WOKE the next morning, Zach was already up. He had some cactus fruits and a few twists of lizard jerky laid out on his bandana. He separated them into two small piles. It wasn't much food, even before dividing it. Our supply situation wasn't looking too rosy.

"That's not going to last us very long," I said, stretching. "How's the water?"

Zach shook both the canteens and they made a pleasant gurgle. For now.

"We need to find those Whitefingers soon," he said.

My head felt better after a night of sleep with accompanying food and water. But it was a good thing Zach had kept my first meal light – when my body got used to food again, it would want more.

Zach and I ate sparingly from his stores and drank as little water as we could manage. Zach gave me more than he took for himself, citing my injuries, but promised that he wouldn't do anything ridiculously heroic to spare me.

Liar.

The heat shimmer swallowed up all but the faintest shadow of Angel City. Between that and the glow of the sun, at least we had a vague bearing. So we moved north. On our left, the Pacific Desert was an endless expanse of blinding white. We kept our goggles firmly fitted over our eyes as we walked. My injured leg was stiff, but working a little better today and Zach didn't have to slow down much for me.

I wasn't at all certain we were going in the right direction, but when I had chased Kiyu out here before, my eyes were more or less glued to the ground, searching for any trace of the pretty White-finger girl. Zach had been watching my back, thankfully, and had a better image of the landscape we had tracked her through.

So I let him do the searching this time, and busied myself scanning the horizon. Maybe someone was still looking for us. I didn't know if Thorn had Greenguard scouring the ruins or if the High Gardener figured that Zach and I were just as dead out here as chained to the stakes. And the Whitefinger man, Jacks, had sent us into the Whisperward with his message. After all the time and effort his team invested in reaching the Angel City Stormsphere, maybe they had stuck around to see what came of their message.

I sure hoped so. If the Whitefingers were already gone, we really were dead.

A glint of light caught my attention. I blinked, wiped dust off the lenses of my stolen goggles and looked again. Something shined out there behind us, flickering in and out of my vision. I whistled Zach to a halt.

"Zee? Do you see that?" I asked.

He turned around and looked where I pointed, but the light was gone now. "What was it?" he asked.

"Something shiny."

"Probably lightning glass or maybe some old metal," Zach said with a shrug.

Fulgurite glass not yet broken apart by the sandstorms some-times gleamed like that. Most metal was so corroded and wind-etched that it reflected absolutely nothing. But some of the scien-tific relics – like I still believed the Stormsphere to be – seemed immune to God's Wrath and maintained their original shine. But whatever I had seen, the light had moved or dust had covered it or something else. There was no sign of it now.

I wondered if it was pretty, maybe the kind of thing that Kiyu liked – something shiny plucked out of the drab sand. I found myself wanting to go back and find the mysterious shiny object for her, but collecting presents for Kiyu wasn't going to do me much good if we died trying to reach her.

Zach let me wear his hat to keep some of the sun off of my pale face and neck. His brown skin was beaded with sweat, but I was turning an alarming shade of red. Zach must have been really worried – I'd never seen anyone wear that hat but him.

Our feet were blistering, too, but our boots held up. Whatever they were made of, it was a hell of a lot more resilient than simple cloth and leather. I was sure I would have walked right through even the best snakeskin boots by now.

At night, Zach and I took turns sleeping. The snakes and lizards were most active during the warm daylight hours, but insects and arachnids could hunt by day or night. We even heard some bats chirping in the dark, but they flew far too fast to hunt. The goggles that Zach had appropriated were better than either of ours had been, a rare model with night lenses. Pressing a small side-mounted button lit up the darkness in shades of green. But we didn't know how much power the goggles had left, so we only used them a few minutes at a time during our watch rotations.

———

ON THE THIRD DAY, Zach found the place where the Whitefingers had captured us.

"Look there," he said. He pointed ahead and I saw several holes burned into the ground. "That's where they used their spears like lightning rods."

"Yeah." I crouched down and peered at the rough glass. "Zee, if a storm comes up, drop that 'bow."

Zach regarded his metal crossbow and nodded.

It wasn't hard to convince him that I should check out the scene alone. Chances were slim that those lightning strikes had created larger glass tubes beneath the sand – bolts that powerful would have melted the Whitefinger spears right down to slag, I suspected – but Zach was in no hurry to take any chances.

So I crept forward cautiously, and when I got close, crawled on my hands and knees. The Whitefingers' spears had channeled the lightning into the earth, but it wasn't particularly sandy here. There were patches of glass splattered across the surface, but the holes weren't deep or large. I called out to Zach and we searched around for any clues about where the Whitefingers had taken us after the fight. It had to be close by, if only because Zach was a big motherfucker and not even Jacks would have wanted to carry him very far.

"Zee!"

I waved Zach over and pointed. There was a pair of shallow paw prints pressed into a thin crust of glass. Two right front paws. Diesel must have stepped in it when the glass was still soft. Not *too* soft. I remembered my surprise at how easily the five-legged dog had trotted after his master. Clearly, Diesel hadn't burned his paws on the glass. The prints pointed northwest, so we began moving in that direction.

Late that afternoon, we found a scorpion burrow. It was a horizontal hole down into the earth, just wide enough for the pincers, Zach told me, and gave us a pretty accurate measurement of how big the scorpion inside would be. In this case, it must have been about as wide as Zach was tall. He shooed me away as he unslung his crossbow.

"Back up, Julia."

"Wait a minute," I said.

I pointed to one side of the burrow. There was something white pinned beneath a small stone there. A scrap of white lace.

"Is that...?" Zach asked.

"There's no way Kiyu dropped it twice." I crept closer.

"Not a good idea, Julia."

But he loaded a bolt into his crossbow and covered my careful approach. I was right. The piece of lace was the same one that I had found at the crime scene in the Houses and returned to Kiyu.

"What are you doing? Julia, stop!" Zach hissed.

I poked my head into the tunnel mouth. "I don't think this is a real burrow. The Whitefingers took us underground and I'm pretty sure this is their hiding hole. Maybe they made it look like a scorpion burrow to camouflage it."

Zach swore and I had to admit that I wasn't precisely thrilled to be crawling headfirst down into the earth and potentially right into the deformed maw of a monster scorpion. But I was right. The horizontal slash in the ground opened up into a carved tunnel better suited to humans than scorpions. It wasn't quite as stony as I remembered and let out into the old basement cave where we had endured the not-so-terrible captivity of the Whitefingers. I held the lace clenched in my fist and realized that I was trembling with excitement.

But the hiding hole was empty. No Whitefingers, no supplies. There wasn't much light, but Zach gave the place a more thorough search with his night-vision goggles.

"They're gone," he said in a flat tone. "Shit."

"Why did they leave?" I asked, fighting to keep the panic out of my own voice. "Where did they go?"

"I don't know. Maybe they were afraid of this happening, that we would find them."

"But they put bags over our heads," I said. I kicked a loose piece of concrete. It bounced across the floor and vanished into the shadows. "They covered their tracks!"

"They don't survive in the wastelands by putting all their lizards in one cage, Julia."

Zach sounded just as miserable as I felt. For all his distrust of the Whitefingers, he knew they were our only chance at survival, too. We agreed unhappily to stay in the burrow for the night.

We didn't know what else to do. Jacks surely had no idea about the lace Kiyu left behind, but if it was supposed to be a clue to where they had gone, I couldn't decipher it.

My partner knelt next to the bigger fire pit and grabbed a rock, striking it against the flat of his knife, but couldn't make a spark before he was worried about damaging the blade. We spent the night in darkness and finished off the last of our food and water. We had to find the Whitefingers soon or our situation was going to get damned stormy.

While Zach slept, I slipped his goggles over my eyes and adjusted the strap from his big head down to fit mine. I turned them on at intervals to peer out through the burrow entrance. I pulled Kiyu's lace out of my pocket and held it, tracing the delicate threads with my fingers and wondering where she was.

———

IN THE MORNING, Zach and I argued for a while about the merits of splitting up our search. We hoped that the Whitefingers were still out there, keeping an eye on Angel City, just from a different vantage point. And if we were wrong... Well, we didn't talk about that. I pointed out that we could cover more ground on our own, but Zach didn't think it was worth the risk.

"Besides, you'll get lost without me," he said.

"Hey, I'm the smart one," I told him. "You just keep flexing those muscles."

But Zach won in the end and we set out together to see if we could find any trace or tracks that the Whitefingers might have left behind. By silent consent, we didn't discuss our lack of food and water. But we did have one piece of luck – the sand around the Whitefinger hiding hole was riddled with scorpion burrows dug into the sandy bank. Most of them were small, just a hand's width or less, and about the same size as those we bred in the Whisper-wards.

There were some bigger burrows, which we steered clear of, but I had to admire the Whitefingers' camouflage skills. Without Kiyu's lace, I might never have picked out the fake tunnel.

Zach and I used a pair of bolts to dig a pit in front of some of the smaller burrows, each about twice as deep as the tunnel was wide, to trap the scorpion. Unlike their spider cousins, scorpions weren't very good climbers and once they fell, if the sides of the hole were steep enough, the leggy little bastards were stuck.

We finished a dozen pits and then resumed our search for the Whitefingers. If we didn't find Jacks and Kiyu and the rest, then we would check the traps on the way back and see how many scor-pions fell into them when they emerged from their dens.

We decided to try our luck to the north first. Kiyu said she had been to Bridge City, which lay in that direction. If the Whitefingers had a home, maybe it was out there. By midday, we had found no sign of them, but I thought I caught another flash of light behind us. Even with my tinted goggles, though, it was too far away to see clearly. Zach saw it this time, too.

"Maybe it's the Whitefingers trying to signal us," I suggested. Desperately.

"But that's back toward the Whisperward," Zach said. He shook his head and rubbed the back of this neck. I think he missed his hat. "Let's keep searching."

An hour later, the distant shine was gone again.

―――――

"Hey, Zee!"

I pointed at a shallow depression in the earth. There was another scorpion burrow dug into the slope. This one was wide enough that Zach and I could have easily crawled in side by side. A few rocks lay scattered around the wide opening, but I couldn't be sure if they had been placed deliberately. Was there something beneath one of them? I hadn't seen everything Kiyu kept in her little pouch of shinies and most of them were small.

"I'm going to take a closer look," I said.

Zach frowned, but he pulled the crossbow off his back, checked the bolt and sighted along it as I scrambled down the slope. I crept up to the burrow and craned my head to look inside, but I could see only dingy shadows.

I began toeing over stones outside the tunnel, and found nothing but boring shale and broken concrete. There was no glass, nothing painted or even very interestingly shaped. Nothing down here would ever have caught Kiyu's eye.

I turned back toward Zach and shook my head. He looked disappointed, too. I only took a single step before I saw his muscles bunch, tensing like steel cables.

"Julia!" he shouted.

I tried to turn away, to look behind me, but something hit me hard in the head. Not the head, I realized a dazed second later, but my *mind*. Dreameater!

It wasn't the gentle Whispers of the Stormsphere, but it wasn't anything like human thought, either. The thing in my mind was hissing with hunger, pain and rage. I saw myself from the outside: a lanky, crude piece of loud meat that had wandered too close. I might have screamed and I definitely fell to the ground, clutching at my skull.

I rolled over and saw the scorpion emerge from the burrow. Its head was a bulbous lump on the front of the pallid carapace and contained at least a dozen eyes. Many of them were dull gray and blind, but more of them glittered malevolently. I choked on a thick, infected stench. What seemed like an entire army of legs scuttled over the sand and stone toward me. The pincers were serrated with jagged teeth along the curved inner edges.

"Leave her alone, you fucking monster!" Zach shouted.

There was a metallic twang and then a bolt sank into the chitinous plates on the huge scorpion's back. Green-blue ichor oozed out around the shaft.

I shrieked again as the massive beast bellowed its pain into my mind. I knew that insects and arachnids bred and mutated fast, but I had no idea they could become dreameaters this powerful.

Zach staggered, too, and struggled to reload his crossbow. He jerked the lever and fumbled another bolt into place as the scorpion scuttled out into the sandy bowl. Its tail arced four feet over my head, but didn't look strong enough to support its massive, swollen brown stinger. Its hooked tip hung low over the scorpion's body and scraped along its back.

Not that it mattered much. Like any other Whisperward kid, I'd trapped a scorpion in a jar with a spider and knew that they hunted primarily with their claws. The scorpion crawled after Zach now, scurrying and staggering past me on too many legs up the sandy slope. Zach fired again, but managed only to impale one of the multitudes of leg joints. More teal blood splattered the ground and my skull felt like it was going to split with the creature's psychic shriek of pain.

Zach fell back, still shouting his own rage and fear, and grabbed for another bolt, but the scorpion was closing swiftly, huge pincers held wide. I hauled myself to my feet, yanked out my knife and ran after it. I reversed my grip, wrapped both hands around the handle and pretty much fell on the scorpion. My knife point scraped along the thick exoskeleton and then found a crease between plates. The blade punched through and sank in up to the hilt. I hung on and braced myself for the psychic scream.

It was even worse than I feared. I screamed, too. Blood ran from my nose and left red spots on the mutant's mottled hide. The scorpion bucked and hurled me back onto my ass. Its multiple legs stamped furiously and I scrambled back, just trying not to be trampled. The tail flexed and the stinger swung. It didn't move very well, but if I got struck, even accidentally, I doubted that it would matter how poisonous it was – that stinger was longer than my knife.

The scorpion whirled on me, awkward but far too fast, and spread its twisted pincers. Either one could have snipped my head from my body like a Gardener pruning the sacred flowers. Zach put another arrow into the scorpion's side and it hissed, the first audible sound it had made the entire time. The scorpion spun toward him again and I hacked at the tail. At its thinnest point, just where the tail met the bloated stinger, it was only as thick as my wrist. My knife cleaved through and the amputated stinger fell onto the scorpion's back, then rolled away. The truncated tail thrashed wildly, spraying blue blood into the air.

I leapt away, but Zach had to put two more bolts through the scorpion's wildly rolling black eyes before it fell into the dust. Zach and I ran until we could no longer feel the dreameater's alien, dying pain in our minds. I sat in the sand, holding my head and trying in vain not to puke until the hissing finally fell silent.

I wouldn't have gone back at all, but Zach pointed out that he had only a single bolt left.

"I need to recover the other ones," he said. "You can stay here."

"Like hell," I panted. "Help me stand up."

Zach did, but we waited ten minutes after the last twitch before going anywhere near the dead mutant scorpion. I kept Zach's crossbow aimed at its head while he jerked his bolts free from the thick carapace.

"Think we could... eat it?" I asked.

Zach shook his head violently. "No way. It was a fucking dreameater. You... heard it. This is exactly why we kill them!"

I nodded wearily. I didn't want to eat the scorpion, either, but I worried about my partner. The Whitefingers didn't hunt or kill their dreameaters like we did, like Zach had spent his whole life doing. If we ever found them and managed to convince Jacks to take us in, Zach was going to have a hard time adjusting.

ZACH and I trudged back to the Whitefingers' old den. Along the
way, we checked the pits we had dug that morning. Eight of them
had scorpions inside. One had a ridge of weird blue spines down its
flanks. This one, Zach crushed beneath his boot.

But we pinned down the other seven, cut off their stingers and
pincers, then threaded them onto a bolt like a kebab. Neither of us
felt good about eating the scorpions and not just because we lacked
fire to cook them. I shuddered as they twitched slowly on the arrow
shaft and tried not to think about their big brother. But by the next
morning, we were both too hungry to object and ate the scorpions
in quick, crunching bites.

We both felt a little better for the food, but we still had no water.
And there wasn't much of the coppery blue-green scorpion blood.
It was getting hard to swallow and my eyes seemed to be shriveling
in their sockets. I began trying to convince my stomach to take
another drink of lizard blood... if we could find a lizard.

Zach and I agreed that we had to search further out and that
meant leaving the basement hiding hole behind. We couldn't live
on scorpions and sand. The Whitefingers were still our only hope
of survival.

So we resumed the search. I was looking for anything drinkable as much as for the Whitefingers, but there was no sign of either. There wasn't much out here at all. Centuries of storms had scoured away what little survived God's Wrath. Only a few megalithic structures remained – superbuildings like the Greenguard base and the Gardeners' headquarters – so Zach and I made for them. The empty husks were just that, empty of anything but long-broken furniture and dust, but one of them still had a final gift to give.

It was noon and the sun's merciless white glare was directly overhead. I could feel it through Zach's hat, hot and itchy. Zach wasn't sweating anymore – which meant he didn't smell as bad as I did – but I didn't think that was a good sign. He had to be getting badly dehydrated.

When I spotted the little smear of green, I thought it was another mirage. But Zach saw it, too. In the lee of a slick white wall, we found the grey-green spot in the dust. When we scraped the sand away, I discovered an oblong tuber of some kind. I didn't know if it was fungus or a cactus, but when I cut off the tip, a milky green fluid oozed out. It was wet and that was all I cared about.

We found a few more of the things and Zach swallowed a single small mouthful before we squeezed the strange juice out into our empty canteen. The stuff was as sour as barrel cactus and too thick to satisfy thirst very well, but it was cool and it was liquid. I felt my body begin forgiving me for the abuses I had heaped on it over the last week.

We dug through the surrounding sand some more, but seemed to have exhausted the patch of mysterious plants, so we finally gave up the hunt and moved on. We had one canteen half full of sour juice and were still thirsty. I took a drink and passed it back to Zach. He made a face as he swallowed and I suddenly laughed aloud.

"What?" he asked.

I imitated his expression and Zach burst into loud laughter too, which only made me laugh harder. I had never been prone to giggling fits, even as a little girl, and it had been a long time since my last attack of them. I was dimly aware that this was weird, but the way that the horizon kept swirling and the ground wouldn't be still was just so *funny*. But Zach was giggling and that was even stranger.

"Zee, wait," I gasped. "Something's wrong. You're not funny."

"No," he agreed. "I'm really serious."

It was hilarious. We laughed so hard that we would have cried if we could.

I was starting to have trouble placing one foot in front of the other. The ground moved up and down like water sloshing in a bucket. When the wind stirred the sand, the earth and sky blurred together.

I tried walking and fell down. I sort of remember getting back to my feet. A feeling of dread crept over me. What if I lost Zach again? We were still going to die out here, probably, but dying alongside my partner seemed okay. I just didn't want to be alone.

I didn't remember falling again, but I was on the ground. I squirmed in the sand, desperate to find Zach. I tried to call for him, but I couldn't find my voice. I found Kiyu instead. She walked toward me out of the distance. Everything beyond arm's length had become as watery and indistinct as heat shimmer, but she was clear. I reached for her and missed. I crawled forward and tried again, but like a mirage, Kiyu remained just out of reach no matter how I chased after her. Didn't Kiyu know how much I needed to find her? She was so close...

"Zee!" I tried to scream. "Help me!"

Wildly, I looked around for him, afraid that I had lost him before Kiyu found us, but Zach was only a few feet away. He knelt, his large hands cupped in front of him and full of a dancing red glow. He made the sign of the teardrop and the flame-colored light left an afterimage like a Halo in the air, a glowing red teardrop suspended before him.

I wanted to reach out to Zach, to feel him real and right there beside me. I didn't want to lose him, but I was frightened of the burning, bloody red tear he had made out of light.

So I turned away, squeezing my eyes shut. When I opened them again, I lay on my back, staring up at the sky. But there was something wrong with it. The sky wasn't white anymore. It was bright and blue, like in the mural on the stairs into the Tear of God. There were patches of more familiar white, but they were fluffy like balls of thistledown.

Something moved against the blue. I squinted. The sun was so bright, but a small, flickering shadow fluttered closer, carried on a breeze as cool and crisp as ay-see against my cheek. Was it a flower? It only had four petals, but they were so beautiful, striped with orange and black and dotted in white.

It wasn't a flower at all I saw as it fluttered by, but something else. Those weren't petals – they were wings. Some kind of insect?

I reached out and grabbed the flutter-by thing and the bright wings tickled my fingers. The bug farms of the Whisperward bred ants and crickets, termites and sand-hoppers. Nothing this beautiful or delicate. But when I opened my hand, I threw the thing inside onto the ground in revulsion. It wasn't colorful anymore. The wings were shriveled and white, the body a dull gray. The flutterby bug wobbled across the cracked earth on twisted, deformed legs, antennae waving blindly.

I yanked off my boot and held it over the crawling little mutant, but I stopped myself before smashing it. The blind white thing was so helpless, defenseless. Carefully, I picked it up again, wondering stupidly if I could fix the tiny creature somehow. It wasn't supposed to be sick like this...

Something grabbed me roughly by the sleeve and jerked me upright. Desperately, I grabbed for the flutterby, but my hands were only full of sand. There was nothing on the ground and the sky was white once more.

"We have to keep going," Zach said in a rough, rasping voice. He pulled on my arm.

"There was a flutterby," I tried to tell him. "I have to find it..."

Zach gave me another hard yank and we staggered on. The sand burned my bootless foot with every other step, but we broke into a trot as we tried to outrun the strange visions.

"Look," Zach said.

I saw square shapes in the ground like drawings. When we got closer, I could see they were the edges of old foundations. How big had Angel City been before the Wrath? Zach found the crumbling remains of a wall high enough to lean against. He steadied himself and then vomited spectacularly onto the concrete. I watched in uncomprehending interest for a moment before a sympathetic wave began in my own belly. And then I was on my hands and knees, spewing sour green juice into the dust.

When I could lift my head again, it was close to sunset. How much time had we lost? But I felt a little better. Edges tended to blur and double at times, but the world seemed somewhat steadier beneath my feet.

"Zee?" I called out.

I found Zach walking unsteadily a few yards away. He stared intently down at the earth.

"Zach? Are you okay?" I asked.

"We've got to find their hiding place."

I nodded. "Thirsty. Where's the juice?"

"I poured it out," he said. "It was bad. Weird dreams."

I frowned at the loss, but Zach was right. Whatever was wrong with us, it was a lot more than just dehydrated delirium and the green juice was probably to blame.

We made agonizingly slow progress through the fading dayglow, searching the ground for more disguised tunnels or openings into long-forgotten basements. White flashes at the corner of my vision kept trying to distract me, but I kept reminding myself that the flutterby had been a hallucination. Unless I wanted that pale and twisted little thing to be my final thought, we *had* to find the Whitefingers.

Zach and I stared too long at every bump and dip in the ruins for potential Whitefinger hideouts. Finally, I managed to grunt his name through dry lips and pointed to a dark crevice. Zach approached slowly, wobbling on unsteady feet. I toed sand into the crack and it vanished into an open space below.

"I found something," I said.

And then the earth gave way beneath me and I plunged down into empty blackness. I grabbed for the edge and my fingers closed on old concrete that crumbled as though rotten. Zach threw himself to the ground and grabbed the back of my jacket. The cloth cinched up painfully under my arms, but didn't tear. For a moment, I stopped falling.

"Julia, hold on–" Zach began as he pulled on the back of my fatigues.

The ancient concrete shattered beneath him and we fell together into darkness.

———

By the time I could make sense of the world again, the sky was black. Not even a wisp of moonglow. It was like looking down into a hole instead of lying at the bottom of one, but the ground under me was reassuringly solid. I felt around until I found Zach sprawled nearby. I gave him a gentle shake.

"Zee?"

Zach didn't move and I shook him harder until he gave a pained but very living groan. Carefully, I removed his goggles and pulled them down over my eyes. The night lenses flickered a few times and I worried that we had broken them in the fall, but the people of the old world manufactured some tough shit before God killed them all. The hole lit up in green and black.

We were in another basement or buried room. Except for the rocks and concrete that had tumbled down with us, it was empty. Wherever my boot was, it was too far away to have fallen in. The ceiling was about twenty feet above us, though, which meant that even standing on Zach's broad shoulders, there was no way for me to reach the surface again.

Zach made another sound, this one louder. "Shit."

"Are you okay?" I asked.

"I... hurt," he gasped. "I think I landed on the crossbow. Something's wrong with my back. My arm's worse."

I looked Zach over with the night lenses and helped pull the crossbow out from under him. I sucked in a breath when I saw his arm. Bolts had tumbled from the quiver as he fell and Zach had the bad luck to land on one. It impaled the thick muscle of his arm. Blood welled up around the shaft.

"Hold still," I told him. "You've got an arrow in you."

"Shot?"

"No. You fell on it, dumb-ass. But I don't think I can pull it out yet. You'll bleed too much. We've got nothing to stop an infection, either."

Zach nodded grimly. "What else did we lose?"

"Don't worry, I still have your hat."

I placed it gently on Zach's head and he chuckled. The laughter died a second later, though, as Zach gave his pockets a panicked pat. But then his expression turned into one of relief and he sagged back into the rubble.

"What?" I asked.

Zach touched the empty canteens and then his sheathed knife.

"Just making sure we have everything," he said.

I frowned. That wasn't true. He stopped his frantic searching at his pocket, not his belt. But he didn't want me to know what he kept there. Some frilly, romantic keepsake? Could Zachary Dias have a girl back in Angel City?

"Can we get out of here?" he asked.

I passed the goggles back so he could have a look for himself. I couldn't see his face clearly in the dark, but I could still read the set of his shoulders and tilt of his head. He didn't see any means of escape that I hadn't. Damn.

"We need help," Zach said.

I saw him touch his pocket again. Did the big religious bastard keep a holy relic in there or something? If he did, no wonder Zach didn't want to tell me. I would have mocked him incessantly.

It wasn't unheard of for people to take stones from the base of the Tear and swear that they brought good luck. I wondered if anyone felt that way about the shards of glass from Byron's greenhouse... I frowned into the darkness. Byron's greenhouse. There was a question there, but my head hurt too much to chase it down and there were more pressing concerns. Like not dying.

If Zach carried some holy charm in his pocket, I didn't think it was going to do much good. God probably wouldn't lift a finger to help the Gardeners, let alone a smart-ass blasphemer like me. What we needed were the Whitefingers. They were out there somewhere. They knew how to survive in the wastes and they could help us do the same.

I felt my own pockets until I found the piece of lace. Kiyu had left it for a reason. She wanted us to find her, didn't she?

"I know what to do," I said suddenly. "I can call for help."

"No one can hear us down here. We're days away from the city," Zach pointed out. "And the Whitefingers obviously aren't nearby."

"Not with my voice, Zee. But yins can hear me with their minds, right?"

"You're... going to call for a dreameater?"

There was a knife-edge of fear in his voice and a shiver ran down my spine, too. What if something *did* hear me, something like that scorpion? We were weak and injured. I took Zach's big, rough hand in mine and squeezed it. If some dreameater mutant came looking for an easy meal, we would fight it off together as best we could.

I wrapped the lace around my other hand and closed my eyes. And maybe, just maybe, Kiyu would come.

WE WERE TOO weak to do much but sleep. When Zach was awake, he was too damned stoic to show his pain, but he groaned in his sleep. I propped him up with some rocks to keep him from rolling onto his arm and jostling the crossbow bolt through his bicep. It grew light again, but he slept on.

Between my own bouts of unconsciousness, I thought of Kiyu as hard as I could, calling for her in my mind. By her own admission, her dreameater powers were more of the physical variety. But Kiyu did say that she could sense what someone was feeling if they felt strongly enough. And I wanted her to find us with all my heart.

I slid in and out of sleep and Kiyu followed me into my dreams. I dreamed of chasing her through the desert, limping doubly on my wounded leg and single boot. Even when I reached her, my arms passed through her body as though Kiyu were only a halo-gram. But there were dreams where I could touch her, too – and I definitely did. I woke from those dreams with my heart racing, but we were still alone at the bottom of the hole.

"Zach, I'm sorry," I whispered.

His eyes remained closed.

———

I HAD SLIPPED BACK into dreams. I was unconscious more often than awake now and I found it hard to keep my eyes open. Kiyu lay beneath me in soft green grass. One of those orange and black flutterbies perched on her nose, beating its wings slowly. I wanted to kiss her, but the fragile wings were in my way. I ran my fingers through Kiyu's shiny dark hair and the Whitefinger girl barked at me.

The rough noise jerked me back into consciousness. It was a dog. There weren't many in Angel City, but it was difficult to mistake that sound, even while dying at the bottom of a hole.

I opened my eyes. The sky was light. What day was it? Not long after we had fallen, I guessed, or Zach and I would already be dead. Shit...! I grabbed Zach's uninjured shoulder and shook him hard. He didn't wake up, but his broad chest was still rising and falling slowly. He was alive. For a little while longer, at least.

The barking grew louder. Three front legs and a long, pointed snout appeared at the edge of the hole. Diesel!

"Go–!" I croaked. I spent a moment coughing and trying to work up enough saliva to wet my mouth. "Diesel, go get Jacks!"

The mutant dog barked once more, then turned and ran away. I really hoped Diesel understood and hadn't just spotted something more interesting to yap at.

I shook Zach again. Harder. This time, he groaned and tried to sit up. I had to help him, which wasn't easy. I might have mentioned that Zach was a bit bigger than me and I wasn't feeling my best. I peeled away the torn sleeve of his Greenguard fatigues and checked his wound. The skin was hot and bright red around the shaft of the crossbow bolt.

"Bad?" Zach asked.

I couldn't lie to him.

"Yeah. Pretty fucking bad. But help's on the way."

"What–?"

Zach fell silent and we both looked up at the sound of voices. Diesel reappeared at the edge of the hole. His pink tongue lolled from his mouth and his ears pricked toward us.

"Careful!" someone shouted in a deep voice. Jacks. "Check it out, but go slow."

Another silhouette appeared at the rim of the hole above us and I recognized Kiyu, even though she was just an outline against the white sky.

"It's them," she shouted. "And they're hurt!"

She slid back from the hole and there was indistinct conversation above us. Kiyu returned to the edge of the pit. Her hair hung down around her face.

"Put your weapons on the ground over there," Kiyu instructed, pointing with one small hand to the dusty floor of our pit.

"Why?" Zach rasped.

"Don't you want to be rescued? We could leave if you like your hole that much," Kiyu said.

"No!" I shouted. My voice cracked.

I drew my knife and threw it to the ground in the direction Kiyu had pointed. Zach stared, took a deep breath and weakly kicked his own blade and crossbow over to join my knife. The quiver rolled over to the heap a moment later.

"Okay. Stand back," Kiyu warned.

I moved away and squatted next to Zach, staring up at her. He gasped and I looked around the hole, worried that the edges weren't stable and that the Whitefinger girl was about to fall in. It wasn't anything in the pit that made Zach gasp, though. At least, not anymore. Our weapons had risen into the air, up and out of the pit. They vanished over the edge.

"Alright. Now you two," Kiyu said.

"No!" Zach shouted. "Just... just throw me a rope or something! I'll climb out."

I put my hand on his shoulder.

"Zee, we have to get out of here and you can't climb with that bolt in your arm." I raised my voice. "I'll go first."

I stood up slowly, but the trembling wasn't just dehydration or hunger. My heart pounded and if I weren't dying of thirst, I would have been sweating right through the carbon microfiber of my uniform. I shrieked and just about passed out when something touched me.

"Hold still," Kiyu said.

It was like the wind made solid. Formless pressure held my arms against my body and my legs together. I couldn't tell if it was soft or hard. The force had no texture. It was just... there. It had no direction either, not like being pulled up by a hand, or even like the pressure against my feet in the Gardeners' elevator. The whole thing was more like being wrapped snugly in a blanket and then lifted. A wave of nostalgia hit me, some half-formed memory of my mother swaddling me and singing quietly.

But I still panicked when my feet left the ground. I screamed and thrashed. Kiyu grunted, but her mind held me tightly and I took deep breaths, trying to get myself under control. The floor fell away and the hole grew closer, then I was out.

"Julia?" Zach shouted. "Julia!"

Jacks and his band of Whitefingers stood off to one side, a safe distance away from the pit. Kiyu moved me over the sand and then lowered me to the ground. Diesel ran circles around us until Kiyu let go, then bounded forward. My legs wouldn't hold me and I fell on my ass, throwing my hands up defensively across my face, but the dog just sniffed me and then licked my fingers. He suddenly stopped and ran back to Jacks. Diesel looked at the Whitefinger for a moment and then, at some silent command, sat down next to his master.

"I'm not going to hurt you," Kiyu was saying. She leaned down over the rim of the hole.

I crawled on my belly to the edge where Diesel had perched. Below, Zach was struggling to stand.

"Julia! Are you okay?" His voice was as tight as a bowstring.

"I'm fine, Zee," I answered as evenly as I could manage with my pulse racing and my lips cracking with dehydration. "Finding the Whitefingers was your idea, remember?"

Zach took a long breath and exhaled loudly. He nodded to Kiyu. I saw him stiffen as she wrapped him in her psionic power.

"Careful of his arm," I hissed.

"I'm trying," Kiyu said. "Shut up."

I shut the hell up. I didn't want Kiyu dropping Zach. His tanned face had gone pale and his jaw clenched so tightly that I could hear teeth grinding. I didn't know if I had ever seen my partner that terrified.

"Hold on, Zee," I told him. "We're going to get you out of there."

I held my breath until Kiyu pulled Zach from the hole and set him down. I ran to Zach and threw my arms around him. He held me tightly for a moment, then pushed me firmly away. Zach spread his feet a few inches further apart, out into a ready stance. He was trembling so hard that I marveled the man was still standing at all, but I took up a position to his left – on his wounded side – and turned my shoulder to protect his back.

"So what do you want?" Jacks asked. "What are you doing out here again?"

Zach remained sullenly silent, so I cleared my throat to speak without croaking. Hopefully.

"We delivered your warning. The Gardeners didn't like it much, though, and tried to execute us. Now we need your help."

"Looks like they just about finished the job," said Jacks, looking pointedly at Zach's arm and then my sliced-up leg.

But he came slowly forward and held out a water skin. Zach and I traded it back and forth a few times. I managed to take it slow enough not to puke in front of the Whitefingers.

Jacks had his spear disassembled and slung on a strap over his back. He held Zach's crossbow and kept it loaded. Some of the others had collected our knives and empty canteens. I clearly hated it less than Zach, but I would have felt better if I were armed. The Greenguard practiced a little bare-hands combat, but the White-fingers had spears and if they decided to kill us, we didn't stand much of a chance.

The Whitefingers selected a stable patch of earth not far from the hole and made camp as the dayglow faded from the sky. They folded their cloaks to sit on and broke out the food. It was a white grain rolled in some kind of leaf around a piece of that tangy meat they had given us before. Fish.

Zach and I were each given one small roll. I guessed they didn't want to spend a lot of food on people they still might have to kill. But it was something.

"What happened?" Jacks asked us.

I glanced at Zach before answering.

"Pretty much what I already said. We returned to Angel City, and told Gregory what you told us. The next morning, we're being hauled out of our beds and taken to Thorn. That's the High Gardener. He asked us a few questions, decided that we'd been corrupted by your dreameater–" Here, I nodded briefly to Kiyu. "–and sentenced us to execution by storm. They staked us out, but we escaped. We tried to find you... Where the hell did you all go?"

"We had to move on," said Kiyu. "There were a bunch of Greenguard searching the ruins. Probably for you. They were getting too close."

"I... didn't see anyone after we got away," I told her. "Are you sure it was Greenguard?"

"Yes, but they went back to the city not long after. Now, what do you want?" Jacks asked.

"We have nowhere to go," Zach said reluctantly between small bites of food. "We... want to join you."

Some of the Whitefingers chuckled. Jacks arched his remaining eyebrow as he looked back and forth between me and Zach. The crossbow rested across his knees, but wasn't pointed directly at us.

"We'll talk about that later," said Jacks. "Are the Gardeners still protecting their Stormsphere with extra Greenguard?"

"Yes," I answered. "Likely more of them after we escaped. Thorn seemed pretty paranoid about anyone getting into the Tear."

"Then there's not much use in trying again." Jacks rubbed his burn-scarred face. "We should return to the warren. Now the question is whether or not to take you with us."

I swallowed hard, struggling to keep silent and still while Jacks considered. The food he had given us sat like lead in my stomach.

"I could give you water," Jacks said. "France could get that arrow out of your arm. You might make it to the Whisperward."

"They'll kill us. We're criminals there. Even if we sneak back into Angel City, we can't hide forever," I pointed out. Probably a touch defensively.

"We lost everything delivering your message," Zach said. "And we want the same thing as you do. We don't want the Stormsphere to fail or anyone to die."

"They were Blackthumbs," Kiyu told Jacks. "They know about the 'Ward. They could have useful information if we ever need to go back."

"If there's even a city there next year. Do you sense anything? Anything dangerous?" Jacks asked.

"Well, not really," Kiyu said. She might have blushed.

"You found them, girl."

"I'm not much of a yin, but they were injured and sky-high on engan. Anyone could find that."

"Engan?" I asked, but no one was listening to me.

"Diesel?" Jacks said.

The dog got up and padded a circle around us. He sniffed, but I knew Diesel wasn't using his nose and tried not to tense. I waited to feel him snuffling through my thoughts or for my brains to start dribbling out of my ears. I still wasn't sure yet which stories of evil dreameaters were true. Next to me, Zach bit his lip hard enough to bruise.

"All I want is for the people of the Whisperward to stay safe," Zach told Jacks.

I had the urge to point out that it was the dog we had to convince, not Jacks. But smart-ass though I am, Zach seemed too frightened to appreciate the remark, so I kept quiet. Diesel finished his circle and sat down beside Jacks again. The Whitefinger scratched behind his ears.

"Very well. We'll take you with us. You wouldn't even be the first to leave the 'Wards and join us," Jacks said. "But you will be the first Blackthumbs. Don't try anything or we will kill you."

"What about our weapons? Can we get them back?" Zach asked.

"Not yet, Blackthumb. Maybe later. Once you see the warren, you're one of us. If you ever try running back to the Whisperwards, we'll catch you and our yins will remove any potentially dangerous memories. It can be hard on a mind."

Apparently dreameaters *could* make your brain dribble out of your ears. I drew a deep breath.

"Alright," I said. "Fuck the Whisperwards. Fuck the Gardeners. Can I have some more food now?"

———

ZACH and I didn't have cloaks and the Whitefingers weren't packing extra bedrolls, so we slept on the ground. I had been doing it for the last week or so, but for most of that time, I was hungry, thirsty, or delirious and hadn't fully appreciated just how uncomfortable it was. Which was *very*.

I guessed that we were on some kind of probation because Jacks organized a watch on us again, though this time, we weren't bound.

I woke every few hours, clawing at the hard earth and reminding myself that I wasn't about to fall, that Zach and I were safe on stable ground. When one of these restless periods came during Kiyu's watch, I sat up.

"Hey," I said.

"Hi," she answered. "Are you okay?"

"Yeah."

Nice start, Julia. Now think of something brilliant.

"Um, this is yours. Again," I said.

I found the scrap of lace crumpled at the bottom of my pocket. It was dirty and looking more than a little threadbare after everything it had been through. Kiyu came closer and took it with a small smile. She didn't seem to care about the dirt and sweat ground into the white lace, though, or the ragged and torn edges. Kiyu traced the tiny loops of thread with her fingertip, just as I had done. Then she pocketed the scrap without saying why she had left it behind.

"Your boss... Jacks," I said. "How did he get that scar?"

"Lightning."

"He got struck?"

"Not exactly. He didn't dig deep enough and some molten stormglass ran down into his pit. Jacks couldn't get up, though, or the storm would kill him. So he just lay there, letting the glass burn him," Kiyu said. She gave me a curious look. "What were you doing drinking engan juice?"

"Engan?" I struggled to follow the sudden change in conversation. Kiyu asked almost as many questions as I did. "Well... uh... I had a very good reason. A very important one."

"You didn't know what it was, did you?"

"I still don't know what the hell it is," I told her.

"It's a plant," Kiyu said.

"Yeah, I guessed that much," I answered. "It was that green goo we drank, right?"

Kiyu nodded. "It's rare, so we collect the juice when we can. Yins drink it to open their minds. It's powerful stuff. Even people without gifts can have visions when they drink engan."

"So it made us... dreameaters?" I asked.

I decided not to tell Zach about that. But Kiyu winced.

"I don't eat dreams, okay?" she said. "Or minds or souls or anything like that. I eat fish and rice and cactus, like everyone else. My gifts aren't a curse or a taint. It's just a thing I can do, like painting or fishing."

"Yeah, but you said you hunt mutants and stuff, just like Blackthumbs."

Kiyu shrugged her slim shoulders. "Sometimes. But that's not all I can do. I go with the hunting parties out into the flats. Sometimes I go with people like Jacks to the Whisperwards. Anywhere dangerous," she said. "...Like a Greenguard, I guess."

"Kiyu? That's your name, right?" I asked.

She smiled. "Yes. What's yours?"

"Julia Reed." Now that I had actually introduced myself to her, I felt a little less guilty about all my fantasies. "Kiyu? Did there used to be more Whitefingers... people like you? Thorn said something, that maybe we didn't always live in the Whisperwards. Do you know anything about that?"

Kiyu nodded and her dark hair bobbed in the moonglow. "Yeah. It was after the meltdown, centuries ago. The cities weren't safe, so everyone left. They migrated southwest to northeast, then back again. Always moving."

"How did they survive the storms?"

"They were protected," said Kiyu.

"By what? The Stormspheres? They're too big to move."

"I don't know," Kiyu admitted.

Damn. At least it was better than Sunday school, where the Gardeners scolded me and called my questions blasphemy.

"So what happened after that?" I asked. "You said that the cities weren't safe. But they are."

"Maybe they are now. Things changed. Some of the people went underground. That's us," Kiyu said, pointing around to the slumbering Whitefingers. "Everyone else followed the Gardeners into the cities, to the Stormspheres. We don't know what they are or how to make them work, though."

"But the Gardeners do," I muttered to myself.

Did they really, though? Two of the Stormspheres had failed already and Angel City would be next unless something changed.

I thanked Kiyu and lay down again. To be honest with myself, I would have preferred to stay up and flirt with her, but my mind was stuck on this new version of history. What Kiyu told me didn't necessarily prove the Gardeners wrong, that God had not wept His great black tears for the suffering survivors of his Wrath, but if she was right, there was a whole other chapter to our past that the Gardeners never talked about.

I rolled over and looked at Zach. His eyes were slitted partially open, but he closed them without saying a word.

As soon as the sky lightened, Jacks wanted our injuries examined. Zach bit down on his belt and nodded when he was ready. The Whitefinger who had taken care of us before – France, apparently – grabbed Zach's thick bicep in one hand, the bolt shaft in his other and then gave it a sharp pull. The crust of congealed blood that had built around the wound tore loose and bright red welled up in the hole.

France said the bolt had missed the artery and that the infection was mild so far. Getting sand packed into an open wound wasn't good for your health, he said, but the desert was actually pretty sterile.

"This is going to hurt," France told Zach.

The Whitefinger sprinkled salt into the hole in his bicep to slow the bleeding. Zach took it better than I would have, but he still left bite marks in his belt that never did come out.

The Whitefinger healer produced more of the salve he had used last time and daubed it over the hole before binding it. Then France turned his attention to me. I bit my lip and let him examine the cut running down the back of my thigh. Thanks to the dressings Zach and I had already tied on, it was still fairly clean. I stopped France when he got out the salve.

"I can put that on myself," I told him.

My cheeks were burning, but France wasn't blushing and his pants were reassuringly absent of bulges. Still, this wasn't really the first impression I wanted to make on the Whitefingers. I might not have minded if Kiyu had volunteered... But she didn't and I managed on my own. When I was done applying the medicine, one of the other Whitefingers tossed me something black and dusty. It was my boot.

"I found that about half a mile from your hole," he told me. "Jacks was going to give it to Diesel, but I guess you'll be wanting it back."

"Yeah, just a bit," I said by way of thanks.

Jacks portioned out the supplies and we had to carry our share, which didn't include any weapons. The Whitefingers set out at a brisk pace, making Zach and I struggle to keep up. We were both injured and had only begun to recover from starvation and dehydration, so we lagged behind. All things considered, though, I'd like to think we did well. Zach and I had been Blackthumbs for years and worked hard to stay fit, but I doubted the Whitefingers were very impressed.

The land sloped away to the west as we crossed the indistinct line between ancient Angel City and down into the Pacific Desert. I pulled my goggles down over my eyes to protect them from the glare off the sparkling salt flats. After a few hours, my boots had picked up a thick coating of white dust and I chuckled to myself. It wasn't going to take long before we were true Whitefingers.

I looked over at Zach to share my thought. He was going to have to accept our new situation. It would be tough on him. The least I could do was help. This was all my fault in the first place. But when I turned to joke with Zach, I saw a flash of light behind us. I stopped walking and found the same twinkling spot of brightness that had plagued us ever since Zach discovered me busily dying in the ruins.

"Hey, do you all see that?" I asked in a loud voice.

One by one, the Whitefingers stopped and peered back.

"It's just the sunlight reflecting off of something," said Kiyu.

"But Zach and I saw it days ago, when we first left Angel City," I told her. "If it's the same thing, then it's got to be moving."

"Diesel," Jacks called.

The dog trotted up from the back of the short column. Jacks crouched, scratching between the dog's pointed ears. Diesel barked once and then loped off in the direction of the light.

"Let's keep moving," said Jacks. He turned west again and resumed walking. "If it *is* following us, let's get some more distance. If not, I don't want to lose a day of travel worrying about it."

"What about Diesel?" I asked.

"If it's something that intends us any harm, Diesel will be able to sense it. He'll catch up and let us know," said Jacks.

I couldn't help a look back over my shoulder every few minutes, though. Kiyu teased me about it.

"Are you worried about Diesel?" she asked. "I thought you didn't keep pets in the 'Ward."

"We don't. It's hard enough to feed the humans," I said. "Can that dog really sense if something wants to hurt us?"

Kiyu nodded and I wished she didn't have her face covered. "Diesel's warned us of a dozen mutants and other predators since we left the warren."

"Was he the one who found us?"

The Whitefinger girl lifted her chin and looked at me. I thought she might be smiling under the cloth covering her mouth.

"No," she said. "I may not be terribly sensitive, but I heard you. You're lucky we were close, though. Distance makes it harder."

"So it's easier to sense what I um... feel now?" I asked. "Since I'm closer?"

"I can pick up strong emotions," said Kiyu. "I could certainly tell if you wanted me dead."

I'm sure I blushed. What had Kiyu felt from me? Oh shit, could she sense my embarrassment? From there, it was a swift downward spiral of thought, making my mortification worse and worse. And presumably easier for Kiyu to pick up on.

"So... Diesel will know?" I asked, desperately trying to think of something else.

"Absolutely. Dogs are very sensitive and empathic. They're almost always yins," said Kiyu. "Seldom yangs. But Diesel can only sense strong stuff, like the intent to kill. Snakes and scorpions out here usually attack on instinct, either to hunt or to protect themselves. So sometimes we don't get much warning."

"Like with Lekan, right? That was his name, the dream– the yin who died?"

"Yeah."

Kiyu fell silent.

Hours passed and Diesel still had not returned, but Jacks didn't seem worried. We had no idea how far off that reflection was. We had to stop for the day and Jacks surveyed the sky carefully before deciding that it would be safe to remain out in the open. There would be no storm tonight, at least. The Whitefingers laid down their cloaks like blankets and began pulling out more rolls of rice and smoked fish meat.

I was hungry enough that I was sure even the most brain-dead yin-empowered dog could have picked that up. Zach glanced at me when my stomach gurgled, but then his did, too. I chuckled and thought of making a crack about our secret Blackthumb language, but not all of the Whitefingers seemed as open to us as Jacks and Kiyu, so I kept my mouth shut. It wasn't easy for me, but my dry tongue served as incentive.

"Here," Kiyu said. She handed me one of her rolls.

"Spread it around," Jacks ordered.

The Whitefingers portioned out the food for seven of us.

"Maybe we shouldn't feed them until we get back to Lago and a real yin reads them," one of them suggested.

"Shut it, Ahmet. I've made my decision. It holds until we get home," Jacks said sternly.

"I'm not saying we should starve them to death. Just enough water to make it back to the warren," Ahmet said.

But he divided up his food like all of the others. I made a point of thanking everyone except Ahmet.

When Zach finally spotted Diesel, I jumped to my feet along with my partner, but no one else did. They just waited while Diesel padded straight to Jacks, who filled a bowl with water and set it down before taking the dog by his furry chin.

"Did you find the shiny thing, boy?" Jacks asked. "Was it dangerous?"

Diesel barked once and stuck his face into the bowl of water, drinking noisily. Jacks nodded and returned to his meal, apparently satisfied.

"Well?" I asked. "What the hell did that mean?"

"Whatever's out there, it's no danger to us," said Jacks.

Zach released a long sigh and sat down again. I reached out and found his hand, giving it a squeeze. He was scared, but we were in this together and I wanted Zach to know I still had his back. That I always would. He looked at me and for a moment, I thought he was going to embarrass us both by crying. I didn't think I had ever seen Zach cry, not even when Thorn pronounced our death sentence. I didn't want to start now.

But Zach just smiled back at me and squeezed my fingers in his. I swore and told the big bastard to ease up before he snapped my hand in half.

———

We walked for days. Zach and I only really had each other for company. Jacks and the other Whitefingers didn't speak much and even though Kiyu seemed to be watching us – or me, if I felt like flattering myself – we didn't talk much after that first night.

The Pacific Desert seemed endless and the dry, salty wind made speaking unpleasant. We walked with our goggles down to protect our eyes from the glare off the salt dunes and our bandanas tied firmly over our mouths. The Whitefingers wrapped cloth around their faces and even wore thin blindfolds to cut down the light.

There wasn't much living out here, but what little there was, the Whitefingers knew how to find. A lone saguaro grew in the shelter of a stand of rocks. I could imagine biting into one of the fruits so vividly that I could taste it. Hell, I was thinking about it so hard that Kiyu and Diesel could probably taste it. But I didn't see a single bud on the cactus.

Jacks used a mirror to look down into the boot that had formed at the base of the cactus. A snake had made a den of the hole, but Kiyu lifted it safely out with a wave of her hand. One blow of a rock later, we had snake for dinner. Jacks reached into the cactus boot and pulled out a pair of water skins. Apparently, the Whitefingers hid caches of supplies when they traveled, and it made sense. No one from the Whisperwards could survive out here and it wasn't even easy for the Whitefingers. I could see why – if we had ever lived in the wastes like this – Thorn had no desire to return to such a hard, scrabbling existence. Not that understanding made me hate the sanctimonious prick any less.

No wonder Jacks and Kiyu had decided to press on with their mission even after losing Lekan. It was a long and dangerous trip back to their warren, so popping home to replace their lost yin wasn't a casual option.

I looked up at Jacks and wondered at how different he was from a Greenguard commander. We reported back to Gregory every day to receive orders from him or guidance from older Blackthumbs.

Gregory consulted constantly with High Gardener Thorn on policy and enforcement – and probably how to tie his own shoes.

Out here, the wastes bred leaders. Given his mission to investigate the Stormsphere's call for help, Jacks had to determine how to get there, how to infiltrate Angel City, what to do when their mind-reader died and when Kiyu got caught trying to finish the mission. Not to mention deciding the fate of a pair of troublesome Black-thumbs. Twice. Even Kiyu had to make her own calls after sneaking into the city and stealing the key from Gardener Byron. Maybe she had made the wrong decision, but I had trouble imagining most Greenguard taking that kind of initiative.

It was really a wonder that I hadn't run off to join the White-fingers sooner. Although that was precisely the point in recruiting me to the Greenguard, wasn't it? Keep your friends close and your enemies closer. Was I truly an enemy of the Gardeners, though? I didn't like them and I hated Thorn, sure. But enemies...? They had tried to execute me and I killed three Greenguard, so I guessed we were.

The white desert was broad and empty. The relentless sun and dry air were threats enough, but on the fourth day, a large shadow swept over us and I looked up. My goggles tinted automatically against the light and I picked out a huge winged shape falling out of the sky toward us. Diesel growled deep in his throat. The White-fingers' blindfolds weren't as good at filtering the bright sun as my goggles and they shaded their eyes, trying to see what the dream-eater dog was snarling at. Jacks and the rest spread out, but couldn't see that the oversized mutant eagle had already targeted Ahmet.

I charged him. If he had been watching me instead of the sky, the Whitefinger might have assumed I had finally turned on them. The eagle dove with a shriek like tearing metal and I jumped, tackling Ahmet to the ground. The wind of the bird's wings buffeted us into the salty earth. I rolled away and scrambled to my feet. There were claw marks in the hardpan three inches deep.

The eagle climbed skyward again, but Kiyu was running after it. Rocks yanked themselves out of the ground and hurled up at the bird. A chunk of stone as big as Kiyu's entire body slammed into its wing and the eagle tumbled down from the sky.

Jacks was on it in a heartbeat. Diesel sank his teeth into its leg above a set of huge yellow talons, but the eagle screamed again and threw the dog off with a single thrash of its foot. Jacks leapt on the bird and put his weight behind his spear. The point sank into the greasy feathers and the eagle screamed even louder than before. Six-inch hooked talons lashed out, but instead of ripping through Jacks, they jerked to a stop in the empty air.

Kiyu stood with her hands out, sweat beading on her forehead where her hood had fallen back. She held the oversized eagle there, pinning it with her will until the other Whitefingers moved in and finished it off.

Zach and I heard the Whitefingers do something similar to the snake while escorting us away from their den, but our eyes had been covered. Seeing Kiyu in action was something else entirely. I liked Kiyu and was willing to try her way of life, but old fears died hard in the face of power like that. I had to wonder why the Gardeners called people like her dreameaters and not rock-throwing-fucker-uppers.

The Whitefingers cut into the bird to see if its flesh was safe to eat. Ahmet dusted himself off – not that his clothes weren't already stained white by salt – and graced me with a reluctant nod. I gave him a smug smirk, but it vanished just as soon as the wastelander turned his back on me. I slipped over to Zach, who stood a few yards off from the Whitefingers. He was staring at Kiyu, too.

"Hey, Zee," I asked quietly. "Are we doing the right thing, trying to join these people?"

"We have to, Julia. This is the only way for us all to survive," he said.

"Are you sure?"

"Yeah. Listen, Julia–"

Zach didn't get to finish whatever he was going to say before Jacks called us over to help carve out any edible meat. We trotted closer and Kiyu smiled at me. It was hard to flirt over the carcass of a giant mutant, but I smiled back a little. If we were going to be Whitefingers – even our carbon microfiber fatigues were turning white now – then we would have to pull our weight.

Zach and I were now apprentices to the Whitefingers that we once hunted. My smile became a smirk. Even if our decision to join the Whitefingers wasn't wise, it certainly was interesting.

———

THE NEXT MORNING, the western horizon was dark. There was a storm brewing.

The Whitefingers were tense and packed up their camp quickly. Zach and I needed no prodding to get moving. My leg was stiff and still hurt like hell, but I didn't let that slow me down. As we walked, I scanned the Pacific Desert through my tinted goggles. There wasn't much cover. I spotted a low ridge of rock worn down into shallow ripples across the crusty white ground, but nothing substantial. Old Angel City was far behind us now, even the ruins refusing to enter the salty and desolate desert. But that meant no shelter from the coming storm. I quickened my pace to catch up with Jacks.

"The storm is coming," I said.

Jacks snorted.

"You have a hiding hole nearby, don't you?" I asked.

"Not here, no," he answered.

"So what do we do?"

"Keep moving. We'll stop in an hour or two."

Jacks was intent on covering as much ground as possible and refused to answer any more questions. Though to be fair to him, it was really just restating the one: how do we not die? I fell back to limp alongside Zach again. My partner looked nervous, too. He pulled his hat down low over his head and leaned into the rising wind. Grains of sand and salt began pinging off the lenses of our goggles.

Jacks called a halt after only half an hour. I guess even he didn't trust the storm to hold off much longer. With a few short commands, the Whitefingers went to work.

"Here, take this," Jacks said.

The big man tossed something to Zach. It took us both a moment to figure out that it was a collapsible shovel.

"That belonged to Lekan," Jacks told us. "Treat it well until we can return it to his family. Now get to work."

Zach nodded and folded out the shovel's handle. The Whitefingers were digging several long pits disturbingly similar to the graves in the cactus fields and orchards. Even Diesel dug frantically alongside Jacks, dirt and sand flying from between his hind legs. Zach fell in beside the others.

"What can I do?" I asked.

Jacks looked up from the ground, but kept digging. He jerked his head to one side. "Set up the spears about twenty yards out toward the storm. Drive them in deep."

"Got it," I said.

Ahmet peered at me suspiciously when I came to collect his spear, but he handed it over and returned to digging without commentary. I made sure that the sections of each spear were screwed tightly together and stabbed them into the ground as hard as I could. One of them leaned precariously and I had to find a new place to set it up. The storm might blow one loose – sand and lightning were dangerous enough without a spear flying around, too. I ran back to Jacks.

"We're rosy," I told him.

"What?" he asked.

"It's done," I said.

Jacks grunted in answer. Sweat beaded on his brown skin. There were no extra shovels, so I just stood in the swirling dust, nervously watching the storm grow closer and wondering how fast it was moving. The sky had turned black and flashed uncomfortably green. Shit. I could only watch for a few minutes before I got down on my knees and dug with my hands like Diesel.

"Kiyu, can't you... I don't know, push the storm away? Like you protected Jacks from that bird's claws?" I asked.

I winced as salty earth bit in beneath my fingernails. Kiyu shook her hair out of her face and concentrated on digging.

"It's too big," she told me in between dumping out shovels full of dirt and salt. "Each grain of sand may be small, but there are millions of them. Together, it weighs tons. And it's complicated, all those moving little particles. It would take a hundred yangs to even try."

I worked up a rhythm with Kiyu, scooping out loose dirt while she emptied out her shovel and the hole slowly deepened. I didn't look out at the storm anymore, but the wind was whipping my braid into my face and thunderclaps echoed across the dunes. The hair stood up along the back of my neck and down my arms. Every breath had a charged, metallic taste.

"Enough!" Jacks shouted.

I wasn't sure I agreed with that, but I didn't think we had much choice.

"France and Peter! Ahmet and Zach," he called out, pointing to each hole in the earth. "Kiyu and Julia!"

Ahmet shoved Zach into the hole they had been digging. Jacks jumped into his own and Diesel climbed in after him. Kiyu grabbed my hand and yanked me down into the earth with her. She pushed me onto my back and lay down on top of me. Kiyu pulled up her hood and wrapped her cloak around us both.

"We're still in the open," I hissed. "The storm!"

"There's resin in the cloaks," she said. "It's non-conductive and insulates us. The spears will draw most of the lightning. Just stay low and the storm should roll right over us."

"...Rosy," I managed to gasp.

"If we don't get buried too deeply," said Kiyu. "Sometimes the storms can lay down a few feet of sand."

I twitched and Kiyu hissed in pain as I jabbed her side. She shifted on top of me, trying to find a comfortable position that kept us both covered. The Whitefinger girl held her cloak wound tightly around us. It smelled strange, half sweet and half musky. That must have been the resin Kiyu was talking about, I decided. Then her elbow poked into my stomach.

"Ow! Would you stop moving around?" I asked.

"You moved first! Besides, would you rather be stuck in a hole smelling Diesel? Or crushed under Peter?"

"No," I stammered. "This is um... fine..."

I trailed off inelegantly. We lay together in the darkness and listened to the wind howl like a demon above us. Kiyu's heart beat fast against my chest and her breath warmed my cheek. She was more or less still now, but I was all too aware of her slender body on top of me, of her legs draped over mine. Her breasts were small and firm against my own, and my nipples swiftly stiffened at the contact. What good was the dark for hiding my blush if Kiyu could feel me poking her?

"Are you okay?" she asked.

"I'm scared," I admitted.

"I'm always scared during storms, too."

We waited quietly again. Kiyu shifted and her breasts moved against mine. Was it my imagination or was she as stiff as me? I was getting awfully wet.

"Can you, um, feel it?" I asked.

"Feel what...?" Kiyu's voice was unsteady.

"What I'm feeling. With your powers? That I'm... scared?"

"Oh." Kiyu's small body shifted on top of me, rubbing lightly and I brutally stifled a moan. "It's hard to tell."

"It is?" I gasped.

Kiyu's lips were right next to my ear in order to make herself heard over the loud hissing of the sand and wind. "It's hard to tell if it's you that I'm feeling... or if it's me."

I turned my head, brushing my cheek against hers. Kiyu moved her head slightly and we struggled with the cloak when a drift of dust blew down beneath the edge of her hood. When we were settled safely under the insulating cloth once more, Kiyu's face hovered in the darkness in front of me. Flashes of green light strobed and backlit her through the cloak. I couldn't see Kiyu's eyes and her face was just a silhouette. My heart slammed inside my ribs.

In the dark, I could see nothing, only feel everything. I lifted my head and gently touched my lips to Kiyu's. She went very still for a moment and I cursed my impatience, but then I felt her lips press back. Her cheeks brushed my skin, as smooth and soft as flower petals. My head fell back into the earth at the bottom of the hole. Kiyu followed me down and kissed me again. I opened my mouth and traced her lower lip with my tongue. She tasted salty and sweet.

I kissed Kiyu and her fingers curled into my sleeves, pulling me tight against her. I shivered and could no longer silence the moan. I wrapped my arms around Kiyu's narrow waist and held her close. For us, in that moment, the storm vanished.

WE WERE TRAPPED THERE in the hole for hours. Kiyu and I didn't
have a lot of room to move around and the weight of sand burying
us eventually put a damper on what would otherwise have been
one hell of a great afternoon. But it was good to be held. Kiyu's
heartbeat was reassuring in the darkness and we kissed as the sand
pressed us together.

The Whitefingers knew the salt desert and had their tricks to
avoid the sandstorms, but the storms could be unpredictable and
prove deadly even to the best-prepared wastelanders. When it was
over, Kiyu and I had to dig through about a foot of loose sand to get
back to the surface. We came up coughing and gasping. For all the
sweetness of sharing Kiyu's breath, the air had grown alarmingly
stale. Jacks and Diesel were clawing their way out of the dust, too,
along with Zach and Ahmet.

"Shovels!" Jacks shouted.

We fell on the fourth hole where the other two Whitefingers
had taken shelter. France and Peter had dug their trench in the lee
of a small boulder, but the storm must have changed direction and
instead of protecting them, the stone had created an eddy in the
howling wind and buried them under several feet of sand.

We dug with shovels and hands and paws. I felt tangled cloth beneath my fingers and gave a shout. Jacks and Zach hauled the other Whitefinger men up out of the hole. Jacks' scarred face was drawn with worry. France and Peter were limp and unmoving on the ground. Jacks put his good ear close to their mouths, listening.

"They're not breathing," he said.

With his fingers, Jacks probed Peter's mouth for sand, but there was nothing. He pinched the other man's nose shut and put his lips over his mouth. Kiyu knelt beside France and did the same. I felt a jolt of jealousy as Kiyu kissed him, but it swiftly faded when I realized that she was actually blowing air into his lungs. In between breaths, Kiyu and Jacks put their hands on the other Whitefingers' chests and pushed rhythmically, working their lungs or maybe their hearts like bellows.

France began gasping and spluttering almost at once, but Jacks worked on Peter for five minutes before the smaller man finally gave a great, retching cough and rolled over onto his side, vomiting into the sand.

I released a breath that I hadn't known I was holding. I glanced at Zach, but he was looking back to the east. His mouth was turned down in a worried frown before he tugged his bandana up over his face again.

"You okay, Zee?" I asked.

"Yeah. Rosy," he said. "That was… I don't know. Something else."

"It was," I agreed and wondered if I was smirking. I doubted Zach enjoyed his time underground as much as I had. He gave me an arched look and I stuck out my tongue.

———

WE HAD SURVIVED a storm out in the open, without the protection of the Stormsphere. But I shared some of Zach's doubts. It would be a while before I forgot the fear on Jacks' face as he pulled his unconscious men up out of the sand. We could survive the sandstorms outside the Whisperwards, but it was dangerous. Two men had nearly died. Life was hard and risky out here.

But when I thought about returning to the Whisperward – assuming that Zach and I could ever prove ourselves innocent of dreameater control – I could only seethe at Thorn and the other Gardeners, their secrets and half-truths... Kiyu and her life may have had their risks, but it still made more sense to me than anything else. I didn't *want* to go back to the Whisperward, I realized.

The sky behind us was still dark and tinged green, but France checked Peter out – and then himself, a bit more awkwardly – and declared them both fit for travel. Peter was wobbly and the other Whitefingers watched him with concern, but after a small meal, we moved hastily on.

"We can manage a few more miles before dark," said Jacks. "So let's get moving."

The Pacific Desert sparkled as if the storm had polished the white dunes. They turned orange and then red as the sun set. Jacks called a halt, but Kiyu told me that we were getting close to the warren now. She was trying to reassure me, I thought. Kiyu smiled and I wanted to take her hand, but I worried about what Zach would think. Or Jacks. I smiled back through the fading dayglow and Kiyu blushed high in her golden cheeks.

It occurred to me that I could have a lot of fun seeing just how much of my mind Kiyu could read, though poor Diesel might get the wrong idea. Would he understand that Kiyu very much enjoyed how I was attacking her?

We slept close together that night, but not under Kiyu's cloak and only brushed trembling fingertips a few times. In the morning, I squirmed back from her bedroll before Zach could wake up and notice. Kiyu was smart, beautiful and resourceful, but she was still a dreameater and I couldn't forget how frightened Zach had been when she pulled him out of the ground.

When we set out after breakfast, I saw that the perfectly polished whiteness of the Pacific Desert was an illusion. The rocks
and ridges were simply so thickly encrusted with salt that from a
distance. And with the white sky and dayglow scrubbing out every
shadow, I couldn't distinguish them from the rest of the desert floor
or even the sky.

Except the fissure. Rolling hills and dunes of salt hid the wide
crack down into the earth until we were almost right on top of it.
The crevice had to be at least a couple miles long and a hundred
yards across. It cracked jagged and black across the stark whiteness
of the desert like the impossible shadow of a huge lightning bolt. It
would take us at least half a day to detour around it and I was really
tired of walking. My blisters and injured leg ached their agreement.

"Uh, Kiyu? How do we cross that?" I asked. "Do you have some
special trick or secret bridge or something?"

"We don't cross it," Jacks answered for her. I guess only one ear
didn't hinder his hearing too much. "We go down."

"Down?" I asked.

"That's the warren," Kiyu said.

"That...?" asked Zach. "A hole?"

Was he thinking of the one we had fallen into? Or about the
trench where we waited out the storm and hoped not to be buried
alive? The Whitefingers *did* seem to spend a lot of time underground.

"It's not a hole," Kiyu corrected primly. "It's Lago Warren and it's
your new home."

Zach's brows knitted into tight, unhappy furrows. "Maybe."

"Come on, Zee," I said with a grin. "It's got to be better than that
squat you called home in the 'Ward. You're a slob, you know."

"Bugshit," Zach grumbled, but he didn't offer up any more con-
structive criticism of the Whitefingers' choice in homemaking.

Jacks led us to the edge of the fissure and along a narrow path
carved into its side, but it only went a few dozen yards down to a

lower ledge. I followed the other Whitefingers at a nervous distance. I couldn't see much down in the black crevice, but it seemed like a long fall. The Whitefingers were visibly relaxing, though. Kiyu removed the wrapping from her face and was smiling beneath. Diesel wagged his tail and practically bounded in a five-legged skip.

At the edge, the Whitefingers disappeared one by one. I approached cautiously and peered over. To my surprise, scaffolding had been erected from the ledge and led down into the shaded depths of the trench. Jacks climbed down a ladder alongside Diesel, who was being lowered in a basket attached to a rope and pulley. The dog leaned his head over the side of the basket, pink tongue lolling from his mouth in excitement. Diesel barked at Jacks as though urging the human to climb faster. Maybe he was – the dog *was* psychic, after all.

"Come on, Julia," Kiyu said. She turned and began descending the ladder.

Zach looked east one last time, back toward Angel City. I braced myself for some final outburst, outrage or pain at being forced away from his home and out into the desert. But Zach just pulled his hands out of his pockets and shrugged.

"I guess this is the place," he said.

I nodded. "Guess so."

I went down after Kiyu, moving slowly on my injured leg. It was a lot like climbing down from the highrises in the Whisperward. A network of ladders, ramps and walkways zigzagged down into the darkness. The temperature dropped rapidly and there was a wet tang to the air like I was standing near the wells in the Houses of Angel City.

As my eyesight adjusted and I removed my goggles, I discovered that it wasn't as dark as I first thought. Sunlight filtered down into the fissure and I could see holes everywhere. There were caves cut right into the sheer stone walls, homes hollowed out of the rock and draped with curtains for privacy. Children played along the walkways and three – three! – of them ran home into one cave.

The Whitefingers kept animals, as well. I saw familiar caged lizards and snakes, but there were birds, too. Diesel barked to another dog padding along a rope bridge behind a dark-haired old woman, a single echoing note that seemed to communicate more than I could understand. A sinewy, slender creature with black fur and mismatched eyes watched us for a moment and then suddenly sprinted away.

"Gone to tell the elders," Kiyu said.

"Is... that thing a dreameater?" I asked. I probably should have used their word – yin or yang – but I had a lot of adjusting to do and vocabulary was pretty low on the list.

"Maybe," Kiyu said. "The smarter ones, like dogs, can sort of communicate to us when they develop skills. But cats like to play it sly."

Voices echoed up through the chasm, overlapping and mingling into a soft murmur so much like the Whispers of the Stormsphere. But these voices weren't in my head. The whole Whitefinger warren was disturbing in both its similarities and differences from the Whisperward.

I guessed that we had made it maybe halfway down the fissure – though I had no *real* idea how deep the trench went – when Jacks stopped us at a line of semi-circular openings that led into small, single-room caves. There wasn't much inside except a hammock strung up between bolts drilled into the rock walls and a flat-topped bucket.

"You can stay here," said Jacks. "We need to talk to the elders, but they may want to see you. Don't go wandering off. And I already warned you about what happens if you run."

Right, hunt us down and rip the memories out of our heads like pages from a book. I nodded.

"I'll see you later," Kiyu told me.

She looked at Zach as an afterthought and said bye. Then she and the rest of the Whitefingers were gone, climbing down into the shadowed depths of their warren.

"We should get some sleep," said Zach.

"Yeah," I agreed. My leg and hip ached. "I feel like I could sleep for about a week."

I poked my head into the second cave and found it much the same as mine. The mottled brown and gray walls were rough, but more or less even. Zach and I made a few tired jokes about the bucket, but then bade each other safe dreams and each went to our own little caves.

I left the door curtain open to let in the weak sunlight and wondered what happened here at night. I didn't see a brazier or oil lamp anywhere in the room. There had to be some kind of light or else I was going to end up walking right off a ledge and falling to my death.

I climbed slowly into the hammock. It took me a few minutes to get the balance of it, but then I was settled. It was a bit like when Kiyu had lifted me out of the hole. I let my muscles finally relax and weariness swept over me.

But I couldn't fall asleep. The sounds and smells of the White-finger warren were too strange, and there were too many questions fluttering around in my head. And you know how good I am at ignoring questions.

Kiyu said that they used to be protected from the storms, something better than lying in hand-dug pits and just hoping not to smother under feet of sand. What was it? What happened to that lost secret? Was it the same thing that was happening to the failing Stormspheres now? Was the old protection that Kiyu talked about the same as whatever was inside the black spheres? I could hardly imagine my ancestors dragging one of those huge black orbs across the desert with them, though. Maybe rolling one...? But even that seemed ludicrous.

High Gardener Thorn had my answers, I was certain of it. I knew now that we hadn't always lived behind the Whisperward walls, but that put me in what I assumed was a pretty small group. Fucking lying Gardeners. Had Byron known? Did he realize that the girl trying to steal his key wasn't some alien monster, but a human woman who might have been his own distant relative?

I squeezed my eyes shut and told myself sternly to go the hell to sleep, but little flowers of color bloomed behind my eyelids and reminded me of something Martin said. Byron had been working on the flowers, breeding them for better nectar. Why? The nectar was just an offering. I had seen the sorting and preparation of the flowers and nectar, seen Torres escort them into the Tear of God.

Was Byron's plant-breeding program somehow aimed at saving the Stormsphere? What about the milkweed? Of all the plants preserved after the Wrath, what could God or anything else want with that poisonous little weed?

The questions swirled around each other until plain old thirst finally ground them all to a halt. I sat up in the hammock and promptly fell out. I landed more or less on my feet and contemplated kicking the damned thing. It didn't seem worth the effort, though. I imagined Zach running over to make sure I was okay and finding me tangled up in the stupid net-bed. I could envision his smirk all too well.

I poked my head cautiously out through the curtained doorway and then walked to the next cave. Everything smelled salty and tangy. Quietly, I called Zach's name a few times, but there was no response from inside. He must have been sleeping – the lucky bastard – so I turned back toward my own cave and just about jumped off the path into that fatal final dive I had worried about earlier. A big white bird with gray wings and webbed feet perched on the rope strung along the edge, regarding me with shiny black eyes and clicking its hooked yellow beak. It didn't try to kill me or anything, though.

"Uh, hi," I said, feeling like an idiot. "Can you go tell the elders or someone that I need help? I don't have any water."

"That's just a seagull. It doesn't understand you."

I jumped again and spun. The bird took wing with an indignant-sounding squawk. I clenched my hands into fists on instinct, but I found my opponent was a small girl of about ten, dressed all in dark green. Her unbound hair was a black puff framing her face, which was cocked to one side curiously. I relaxed my hands.

"Um, hi. Who are you?" I asked.

"I'm Angelica. What's your name?"

"Julia."

"You must be new," Angelica said. "You have funny clothes."

"Yeah, I guess so."

"They're ripped. I can see your butt."

Angelica giggled and then laughed again as I turned a circle trying to see my own ass. My fatigues were still slashed open down the back of my leg where Woods had cut me and I wished I had thought to grab a pair off one of the other Blackthumbs.

"Yeah, well, I don't have any other clothes," I said.

"You need help, right?" Angelica asked.

"Uh, yes. I need some water."

"That's all? Follow me."

The girl ran off along the nearest bridge, heedless of the huge drop just a few feet to either side. I hesitated. Jacks told us that we weren't supposed to wander. And what if Zach woke up and found me gone? But I was so thirsty... and maybe a little curious. I started off after Angelica and reasoned that I could bring back some water for Zach. That made the trip important, didn't it?

Angelica made her way along the ledges and bridges that crisscrossed the fissure, confident as a lizard. Her home was on the other face of the wide stone chasm. I slowed as I crossed the narrow rope bridge. Assuming I hit the next one down, it was still a thirty-foot fall if I went over. Considerably longer than that if I missed any of the other walkways and went all the way to the bottom. Angelica was already on the far side. The bridge creaked beneath my weight, but seemed stable enough and well maintained, so I hurried to catch up.

I glimpsed Angelica slipping through a curtained doorway. A few more paces behind her and I would have missed it entirely. All of the cave holes looked pretty much the same to me. Hell, chances were bad that I would even be able to find my way back to my own cave alone.

"Hello?" I called, knocking on the stone.

"Come in!" said Angelica's voice from within.

I pushed the curtain out of my way and ducked inside. Angelica's cave was much bigger than mine and I wondered if I should be jealous. The stone floor was covered with a thick rug. There were chairs and tables, with food and dishes stored in shelves carved into the rock or in nets hanging from the ceiling. They seemed to be woven from the same dark green-black fiber as the bridges. Something like lamps lay nestled in smaller hammocks and wall niches – they were cylindrical, but there was no flame. Instead, they glowed with a soft blue-green radiance. There were two more curtained entrances off the central room.

Angelica stood on her tiptoes to pull down a lidded jug from a high shelf. One of the door hangings parted and a tall man stepped through. He had Angelica's dark skin – or she had his, I supposed – and long-fingered hands white with salt. His brow furrowed when he saw me. I gave him an apologetic wave.

"Angelica...?" he asked.

"The new lady needs water, Dad," she said.

Angelica's father hurried to help her with the full pitcher. Some water splashed on the stone floor before he managed it and I gasped at the loss.

"Just... just a drink," I said in a tight voice. "If that's alright."

"And a bath. She's all dirty," added the girl.

"Angelica," her father admonished gently.

"She's not wrong," I said.

He poured clear water into a metal cup and passed it to me with a smile.

"Here you are," he said. "I'm David. I hope Angelica didn't drag you away from anything important. She's quite the handful."

"So was I at her age." I winked at Angelica.

"You *are* new, though?" David asked. "Some of the people from Bridge City ended up here. Are you one of them?"

I blinked and almost choked on the water. I had thought Zach and I were the only 'Warders here, but now I vaguely recalled Jacks saying something about it.

"There are people from Bridge City here?" I asked.

"A few. The hunting parties have rescued a few and they decided to stay."

"I'm from Angel City. Me and my partner came in with Jacks and Kiyu. We were..." I hesitated. "We were sort of banished from the Whisperward. They were going to execute us."

I wasn't sure why I was telling David – and a ten-year-old girl, no less – all of this, but it felt good to say it to someone. For a while, I didn't have to worry about upsetting Zach or looking weak in front of him.

David waited for me to go on, but any more and I would start crying. I didn't think I wanted to share quite that much. I gulped down the water instead and after a moment, David nodded and gestured to one of the other doorways.

"I'll draw water for a bath and you can clean up."

"Thank you," I said. I cleared my throat and rubbed my eyes until the sting of tears subsided.

"It's much better here than the cities," Angelica told me. "You'll like it."

"How do you know?" I asked a little too sharply.

Angelica shrugged. She was still young enough for that absolute certainty in matters she knew nothing about.

"I like it here," Angelica told me. Clearly, that was all the reason she felt I needed. "Are you going to stay?"

"Yeah," I said. "I think so."

"Maybe if you're nice, I'll be your friend."

I accepted her offer as the gracious gift that it was.

Twenty minutes later, I thought that David had made a mistake with the bathtub, or had done something stupid like spend his whole family's water rations for someone who wasn't even really a guest in their home – the tub was full nearly to the brim.

"Go ahead," David told me. "Take a soak. It's just salt water."

Before I could ask what the hell that meant, David left and let the curtain fall down over the door. I kicked off my Greenguard boots and flexed my blistered toes. They had been trapped in those shoes for something like a week now. Well, one of them had.

I held my breath and bravely removed my socks. My fatigues were full of salt and sand. My slashed and bloody pants went into the dirty pile, too. Biting my tongue, I unwound the bandages around my leg carefully. Blood stuck to them and pulled at the tender skin beneath, but it felt good to finally uncover the cuts.

I shed the rest of my clothes and then eased into the bathtub. I hissed as I stepped into the cool water. My skin pebbled as a cold shiver went up from my knees to my back. I sat on the rim of the tub and scooped handfuls of water over my legs and arms, then bit my lip nervously and slipped into the bath. I almost screamed aloud when the water hit the back of my injured thigh, but I guess it was healing because the burning subsided after only a minute or two.

I had never been immersed in water before. It was harder than it looked. I kept bobbing up in the tub, but it felt fantastic to have the weight off my feet and the water was wonderfully cool on my wounded leg now. Next, I went to work on my hair, scrubbing and combing my fingers through the dark tangles until I had undone the worst of the damage.

The water had turned a revolting brown, but I floated there, reluctant to climb out. I could get used to this... I lifted my hands out of the water to examine my nails and gave a little shriek. My fingers were shriveled and pale like those of a corpse.

I jumped out of the tub and scrambled away, gasping. I quickly examined the rest of my body. The wrinkling seemed limited to my fingers and toes. There was no pain, but I worriedly rubbed my hands together until I spotted the towel David had left for me. I scrubbed my body briskly, even my wounded leg. I didn't want whatever poison was in the water to do any more damage. I dressed hurriedly, suddenly unsure if David and Angelica were as friendly as they appeared.

I found them in the front room, talking to a woman with angled eyes like Kiyu's, as well as Kiyu herself. The yang girl stood up when she saw me.

"I brought dinner and some things for you and Zach," Kiyu said.

"How did you know I was here?" I asked.

"There's only a few thousand people in Lago. Everybody knows each other here, so it's not hard to find anyone. Come on, I brought some food."

"Kiyu, they tried to poison me," I hissed.

"What?" Kiyu asked.

David blinked and his wife's face turned bright red.

Angelica just looked confused. "Dad, what's she talking about?"

I held out my pale hands. Kiyu laughed and took one of them. Her touch was soft and warm.

"That?" she asked. "That's just what happens when you're in water too long."

"It... is?" I inspected my wrinkled fingers. The damage didn't seem so bad now. My skin had smoothed out and the color was returning to a healthy pink.

"It goes away after a little while," Angelica told me. "You really thought we would poison you?"

"Um…" I said eloquently.

"You've never been swimming, have you?" Kiyu asked.

"No." I ducked my head and looked back at David and his family. "I'm sorry. I didn't realize…"

David still looked shocked, but Angelica and Kiyu laughed. Her mother smiled indulgently and invited me back for dinner sometime. My cheeks were flaming as I agreed and hurried out the door after Kiyu. She was still laughing. I followed in silence, half embarrassed and half just concentrating on crossing the tangle of swaying rope bridges. I never thought that a ladder leaning up against the twentieth story could feel so stable by comparison, and I found myself holding my breath as I crossed the fissure.

"So, what do you think of Lago Warren?" Kiyu asked when her giggles subsided and we reached the far end of the bridge.

"It's a lot like the Whisperward," I said.

"What?" Kiyu protested. "No, it's not! You have Gardeners and Greenguard and the Stormsphere."

"Yes, but you have your elders and your yins and yangs. Your job is the same as mine. Well, as mine used to be."

"I only fight to protect the warren, though. Or sometimes the hunting parties."

"That's what I thought we were doing, too," I said. "Zach and I only wanted to help."

Kiyu left that in silence for a moment. She brushed her hair back behind her ears. "Yangs don't just fight, though. We help clear rocks away and bring up water, too."

"We didn't just fight, either," I said. I wasn't sure why I felt the need to defend a profession that I made no secret of hating. "There really weren't all that many mutants to kill. There was birth control, too. And mostly we protected people from ordinary criminals. Zach and I investigated them. Not that our last case ended well…"

Kiyu stopped outside a cave entrance that I assumed was mine, but it looked identical to a dozen others. I gave it a closer inspection this time, searching for some distinguishing characteristic. There was a cracked stone above the curved opening that was patched with reddish clay. Okay, I thought I could pick my place out of a lineup now.

Kiyu went inside to begin unpacking the woven bag she carried. I went to the next door to wake Zach and banged on the stone.

"Hey, Zee!" I called out.

I heard a grunt from inside and then bootsteps before Zach appeared at the door, blinking. There were dark circles under his eyes. Had he slept at all?

"What is it?" Zach asked. "Are you okay?"

"Yeah. Come on, Kiyu brought us some stuff."

Zach followed me slowly along the roped-off ledge to my cave. Kiyu's sack contained several jars of different sizes and I wondered how the small woman had managed to carry so much. Had she used her psychic powers to take the weight? There were jars of food and a big, lidded jug of water for each of us. A third one was frothy with soap that Kiyu told us was to wash our clothes. I picked up a smaller glass jar full of cloudy water and started to unscrew the top.

"No, not that one," Kiyu said. She took it from my hands and gave it a brisk shake. The water inside began to glow a pale blue-green, like the lights in Angelica's cave. "It's a phosphorescent algae. For light."

Kiyu set the jar to one side.

"Algae?" I asked.

"From the sea." She saw my face and held up a hand to stop the next question. "The water. You'll find out all about it. Just use this stuff for light. Oil is hard to get out here and we can only use it in the front rooms where the smoke can escape."

"Well, we've only got the one room and one door," I pointed out.

"These are just temporary," said Kiyu. "We can get you moved somewhere bigger in a little while."

"Then maybe you can take me on a tour and tell me about this sea?" I asked.

"I'd love to."

Kiyu smiled and blushed a bit. I badly wanted to kiss her again.

"...Both of you," she amended. "I mean, I'd like to give both of you the tour."

"So what happens next?" Zach asked.

He scratched his cheek. Dark stubble covered his jaw. He could really use a bath, too. I made a mental note to warn him about the shriveling finger thing so he wouldn't freak out.

"Diego will likely want to talk to you," said Kiyu. "We've never had Blackthumbs out here before. And you're the only ones who spoke to Thorn about the Stormspheres."

"Okay, we'll tell him anything he needs to know," I said.

"As long as it doesn't compromise the safety of Angel City," Zach added quickly.

"Zee, they don't want to hurt anyone. Thorn was the one who tried to have us killed."

"I remember. But that doesn't mean I want anyone back home to die," Zach said. "It was Thorn, not the people of Angel City who sentenced us."

"They didn't try to help, either," I said more bitterly than I intended.

"Julia," Zach admonished. "They didn't know what was going on. They saw Greenguard doing their job, even if it meant staking out their own."

I stared down at my hands, twisted up together in my lap. The wrinkles were gone now. Zach was right, of course. When I thought about the Greenguard I killed during our escape, it didn't feel good. I couldn't stop thinking of Woods struggling to get away as I tried to choke the life out of him. I hadn't felt any loyalty to the Gardeners, even when I was their official enforcer, but I didn't really want them to die.

Except for Thorn. God could call that prick home any time He wanted.

Kiyu had fallen silent, but now she smiled at both me and Zach. "That call is still going out from the Stormspheres. Diego and the other elders may have another idea about how to help."

"You Whitefingers don't know anything about the old science," Zach said. "I don't think you can help."

"We can try," Kiyu told him.

She shook the sack to make sure it was empty and stood. With a nod to Zach and one to me, she stepped outside. I followed. Kiyu turned and regarded me, looking nervous but still smiling. Maybe she wondered if I would kiss her. I wondered the same thing, but I had something important to tell her.

"Thanks for trusting us, Kiyu. And for saving us. We would have died out there if you hadn't heard me."

"I'm glad I did," she answered. "Maybe you know something useful about what's happening in the Stormspheres."

"I doubt it. We've already told you everything we know. Will I see you tomorrow?"

"Yes. I'll bring you some more food and water."

"And maybe that tour?"

"I'd like that."

I inched in closer. Kiyu fidgeted with the sack in her hands, picking at the drawstring. I leaned in. And then Zach stepped out of the cave and I straightened up quickly. Kiyu jumped back and then hurried away without waving.

"What was that?" Zach asked when I glared at him.

"Nothing," I answered too fast.

He stood in the door, thick arms crossed over his thicker chest. "You like her, don't you?"

"So what if I do?" I socked him in the side since my favorite punching arm was still bandaged up.

Zach watched Kiyu climb nimbly down a ladder to the lower depths of the warren. "Julia, you don't want to get involved with that girl. She's a Whitefinger–"

"So are we. We're sure as hell not 'Warders anymore."

"–and a dreameater. She'll hurt you," Zach finished.

"You don't know that, Zee!" I protested. "Kiyu's done nothing but help us."

"After she murdered Byron and ran away. Twice," Zach said. He grabbed my arm in a gentle but firm grip and pulled me back into my cave. "Julia, listen to me. Kiyu... seems nice enough. But don't forget what she is, what she can do."

"What she can do pulled us out of the ground after my stupidity nearly got us killed," I argued.

"And that's... I don't know what that is. Good, I guess. But what if she gets frightened? Or angry? What if you two have some argument and Kiyu smashes you into one of these walls with her mind? Or throws you right over the edge? She could kill you without even trying, Julia. I don't want to see you hurt."

I sat down and grabbed one of the jars, twisting the top. Zach had a point, but I couldn't bring myself to tell him so. I poked the round, pale green things in the jar. They smelled strange, but Kiyu had said they were food.

"Come on, Zee," I said instead. "Let's have dinner and then I'll take you to meet Angelica. Maybe her parents will let you take a bath."

Zach lifted his arm and wrinkled his nose. "Yeah, okay."

KIYU RETURNED the next morning with breakfast and some more water. There was needle and thread to mend the long tear in my pants, too. Angelica had informed her of the problem, Kiyu said.

"You didn't notice before?" I asked.

Kiyu shrugged, but she was smirking as she set out breakfast. It was familiar prickly pears and lizard eggs. The eggs were scrambled and had gone mostly cold, but just eating something that I recognized was a pleasant change of pace. I asked Kiyu where she got this stuff and she rolled her eyes.

"We have scale farms here, too," she said. "I'll show you."

Kiyu told us to bring the buckets if we had used them. Blushing furiously, I grabbed the pail and Kiyu provided a lid. Zach followed suit and then she led us out. Navigating up the ladders was a bit of a challenge while balancing our buckets, especially with my injured leg and Zach's wounded arm, but Kiyu let us go slowly and offered me her hand at the top. She did the same for Zach, but their size difference made it a token gesture at best.

The upper caverns that we had climbed past the day before were deep and, to my surprise, bright with dayglow. Huge polished metal mirrors had been set at the entrances to reflect sunlight into the caverns. The sun shone from the mirrors and bathed cactus patches in horizontal beams of sunlight. There were saguaro, barrel cacti, agave and prickly pears. A couple of young women took our buckets away to fertilize the sandy soil.

"Come on. I want to show you the water," Kiyu said.

She grabbed my hand and tugged me back out into the fissure. Kiyu didn't release my hand until we reached the first ladder, but took it again at the bottom. I think she may have even passed up some ladders and taken a longer route down ramps and across bridges so she wouldn't have to let go.

I could feel Zach's eyes on us and my hand went a little clammy in Kiyu's grip as I remembered his warning. If she wanted to, the pretty yang girl could fling me off the bridge with her mind and send me plummeting to my death. She might not even mean to. It could be an accident, like with Byron.

When we reached a solid and relatively wide path, I looked back at Zach. I had to admit that my partner was an impressive man. He was tall and kept himself in peak physical shape. It was hot down here, and away from the harsh, burning sunlight, Zach's shirt was unbuttoned to show off a remarkable expanse of tawny muscle. Maybe Zach would find a nice Whitefinger girl to help him adapt to our new lives here. Maybe I could help him out, too. I bet Angelica could tell me about all the eligible girls in the warren.

I was still thinking about Zach's body. I'm sure it was attractive enough, but that wasn't the point. My partner was strong, powerful. If it ever came down to a fight between us, my bet would have been on Zach. He was strong and well trained. He could throw me right off a bridge, too. Kiyu's power may not have relied on what had to be at least a hundred push-ups a day, but was it really that different from Zach's purely physical strength?

We climbed back down the fissure, past the loaner caves until the light started to dim. Jars of phosphorescent aqua hung from the crisscrossing bridges and from ropes strung over the walkways. The blue glow was strange but beautiful, and I walked close beside Kiyu through the light. There was nothing like this in Angel City.

The air began to change, too. The salt smell we had left behind on the surface of the Pacific Desert returned on damp air, accompanied by a sharp tang. And there were whispers.

Kiyu winced as I squeezed her hand too hard and stumbled to a halt, grabbing the rope railing of the bridge. Zach froze beside me, listening. It was a susurrant murmur like the wind through cloth, but somehow softer and harder at the same time. The sibilant hiss grew rhythmically louder and quieter, ebbing and flowing.

"What's that?" Zach asked.

"The water," Kiyu answered. She squeezed my hand gently. "I'll show you."

Rocky pathways and swaying bridges spiraled down to the bottom of the fissure. It was lit by more of the aqua algae lights and their reflections on... water. So much water. The entire fissure was like an immense well. Dark water rose and fell in gentle swells, so deep that I could see no sign of the bottom. The stone all around the edges was stained a sparkling white. Salt water.

"What is this?" I breathed.

Zach pulled off his hat and made a teardrop over his heart. "God, I've never seen anything like it."

"This is what's left of the ocean," Kiyu said. "At the bottoms of trenches like this. All of the water is underground now. It used to cover the entire Pacific Desert. It was the biggest ocean in the world before the meltdown."

Before the Wrath. But I remembered the vast white expanse above us. It stretched from horizon to horizon. Could that truly all have been water once? I couldn't even imagine it.

Bridges were strung all across the cave and scaffolds had been added to ledges that extended out over the sunken ocean. Women and men clustered along them, holding long rods tipped with strings dangling down into the water. I saw two of them pulling up one of the lines with a silvery creature hanging from the end. It had no legs, like a snake, but was shorter and wider.

The sounds of children laughing drew my attention. There was a small rocky bowl on one side of the cavern, shallow and filled with water. Children splashed through the pool, laughing and playing. I thought I recognized Angelica.

Kiyu dropped my hand and ran forward as some of the other Whitefingers shouted. One of them – a man with a twisted arm who would have been left for the storm at birth in Angel City – struggled with his taut line. A woman helped him hold the bending rod steady and a shiny water-creature the length of my leg breached the surface, thrashing on the end of the string. To my astonishment, the two Whitefingers wrestling with the pole and line were *laughing*.

Kiyu leaned out over the edge of a bridge. She gestured and the beast rose up from the water. Its silver body flexed and rippled, but it couldn't flail out of her mind's grip. The men with the rods gave a shout as Kiyu floated the beast to the ledge and they fell on it. Deftly, they pinned the scaly animal down, removed a hook from its mouth and wrestled it into a large sack attached to a post by a rope. They dropped the sack into the water and Kiyu waved at them cheerfully.

"What the hell was that thing?" I asked.

"A lingcod," Kiyu answered. "It's a kind of fish. Look, I need to help the fishers out down here for a while. We all have work to do. We've got new mouths to feed, after all. You should start thinking about your contribution."

"Can I... stay down here for a while?" I asked. I wasn't ready to leave this amazing place just yet.

"Yeah," Kiyu said with a smile. I guess she liked my idea. "Stay out of the way, though."

Zach and I sat down on a bridge, feet dangling over the edge. The water lapped just a few feet below, but this time I wasn't scared. This place was too astonishing to be scared.

"What do you think, Zee? What could we do around here?" I asked. "Maybe I'd be good at catching those fish things."

"They don't have Greenguard."

"But they have hunters. And people like Kiyu. Blackthumbs, I think, if not Greenguard," I said. I glanced back at Kiyu, who perched at the edge of the little piece of ocean. Occasionally, she pulled a fish up out of the water with her mind. "Though I guess they still need to help out with other stuff sometimes."

"Could you really do this, Julia? Stay here for the rest of your life?" Zach asked.

"All this water? Those fish? I could stay down here forever and never get bored," I said.

"It's lonely here. The population here is less than a tenth of the Whisperward. It feels so... small."

"That's okay."

"They don't have any of our technology. No lights, no Halos or... robots." Zach trailed off, looking uncomfortable. He pointed surreptitiously to the man with the withered arm. "There are mutants and dreameaters here, too."

I looked where Zach was pointing. The fisherman limped, too, but was working just as hard as any of the others. And they seemed to treat him no differently.

"It's not his fault, Zee," I said. "He can't help how he was born. Neither can Kiyu. And he's doing just fine, seems like."

"I know it's not his fault." Zach hesitated. He replaced his hat and turned to look at me. "You hated birth control as much as I did, Julia. But it was for the good of the Whisperward."

"You let the Garzas off."

"I know. But a man like that–" Here, Zach nodded to the one-armed fisherman again. "–allowed to live? To breed? What would that be like? And what about his children? How many generations until everyone in the city was like him? He might even be sterile.

Some mutants are. What if that happened to an entire generation? Humanity would die out."

"I'm not too fucking likely to have kids," I told Zach. "Doesn't mean I can't help out, Zee. Maybe I could even take in children like that little Garza girl."

Zach smiled, though his eyes remained unhappy. "If you could curb that mouth, Julia, you would make a great mother."

"You bet your ass."

I couldn't be bitter. Zach was a good man. As soon as he learned to think of the Whitefingers as his own people, he would be the first to lay down his life for them.

"In any case, we'd better get used to it," I told him. "We're never going back to Angel City."

"Maybe," Zach sighed, the word nearly lost in the hiss and rush of the water below.

The fishers took a break for lunch. Kiyu brought us food a lot like what we'd eaten on the long trip to Lago Warren – rice and fish meat rolled in a dark green leaf. Kiyu called the leaf *seaweed* and said it grew underwater. This time, all of the ingredients were fresh and I was getting used to the fish flavor. The meat was much softer than lizard or snake, almost flaky. It was delicious and even Zach didn't complain about the food.

"Kiyu!"

We looked up to see Jacks and Diesel. The dog trotted out ahead of his master and sniffed us. I scratched him behind the ear and he licked my nose. His breath was terrible. Jacks waved briefly to me and Zach, then pulled Kiyu away to one side. They weren't speaking particularly softly, but with the constant echoes of the splashing water, I couldn't make out a word.

"What was that all about?" I asked when Kiyu came back.

"Diego and the elders have been talking with the other warrens. They're going to attempt to make contact with the Stormsphere directly and commune with whatever is inside."

"Who's Diego?" I asked. "Is he your leader or something?"

Kiyu laughed. "No, he's just one of the elders."

"Is he a yin?"

She shook her head. "Not all the elders are gifted. They're just the oldest and wisest people in Lago. Diego has the respect of the other elders. He's strange, but most of the elders are. Probably because of all the engan they drink. But he's intelligent and we listen because he's almost always right. And Diego isn't above gloating if we ignore his advice."

"What's communing?" asked Zach.

"Well, the elders all drink engan and the yins join their minds together," Kiyu said. "The engan helps them reach out with their thoughts to the other warrens. That's how they can communicate with one another."

"Other warrens?" Zach's eyes widened.

"Sure. You didn't think Lago was the only one, did you? There are more warrens than Whisperwards. When the elders commune, they can speak to warren councils all across the world and pass along information. That's how we learned that the other Whisperwards are failing, too."

"How many of them?" I asked.

"Apple City's protection is beginning to shrink and Wind City is trying to build a bigger wall to stop the storms."

That wasn't going to work. Maybe for a while... but the sandstorms had torn ancient Angel City apart. How long did Wind City think their wall would last?

Zach actually growled in anger. "They need to do something!"

"And that's why the elders are going to talk to the Stormsphere," Kiyu said. "All of the most powerful yins in the Pacific will join their minds and reach out to whatever's inside the Angel City sphere."

"Then why did they send you out to our Whisperward?" I asked. "The 'Ward, I guess. It's not ours anymore... Why steal a key and try to break in if yins could just talk to the Stormsphere?"

"Because it's really dangerous," Kiyu said. "That call for help was so powerful that it... affected our yins. Some died from even brief contact. More killed themselves afterward."

"And that might happen again?" I guessed.

"It could be even worse this time. Elders from dozens of warrens will be communing together. It will make them more powerful, but if something happens, if someone died, the effects could spread through the whole communion."

"Spread?" I repeated. That didn't sound good.

"A dozen warrens could all lose their elders. That's why they've never communed on this scale before." Kiyu helped me to my feet and then motioned for Zach to stand up. "Come on. Diego wants you there during the communion, so we better get moving."

"Does he want us to... uh... join in?" I asked.

My heartbeat sped. This seemed every inch as bad as any of my mother's dreameater horror stories. Zach and I fell into step behind Kiyu.

"No, but you were both Greenguard," she said. "You know Angel City and even saw the Stormsphere up close. Diego just wants you on hand to answer any questions."

"What about you?" I hoped I didn't sound too worried about her, but I guess I wasn't schooling my tone very well. Kiyu smiled and blushed a little as she answered.

"I'm not a strong yin. There are much better ones among the elders," she said. "But I'll be there with you."

Kiyu took my hand and led us up through the blue light.

KIYU GUIDED us up from the little ocean, but we didn't go far. The lower reaches of the crevice were pocked with more caverns, each with wide entrances hung with the best – though still salt-whitened – hangings I had seen anywhere in the fissure. These must have been the homes of the elders and the other important folk of Lago Warren. No society was totally equal, I supposed, but so far the elders here hadn't done anything to make me resent them.

I wondered if you actually had to be old to be an elder. I had a lot of great ideas that the Gardeners never listened to. Maybe the Whitefingers would. But call me vain – I wasn't sure I wanted anyone thinking of me as *elder*.

Zach had his hands buried in his pockets and fidgeted. I teased him for acting like Gregory and managed to get a chuckle out of him, but I was nervous, too. If these elders really reached their thoughts into the Stormsphere, they could answer questions about the Tear of God that I had been asking since my first time in Sunday school. And maybe we could finally discover why the Tears of God were dying.

Diego's home was one of the larger canyon caverns. The central chamber was as big as Angelica's entire cave and several openings led off in different directions. Blue-green algae jars sat on every surface and dozens of them hung from the ceiling. Kiyu gave some of the dimmer ones a brisk shake as she took us inside.

Ten old men and women reclined on cushions strewn around the floor, but I picked out Diego easily. Either because this was his home or just out of respect for his wisdom, Diego sat on the nicest, fluffiest pillow, and though the others were arranged in a circle, they all faced him slightly.

Elder Diego wasn't old. He was ancient. His back was hunched and his face as wrinkled as an old shirt. Diego's sun-browned skin dangled from his frame and gathered under his chin in waddles. His long hair was as fine as spider silk and hung around his prominent ears in gray wisps. The elder's eyes were bright, though, and caught my gaze from across the room. He waved Zach and me over with a withered and age-spotted hand.

"You're the two Blackthumbs?" Diego asked in a quiet, wheezing voice. "How are you finding Lago Warren?"

"It's... different," Zach answered diplomatically.

"Will you help us today?"

Zach shuffled his feet like a chastened schoolboy, his hands still in his pockets. I smirked in the turquoise light, but it didn't feel right teasing him in front of Diego. I would give Zach hell later, I decided.

"Yeah," I said for us both. "We'll help if we can."

Diego inclined his head and it looked like an apple on the end of a stick. Shit, I hoped no one heard me thinking that. Diego may not have been a yin, but how many people in this room were?

The front door hangings rustled and the tall shape of Jacks ducked through, followed closely by Diesel. Kiyu put her finger to her lips. Diesel and his burn-scarred master remained silent as a teenage girl who looked like she might have been Diego's grand-daughter – or maybe great-granddaughter – walked around the circle of elders. She carried a heavy water skin and stopped in front of each elder to squeeze some thick, murky liquid into a bowl. I smelled the sour stench of engan, which I wasn't likely to forget any time soon. I was glad that I didn't have to drink any. Once was more than enough.

"Tell us what you saw of the Stormsphere," Diego said. "Perhaps it will prepare us for what awaits us there."

I couldn't help thinking that I was betraying the Whisperward. The feeling surprised me a little... But we had promised to help, sold ourselves to Jacks based on the value of exactly this kind of information. Maybe we could even help the Whisperward that had disowned us. It went against a lifetime of habit, though.

"The Gardeners gathered offerings of nectar and flowers, then carried it down a staircase," I said. "There were paintings along the walls of milkweed and some trees I've never seen before."

Diego nodded, but didn't ask me any questions. The other Lago elders held their engan bowls, waiting and listening.

"I think there used to be more to the murals," I went on. "Parts of them were painted over, like the Gardeners might have covered something up."

"It was just repairs," said Zach. His hands were balled into fists in his pockets.

"Maybe," I agreed reluctantly. I doubted it, but didn't say that to Diego. "At the bottom of the stairs was a black door. It was shiny and curved like the outside of the Stormsphere. Torres – one of the other Gardeners – opened it with a card-key. Just like the one Kiyu stole. Hey, do you still have that?"

Kiyu nodded. "Yeah, I do."

"I didn't see much of what was inside, though," I admitted. "It was... white. That's about all I can tell you."

"Thank you both. Please wait while we commune," Diego said. A smile creased his wrinkled face. He was missing a lot of teeth. "Quietly. We may have more questions for you. Until then, you can just watch us all drink this vile stuff."

Diego held up the bowl of slimy engan and winked at me. Kiyu tugged at my sleeve and we retreated back to one side of the cave. I leaned against the wall next to her. The other elders mimicked Diego, raising their bowls and then the whole circle drank deeply. They didn't even wince at the taste.

Two by two, the elders' eyes drifted closed. Their breathing began to even out until they all inhaled and exhaled together. I had to concentrate not to time my breath to theirs. It was eerie. A faint thump echoed from somewhere outside Diego's cave, but there was no other sound.

We all waited in silence. Zach restlessly shifted his weight from foot to foot. I was getting bored, too. The only thing to look at was the ring of old people, unless I let myself stare stupidly at Kiyu. But I didn't want to start drooling in case Diego needed to ask about anything else, so I kept my eyes to myself. There were more muffled thumps and I thought I might have heard voices. I listened, wondering if a storm was blowing over us and I was hearing thunder echo down the deep stone fissure.

Jacks frowned. Diesel followed him to the cavern entrance. Jacks pulled the hanging aside and looked up, his frown deepening.

"What the hell?" he muttered to himself.

"Can you hear it?" Kiyu asked.

For a moment, I thought she meant the distant booming sounds outside. I wondered if Jacks was going to climb up and quiet whoever was making the ruckus. I would have assumed that the White-fingers would be more used to storms passing over them out here. It must have been a bad one and I hoped the underground warren was safe. Jacks waved his hand in front of his face as dust filtered down from high above.

But then I heard what Kiyu was talking about. Whispering. I put my fingers in my ears and shuddered when that did nothing to stop the sound. It was inside my head. Was that the Whispers? All the way out here? No, I realized a moment later. There were snatches of words I knew, songs that I didn't recognize, but that were definitely human.

"That's the communion of the warrens," Kiyu said very softly. She stood up on her toes to whisper into my ear. Her lips brushed my skin and I shivered. "The Lago elders have joined their thoughts to those of the other warrens. Now they'll reach out to the Stormsphere."

"This is it?" Zach asked. His voice cracked. I couldn't even imagine how scared he was, surrounded by dreameaters.

"It's okay, Zee," I said. I considered taking his hand, but I didn't want to embarrass him.

Kiyu put one slim finger against her lips. Tell that to the storm outside, I thought. And the people. The voices were louder now and I could discern a note of panic in them. Another boom sounded, this one shaking the stone walls. At the door, Diesel whimpered. I wanted to ask Jacks what was going on – despite Kiyu's admonitions of silence – but then the elders spoke.

"Are you there?"

Diego and the other nine spoke at once, each voice a little different in pitch and resonance, but all in perfect unison. Their question echoed through my head and I felt my teeth clench too hard as my whole body tensed reflexively. An icy chill slithered down my spine. I didn't need Kiyu to tell me what they were talking to. The Whitefingers were reaching out to the Stormsphere. Now would it answer...?

"Are you there?" the elders asked together. "Can you hear us?"

"What's going on out there?" Kiyu whispered.

She slid away from me to the door and looked past Jacks and Diesel. I followed her, grateful for the excuse to put a few more feet between myself and the circle of Lago elders engaged in their otherworldly conversation. Zach was right behind me, close enough that I felt his breath against the back of my neck.

"Come on..." he whispered.

We stepped outside the cave and into the open warren. At first, I couldn't see anything through the smoke overhead. Smoke? And then I saw the flames. Bridges were burning, door hangings smoldering and falling away to ash, even stone blackened and cracking with thunderous sounds. People ran along ledges and slid down ladders, crying and screaming as they fled. Something fell past us, streaming bright fire and dark smoke. Zach grabbed my arm and pulled me back against the rock wall of the ravine.

What the hell was going on? A beam of red light stabbed out of the black smoke and streaked across the cavern. Soundlessly, it sliced a bridge in two and dumped a dozen running Whitefingers tumbling and screaming down into the abyss. Kiyu made a strangled sound and she lurched, hands stretched out as though she could catch them.

Which she could... but only some. Three of the flailing bodies stopped midair and sweat broke out across Kiyu's forehead as she pushed them onto another ledge. The Whitefingers grasped for the rocks as soon as they were close enough and then scrambled into the nearest cave.

"What is this?" Jacks bellowed, whirling on Zach and me.

My mouth was as dry as dust. I had seen that kind of light only once before – eleven years ago when I stood on the Angel City walls and watched the destruction of the swarming mutants. Another silent, blood-red light slashed through the cavern. It glowed like a halo-gram, but so unlike a Halo's projection, which I could pass my hands through, these beams incinerated everything in their path. Where the light met flesh and bone, there were little flashes, then red smoke and black ash. Where the beam hit stone, it burned instantly orange, burst briefly into flame, and then exploded with a sound like a gritty thunderclap. Only one thing in the world was armed with weapons like that, and only the Gardeners could order them into action.

No.

I was still trying to understand how there could be a robot out here, so far away from the Whisperward, but Kiyu sprinted for the closest ladder. Before I realized what I was doing, I chased after her.

"Julia, don't!" Zach shouted after me.

"We have to stop that thing!" I cried.

I found part of a Whitefinger's spear rolling on the ground. I had to dive to catch the pointed metal tube before it went over the ledge and fell far out of reach. I scrambled up and sprinted after Kiyu. I wasn't sure how to stop a robot with half a spear, but I was sure as fuck going to try.

Kiyu waved her hand and burning rocks flew up off the ground, sailing across the chasm. I heard them crunch into the far wall, but something rang off of metal. For a moment, the smoke cleared and I saw the bristling cactus of machinery that was the robot. It had as many glistening, jointed legs as the most horrifying mutant spider. It crawled along the warren's sheer stone wall, spined with metal tubes and slender, upthrust wires. Fading dayglow and the light of flames shined on the chassis and I knew that this was what we had seen in the desert. It followed us all the way from Angel City.

We brought it here.

My knees turned into water and I felt sick, but there was no time for my guilt. The robot's sections swiveled across the cavern and weapon nozzles lit up with red death. The machine rocked as something struck the reinforced metal. A group of Whitefingers charged toward the robot. I saw Jacks' burned face in the lead, mouth open as he shouted orders. Diesel raced after him, ears back and teeth bared. A Whitefinger that I didn't recognize gestured and hurled a boulder still glowing along one side where the robot's death ray had carved it off the wall. The rocky missile clipped the robot and made it sway on top of its cluster of shining silver legs.

A hatch popped open and something streaked out of the robot on a tail of fire. It hit the ground and exploded. Stones and bodies flew.

I heard Diesel barking, but couldn't see the dog anywhere in the smoke. I was running a dozen yards behind Kiyu. She psychically flung rocks at the robot as she sprinted, barely watching where she was stepping. I was terrified that Kiyu would fall to her death before she did any good. There was nothing I could do with my spear from this distance, so I concentrated on catching up with her.

One of Kiyu's flying stones slammed into what seemed to be the robot's head. Weapon arms whirled and pointed. I leapt at Kiyu and grabbed her around the waist, smashing us both down onto the narrow ledge. I was only a second ahead of the robot. A red beam raked the wall over our heads. I covered Kiyu with my body as chips of burning rock rained down on us. I grunted when a rock thumped against my back, but nothing seemed broken.

I seized Kiyu around the waist and dragged her into the nearest open cavern. Zach threw himself through the door after us. A dripping line of melted stone scarred the wall where a beam had passed through the open doorway and scorched everything inside to ash. A single white hand lay curled in the center of the room, the wrist just a blackened stump.

"What... what is that thing?" Kiyu cried. Her voice shook and I could barely hear her over the sounds of death just outside.

"Robot," I answered. "The Gardeners sent it. It must have followed us. I'm so sorry, Kiyu. I never wanted this to happen."

"Maybe it's for the best, Julia," Zach said. "Our faith has to be in the Gardeners."

"What are you talking about? You don't mean that, Zee!"

Why the hell was Zach chasing after me, anyway? He didn't just watch people die. He just didn't. Why wasn't he fighting? I couldn't understand any of this.

I leaned out of the doorway. The robot skittered down a steeply descending ramp, methodically blasting every level of the warren as it went, or at least trying to. Half of its weapon nozzles rotated, took aim, and then turned toward a new target without actually having emitted one of its deadly beams. But even at half capability, the damage was terrible. That hatch – or maybe it was a different one – opened again and released another flying missile. It detonated against the warren's far wall and hurled stones and bodies up into the air. I grabbed Kiyu's sleeve when she tried to run out past me.

"Let go! I have to try to stop it," she shouted.

"I know. Take this," I told her. I handed her the half of a spear I clutched. "See that hatch?"

I pointed to the port as it closed. We caught a glimpse of small white shapes inside, the things that the robot fired.

"Can you hit that?" I asked.

"Yeah," Kiyu panted. "So?"

"They explode."

Kiyu's dark eyes flicked up to the crater blown out of the stone across the ravine. She nodded and took the spear from my hand. Kiyu dashed out of the cave, moving in a low, ready crouch. I don't know why I followed her. It wasn't like I could help. Even if I had my crossbow, I didn't think it could pierce the robot's thick armor. But I wasn't about to send Kiyu out there alone. Zach shouted my name, cursed and then chased after us. We had to climb down to find the robot again. I could see water below us.

"I need it to open that panel again," Kiyu hissed.

"Got it," I said.

Kiyu looked confused, but Zach knew exactly what I had in mind, of course.

"No!" he shouted. "Julia!"

But it was too late. I was already running out along the ledge. I scooped up a rock and felt the heat of it burning my hand. I wasn't as good a shot as Zach, but I liked to think that I was still one of the best Blackthumbs in Angel City. I aimed and sent the stone soaring at the robot. It bounced off the metal with a sound like a struck bell and the machine pivoted on its cluster of legs. The insectoid antennae twitched toward me. Weapon barrels rotated to take aim.

Come on, shoot me...!

And then Zach slammed into me and I went sprawling to the ground. Zach waved his arms at the robot, holding something out toward it.

"No!" he shouted. "Not her! Thorn said you wouldn't–!"

Zach fell silent as the beam of light sliced through him. Everything between his knees and ribs was gone in a burst of hot, sticky mist. What was left of my partner hit the ground beside me. The edges of his fatigues were on fire and the flesh beneath sizzled.

"Zee!" I screamed.

But there was still another target. Something inside of the robot whirred and one of the middle segments spun to aim its round hatch at me. The cover plate slid back and then something dark streaked through the smoke like an oversized crossbow bolt – the spear. Kiyu clung to a ladder below me, one hand held out. The spear's course arced up against gravity and the point slammed itself into the open missile port.

There was an instant of relative quiet as machinery grated inside the robot, shattered and broken. And then an explosion tore through the metal skin. The shockwave blew hair back from my face and the afterimage of fire glowed in my eyes like a vision of a burning flower.

Some of the explosives inside had either been duds or else the ancient robots were even stronger than the Gardeners claimed. Several weapon-studded limbs lay scattered across the stone or tumbled down into the seawater, but the robot twitched and scrabbled at the ground with its remaining legs.

Jacks leapt down on it while Kiyu and at least one other yang attacked the robot with brute mental power. It fired off a single strobe of red light that vaporized the man standing next to Kiyu before she raised her hand, clenched it into a fist, and shouted a warning to Jacks. The scarred man jumped clear just before Kiyu brought a wall of laser-scorched rock crashing down onto the robot.

The avalanche crushed another arm off and then swept the robot over the edge. It smashed through a bridge and then splashed into the black waters far below. Sparks lit up the shadows and then the ruined metal monster sank out of sight.

I crawled to Zach. His face was pale and dark blood stood out starkly against his skin. His eyes were open wide... but they were empty, already beginning to cloud. In one hand, Zach clutched a small cylinder of metal. A red light blinked on the top.

"Oh, Zee," I said. "What have you done?"

I was grabbed, tied up and dragged away. I resisted only because they were trying to take me away from Zach. I fought and screamed and bloodied a few noses, but it didn't take long to get me under control. The Whitefingers dumped me into a lightless cave where they had bolted an actual door into the entrance and left me there alone. They brought me just enough water and food to keep me alive, and occasionally emptied my bucket. Each time, they kept me at spear point until the door bolted shut again.

I think I was there for two days, based on the number of visits to feed me, but I wasn't really counting.

Zach was dead. My partner. That was something that happened to other Greenguard, not us. Zach and I were smart. We were good together. We were careful... Okay, not as careful as we could have been, but when things turned stormy, Zach and I were always there to get one another out of trouble. Always. No questions, no quibbles. We could tease each other, but Zach was *always* there to save me. How could my world keep going with Zachary Dias dead?

But he was gone. Zach was my rock, the wall I could always put my back against when things got stormy. The only person in the Whisperwards I cared about... He died and left me alone.

Zach had kept secrets. He had betrayed me. The thought was too big, too ugly. It made the whole world twist in on itself, but drew me back again and again with its terrible gravity. Zach had been holding that little blinking device and I knew instinctively that the red light brought the robot. It was some kind of beacon... No wonder Zach had dismissed the distant metallic shine as unimportant, too far in the wrong direction to investigate. Of course Diesel had felt no malice or danger. Robots didn't hate anyone. They just followed orders.

When did Zach get the beacon? I didn't think he had it when Woods and the rest were staking us out.

But then we were separated. I remembered the indistinct figure being dragged back toward Angel City. Two of the Greenguard had come after me. That meant five to chase down Zach. I just assumed he was good enough to take on those kinds of odds... But what if he wasn't...?

They must have caught Zach. Then why didn't they kill him?

And what had he shouted at the robot? My eyes felt full of glass sand and it hurt to think, but I couldn't forget. *Not her. Thorn said...*

Zach had cut a deal with the High Gardener. What was it? Kill the Whitefingers and all was forgiven? But not me. Zach would never hurt me. I sobbed in the darkness. Zach's deal wasn't just for his own life. It was for mine, too. I hated and loved Zach so much that I felt like it might tear me apart.

He never believed that the Whitefingers could help us, or help the Whisperward. His faith had always been in the Gardeners. Zach and his fucking unshakable faith...

How could I have missed it? The food, the extra water... It came from the Gardeners. And Zach's hat. He hadn't been wearing it when Woods dragged me into Thorn's office. But I was so used to seeing Zach in it that I never questioned its presence.

It was all Zach's idea to find the Whitefingers... I should have known. He always hated the wastelanders, feared their alien ways and dangerous dreameaters. He believed in the Gardeners and the Whisperward. But I had clung to the idea so eagerly, accepted their ways and life so much more easily than Zach, that I almost forgot the plan had been his.

Now I knew why Zach had kept checking his pockets. I understood and I had never wanted my curiosity satisfied less. Zach had betrayed me. He had tried to save me. I grabbed the bucket and heaved into it. It didn't matter that they hadn't fed me much. My stomach went on convulsing, trying to vomit out this feeling long after the thin, acidic spittle stopped coming up.

————

WHEN THE DOOR OPENED AGAIN, I didn't look up. I didn't want to eat or drink anything. But spears prodded me to my feet and someone bound my hands once more. Whitefingers marched me out of my cell and I blinked even in the shaded interior of Lago Warren. I wanted to screw my eyes tightly shut, but not to keep out the light – I didn't want to see what had become of the warren.

I didn't want to see what Zach had done.

But I couldn't walk with my eyes closed and my Whitefinger escorts set a brisk pace. I had to look. The air was clear of smoke now and there were no more fires, but the scars of the attack were terrible. Most of the rubble had been swept away, but there were blackened and melted holes in the stone. Caves had collapsed and severed bridges hung from the ravine walls like dead limbs. There was a rough gash of pale, fresh stone where Kiyu and the other yangs had ripped down tons of rock to bury the robot.

There were fewer people, too. I saw only a handful of Whitefingers repairing and crossing the remaining bridge. The hum of voices that had so reminded me of the Whispers was nearly silent now. The survivors of Lago Warren moved quickly, without speaking. I didn't see any children playing anymore.

The Whitefingers led me deeper into their warren. We had to climb down ropes in places where the ladders and bridges were gone. It grew darker as we descended. Only a handful of their blue-green algae lights glowed here, illuminating more black craters and melted scars. How many people had died? How many homes were destroyed?

Water hissed beneath us, as black as tar in the thin aqua light. There was no one fishing, no children splashing in the shallows. Was the robot still down there in the remains of the sea? Would I be sent to join it? Was that how the Whitefingers executed traitors? I remembered floating in the bathtub and wondered if drowning would hurt.

We edged along a broken path. The stone ground ominously beneath my feet and I worried it was going to save the Whitefingers some trouble by unceremoniously dumping me down into the salty water. But the ledge held and the Whitefingers pushed me through a cracked hole in the rock, into a cave.

It took me a moment to recognize Diego's home. There were fewer watery lights in here, too, but I could still see that something was wrong. Only four of the aged Whitefingers sat in the dim cave now. Diego was there, but the old man sat crookedly, propped up with the empty floor cushions. One half of his face hung slack and the eye on that side drifted, unable to focus.

Jacks stood beside Diego. The unburned side of the huge man's face was twisted with pain and he held the crossbow he had taken from Zach. It was loaded.

I didn't see Diesel anywhere.

Kiyu waited just behind Jacks. Her mouth opened and she took a half step forward when she saw me, but Jacks shoved her back. The girl's face was stricken and pale, her beautiful eyes rimmed in red.

"What happened?" I asked. My words were withered to a croak by too little water and too much crying.

"Your robot interrupted the warrens' communion," Diego said. "The deaths tore through us before we could make contact with the Stormsphere. Fifty-seven elders are dead across the desert. More are damaged."

Diego raised his stick-thin fingers to the sagging side of his face. Hundreds were dead in Lago. Warrens all across the salt desert had lost their elders. And we knew nothing more about the Stormspheres than we had before. I fell to my knees on the cave floor. I wanted to go back to my cell.

"Are the Whisperwards going to war with us?" Diego asked. His words were slurred.

I shook my head slowly. My hair was hopelessly tangled and appeared black in the wan blue light. "Not the 'Ward."

"Then why were we attacked?" It may have been hard to understand Diego's words, but not his question.

"The people of Angel City probably don't even know that this happened. Zach said... I think Thorn did this," I said. Diego waited, head wobbling on his thin neck while I cleared my throat painfully. Even saying Zach's name hurt. "Only Thorn and Gregory have the codes to activate the robots. One of them must have given Zach the device that the robot tracked."

"Did you know?" Jacks growled. The rage and pain on his face was far uglier than the twisted burn scars. "Did you know that... thing was coming?"

"Does it matter?" I stared down at my hands. "No, I didn't know. But I should have. Zee..."

My eyes stung and I pressed my fingers into the lids until they ached, but my tears remained in check. For now.

"Leave Julia alone!" said a strained voice. "This isn't her fault!"

"Shut it, Kiyu," Jacks barked.

I opened my eyes again and found the remaining Lago elders regarding me in the wavering blue light.

"We believe her, as well," Diego said. "She didn't know."

The other elders all nodded together. They had communed so much over the years that they didn't need the engan or yins joining their minds to think alike.

"Will you still help, then?"

I didn't even realize that I had asked the question until Jacks snarled at me. "Help you? Why shouldn't we kill you now? More than a thousand people died! Diesel's dead–"

"Jacks, please." Diego's mushy voice silenced the big White-finger. "What do you mean, Julia?"

"People will die," I said. The ropes around my wrists chaffed as I shifted my weight. "More people. You can kill me, but it's not going to change what's happening to the Whisperwards."

"Let the Gardeners protect their cities," Jacks said. Zach would have agreed. "If Thorn commands things like that robot–"

"Robots can't stop a storm. And sending a machine was Thorn's decision," I argued with passion that surprised even me. I had left Angel City behind, but I couldn't just abandon the people there. "All of the 'Wards are failing. Don't condemn entire cities to die because of Thorn and Zach!"

"She's right," Kiyu said.

She stepped around Jacks fast enough that he couldn't grab her this time and came to stand beside me. Still down on my knees, I stared up at Kiyu. So many of her own people were dead. Why would she defend me?

"None of the warrens are nearly big enough to take in all of those people if the Angel City Stormsphere fails. Can we really just let them all die?" Kiyu asked.

"Their Gardeners would do it to us," Diego pointed out. "They didn't even wait for the storms. They sent their machines to kill us in our own homes."

"And what about the cry for help? Even if you don't care about saving the people of the city, what about the thing in the Storm-sphere?" Kiyu asked. "It needs our help, too."

She stood her ground with hands on her hips, half Jacks' size and utterly defiant. Had I ever looked like that when I argued with Thorn? The elders traded long looks and then nodded together once more.

"We will try again," Diego decided. "But all of the warrens have lost their most powerful yins. We'll need more minds to make up the numbers. That means you, Kiyu."

She gulped audibly, but she set her jaw and nodded. My heart sped. The communions were dangerous at the best of times. Diego said that the mysterious entity in the Stormsphere presented unknown threats. And what if there was a second attack while they were communing?

"What about Julia?" Kiyu asked.

Diego regarded me with his one clear eye.

"She's free to go," the elder mumbled. "For now. But I want her here tomorrow when we try to communicate with her Stormsphere again."

Kiyu nodded and waved back the two Whitefingers guarding me. She knelt and untied my hands. I flexed my fingers a few times. They hurt, but I just couldn't care that much.

"Come on, Julia." Kiyu helped me to my feet and led me out of the cave.

KIYU DIDN'T TAKE me back to my cell or even to the cave where I had stayed before the attack. Instead, she led me up the opposite wall of the fissure and held aside a curtain that looked new.

She didn't have to tell me that it was her own home. I knew. The cave was smaller than Diego's spacious cavern, though still much larger than my loaner or cell. There were a few cushions and a low table, but what caught my eye and made Kiyu's influence unmistakable were the shelves and niches carved into the walls. Every one of them was full of pieces of glass, colored stones, cloth, bits of sand-scoured wood, painted scraps of precious paper and even toys.

I drifted over to the shelves. My numb fingers stole out of their own accord, touching plastic and glass and wood and metal. Some of Kiyu's prizes really were beautiful, but others were shoddy and cheap, remarkable only in that they were shiny or brightly colored. A shield-shape of metal leaned in one corner, painted red at the top and then blue beneath. I couldn't make out the words, but even through the peeling paint, I saw a large number five printed there in white.

I found the tattered piece of lace that Kiyu and I had exchanged so many times.

"Why... why do you keep all of this?" I asked.

Kiyu let the door curtain fall shut and shook a jar of algae. Even in the aqua light, her blush was dark. "I told you. They're pretty."

"Is that all?"

"Is that all?" Kiyu repeated. "Julia, there's nothing up there but sand and salt. Everything in the world is worn out or broken, but there are still beautiful things all around us. Little things. Unimportant things. But they're important to me."

She touched the lace I held. Her fingers brushed mine.

"Why?" I asked. "Why do you care about any of it?"

"There has to be beauty left in the world. Otherwise we have nothing."

"Kiyu..." I squeezed the lace in my hand, wanting to crush it. Everything inside me felt so broken and ugly. "You told Diego that you wanted to help the Whisperward. The people. Not the mural in the sorting shrine. Not some shiny bit of glass."

"But I did find something beautiful in your city," Kiyu said. She closed her fingers over my clenched fist. "It wasn't a painting or glass, though."

"What, then?"

Kiyu sighed. "You, stupid. That's why I left the lace after we took you back to Angel City. I... hoped you'd find me again."

She stood up on her toes and kissed me gently. Her lips were so soft. I turned away and replaced Kiyu's lace on its shelf.

"I'm sorry about Zach," she said, still standing close.

I leaned against the wall, staring down at the little shred of lace. It was rumpled, so I smoothed it out as I looked over the shiny, bright collection again. They *were* beautiful, and I was unexpectedly glad to know that Kiyu had all these pretty little things. That they were as important to her as answers were to me.

"We all have our own truth," I said. I couldn't stop the tears anymore. My best friend was dead. "Zach... Zee wasn't a bad guy, Kiyu. I knew him. He was a highriser like me. He wanted to help people.

He saw what they did to each other in the 'Ward and he worked so hard to join the Greenguard."

The lace and shelf full of shinies blurred and tears stung as they rolled down my raw cheeks.

"Zach just needed more time," I whispered. "He thought you were a monster. He thought you would hurt me. He only wanted to protect me, protect Angel City. That's all."

"I believe you," Kiyu said quietly. "I'm not a powerful yin, but I told you that I could read people when they felt strongly enough. All I ever sensed from Zach was fear and love. He would have done anything for the people who mattered to him."

I crossed my arms over my chest and hugged them around myself, weeping bitterly for Zach. The sobs shook me so hard that I couldn't talk anymore. I couldn't see anything. I just wanted Zach back. Just for a minute to tell him that I understood. I could never agree with what he did, but he only wanted to save me, save the people he loved. I could never hate him for that.

Kiyu's slender arms wrapped around me and she held me close. I fell against her, crying into her hair. Kiyu stroked my back and didn't say anything. She held me and kissed my wet cheeks, then my lips. I tasted my own tears on her kiss.

———

WE SLEPT TOGETHER, though not the way I had wanted to so badly since first seeing Kiyu in Angel City. By the time we made it to her bed – thank God, they actually *did* have beds in the warren, not just hammocks – I was cried out and exhausted. Kiyu let me hold her and I fell instantly into a deep, dreamless sleep.

Kiyu woke me in the morning with breakfast. Eggs and tea with a slightly different flavor than what we brewed in the cities. Kiyu had poured me a bath so I could clean up after my imprisonment. She gave me some privacy to bathe.

The salty water was cold and still stung my leg, but other than the eerie, wrinkled white corpse-fingers, it felt nice to scrub myself all over. When I was done, Kiyu brought some clothes that were large enough to fit me and clearly not her own. She must have borrowed or bartered them from someone else. There were far fewer people in Lago Warren now, I reflected sadly. Was I wearing a dead woman's clothes?

There were some woven pants and a loose shirt of plain white cloth. I cinched it around my waist with my Greenguard belt, to which Kiyu had returned my knife. I slipped my feet into my old boots and tied my hair back with a ribbon borrowed from Kiyu. It was damned good to be wearing clean clothes again and I felt a little more capable of dealing with the world today.

Zach's betrayal and loss was a weight inside my chest, still unfamiliar and prone to knocking me off balance if I bumped up against the wrong memory. But I would learn to live with it. I would remember Zach for the man he was, even if no one else did.

"You look nice," Kiyu said.

She stood up on her tiptoes to kiss me and I returned her affection eagerly. I was beginning to think that putting clothes on might have been a waste of time when someone called from the cave door.

"Kiyu?"

She pulled away, opened the curtain and waved Jacks inside. His eyes darted to the knife on my hip, but otherwise, he ignored me. Diesel had dragged Jacks clear of the blast and then charged the robot, Kiyu told me the night before. The dog was found only a day later, cut almost in two.

Jacks and I had both lost our best friends in the attack. I wondered if we would ever be able to talk about that.

"The elders will try the communion again at noon," Jacks said.

"I'll be ready," Kiyu said. "I can do this, I promise."

Jacks nodded unhappily and left. Kiyu asked me to go down to the water and wait for her there. I wasn't sure I was ready to be on

my own yet, but if Kiyu needed some time alone to better prepare herself for the communion, then I wanted her to take all the time she wanted. Enough people had died already and I didn't want Kiyu to be one of them.

I made my way cautiously down the fissure. At least I couldn't get lost. All I had to do was take every downward ramp or ladder, though I had to retrace my steps a few times as I found my way barred by broken stone or missing bridges.

I finally discovered an empty ledge overlooking the water and sat, dangling my feet. Some men and women were back at work, pulling up fish and seaweed. Not everyone was dead in Lago Warren and for those who remained, life went on. I saw the mutated man with the crippled arm. He sat patiently with his fishing rod cradled in his good arm, waiting for a bite. It hurt to smile, but I was glad he was alive.

On impulse, I found a rope bridge still intact that led me across the water to his fishing spot. Everyone else was working, trying to keep the warren going. It was the least I could do to help.

"Hi, I'm Julia Reed," I said.

I offered him my hand. It was trembling. The fisherman shook it with his bent arm and I couldn't be proud of myself for not flinching. He wasn't a mutant like the scorpion had been, I reminded myself. He was just a man.

"Joshua," he introduced himself. "You must be the one from Angel City."

I nodded. I braced myself for the onslaught of accusations, but Joshua patted the ledge next to him.

"I saw you running after that death machine. You threw a rock at it," he said. "That was pretty stupid."

To my surprise, I laughed. The sound was raw and painful, but it was real. Yeah... For a woman who prided herself on her brains, I could be *really* stupid. As Zach had never hesitated to remind me. And protect me from.

"I was just the distraction," I said. "It was a crucial part of a very clever plan, you know."

I waited with Joshua until his line went taut and then helped him pull in the catch. He showed me how to tire the fish out before towing it up. A big fish could easily snap the line.

"If it's not big enough to break your line, then it's not worth bringing in," Joshua told me. "Especially the tuna. We let them get nice and big. A full-grown adult can feed a family for a week."

When Kiyu came to find me, we had nearly filled up Joshua's basket, though not with any of the huge tuna he had told me about. Maybe next time.

"It's time to go, Julia," Kiyu said.

I thanked Joshua, then followed Kiyu up through the warren to Diego's cave. The remaining elders were seated in a circle of blue algae light, the rest of the cushions occupied by younger psychics of the warren. I recognized one of the yangs from the robot's attack.

Kiyu squeezed my hand and then took her place in the circle. Jacks stood protectively over them, the crossbow he had taken from Zach cocked and loaded. The business end drifted toward me a few times and I kept my hands well clear of my knife.

The girl with the engan made her circuit of the volunteers once more and filled a bowl with thick, cloudy juice for each of them. She knelt next to Diego and poured.

"Grandpa, please let me help," she said quietly, but not so softly that I couldn't hear the worried note in her voice. "I'm a yin. I can do it."

But Diego held up a thin hand. "You're too young, Hannah. And if something else goes wrong, we can't leave the warren entirely without gifts."

Hannah bit her lip, but helped Diego raise his bowl. His left hand remained limp in his lap and engan dribbled out of the slack corner of the old man's mouth. Hannah wiped Diego's chin with a cloth and eased him back into the cushions.

The others drank, too. Kiyu squeezed her eyes closed as she choked down the sour juice. It was obviously her first time and she wasn't the only one. A man with violet patches on his skin retched and vomited. Jacks and Hannah carried him out of the circle.

The Whitefingers settled into silence, eyes closed and bodies slowly going limp in the wavering blue light. After a few minutes, their breathing synchronized and then I heard the whispers as Lago Warren reached out and touched minds with the remaining White-finger yins across the Pacific Desert. The whispers were quieter this time, barely perceptible at the edge of my mind. I thought I heard Kiyu in the muddle of voices.

I stood in the swirling, watery light, and watched with my heart in my throat. Without Kiyu to tell me what was going on, the whole experience was even stranger and more alien. I picked nervously at my fingernails and felt warm, sticky wetness as I cracked one of my dry cuticles. I was working up the nerve to ask Jacks what was happening when the circle of psychics suddenly moaned in one choral voice.

"So weak," they said together. It was eerie to see Kiyu's lips form the words but speaking in that shared voice. What did the communing psychics mean, though? Were they too weak to contact the Stormsphere?

"So many. So weak," the voices moaned. "Who are you?"

"Help. Help us!"

It was the same voices, those belonging to the thirteen men and women filling Diego's cave, but the mingled voices were louder now. Something had been added to the group mind, new thoughts joined in communion. Thousands of voices spoke through a dozen mouths.

"What happened?" the circle asked themselves.

"Our journey was... interrupted," came the answer, hissing and quiet despite a dozen voices. I knelt with my head cocked at Kiyu to catch the words. "The journey of generations. The migration.

You traveled in our shadow, followed our path, under our protection."

So many, they said. *Our.* There was more than one mind inside the Stormsphere. A hell of a lot more than one.

"But you stopped us. Caught us. Caged us," murmured more voices than mouths. "The seasons and the generations passed, but the journey could not continue. We're dying. You're dying. We can't protect you anymore. We're too weak. Release us! Free us!"

"What?" I said. "No! If you leave the city, everyone there is going to die!"

Jacks hissed for me to be quiet, but the strange psychic voices from across the desert were asking us to let them go, to let them abandon Angel City.

The circle was silent. The whispers of their joined minds still hovered at the edge of perception, murmuring. Thinking...? I remembered Thorn's shouted words, the High Gardener swearing that his people would never return to wandering the desert like beasts. What else had he said?

At the mercy of mutant abominations.

The contents of the Stormsphere still hadn't identified themselves, but they were obviously dreameaters of some kind. Just like the dreameaters the Greenguard hunted down and killed. For all the lives those in the Stormsphere had saved – even if they no longer could – Thorn didn't have much reverence for the Tear of God he served. Hypocrite.

Finally, the circle spoke again.

"Free us," they said. "Let our journey continue. Come to us and we can show you how to live. Hurry... We are dying. Save us, and save yourselves."

TWO MORE HOURS passed before the Lago elders and their assistant yins and yangs finally blinked their way out of the engan trance. Diego rubbed his bent back while the younger ones clutched at their heads and stomachs. A few more Whitefingers were summoned to help the worst off stagger outside into the fresh air and to keep them from falling into the water. Diego watched them with a faintly amused expression on half his face. I guess there was a lot to say about experience over youth.

I went to Kiyu and pulled her gently upright. She groaned and did her faltering best not to throw up on me. Hannah poured cups of water and I helped Kiyu to drink.

"Now what?" I asked.

"They're not human," Diego said. He stood and didn't seem at all unsteady after the engan. "The Whispers are something else, and there are a great number of them. It was like nothing any of us have ever felt before. Each mind is tiny, simple and innocent, but they live in a state of constant communion. Their understanding is immense and their memory spans generations."

"Animals of some kind," Kiyu groaned. She held her head like it might break. "They were... pretty."

I thought of Diesel and tried to imagine thousands of dogs living inside the Stormsphere. Dying in the Stormsphere, and when they were gone, the Whisperward collapsing. It had already happened in Sun City and Bridge City.

"What was all that about a journey?" I asked.

Diego looked at the other surviving elders, but only shook his head. "I don't know. But ending it seems to have directly contributed to the failure occurring now."

"The Gardeners captured them," I said. Kiyu coughed and I rubbed her back, much like she had done for me the night before. "Trapped the Whispers inside the Stormspheres, right? All of those flowers and nectar... They're not offerings at all, are they? They're food."

"That makes sense," Diego agreed. He looked tired and Hannah hurried to bring another pillow for the old man.

"That's why Byron was trying to breed a better nectar," I said. "Because the things that they're feeding are dying."

It made sense and I hated Thorn for his secrets. Kiyu leaned against me.

"Diego, do you really think that the Whispers will help us if we save them?" I asked.

"We were in communion, Julia," Kiyu answered. She coughed again and continued. "We shared minds. The Whispers couldn't have lied to us. We don't understand everything they told us, but they couldn't hide anything."

"If we can free them, they'll help," Diego said. "They only want to resume their journey, but anyone who wants to will be welcome to join them. We can travel with the Whispers and rediscover our world, if we wish."

"Thorn's not going to like that. But if we can learn to protect our own cities without a bunch of trapped animals, Thorn can um... eat thorns." I moved hastily on. "So how do we do it? How do we free the Whispers?"

"I still have the key to the Stormsphere," said Kiyu. "I can get back into Angel City. I've done it before."

"That didn't end very well the last time," Jacks pointed out. "If the Gardeners are still keeping a close watch on that Stormsphere, we're going to need more people. At least fifty. You're a good yang, Kiyu, but even you can't tangle with the Greenguard alone."

I shook my head. "You'll never get that many people through the greenhouses, to say nothing of getting close to the Stormsphere before the Blackthumbs notice. Thorn knows the Tear is failing and he knows that we want in. He'll be protecting it with every man he's got."

Jacks' half-burned brow creased in thought. "We could try approaching in small groups, increase the chances of a few getting through..."

"What about Thorn's plan?" I suggested.

"Which plan?" asked Kiyu. "You mean the robot?"

"We don't have any of your killer machines," Jacks said.

"No," I agreed. "But Angel City does. We don't go straight for the Stormsphere. We get a yin close enough to Gregory to retrieve the codes for the robots, then we turn them on."

Kiyu took my hand and squeezed my fingers gently. "We can't do that, Julia. You're the one who said that it was Thorn trying to kill us, not the rest of the 'Warders. That robot killed so many people. We can't do that to Angel City."

For the first time since Zach's death, a warmth filled my chest. Kiyu's compassion astonished me. I pulled her into a fierce kiss and didn't care if Diego or Jacks objected. If they did, neither man said anything. I could feel them staring, though.

"No," I said when I needed to breathe again. "The robots follow their orders, regardless of what they are. Machines won't care what the Blackthumbs do to them. If we order them to clear the area but not to kill anyone, they will. No matter how many robot parts we're scraping off the ground when it's done."

"That's a good idea," said Diego.

It was hard to tell with his weak, whispery voice if he was surprised about that. I decided not to be offended.

"Kiyu, how close would a yin have to be to get into someone's head?" I asked.

"Depends on the yin."

"There are some who survived the robot who could do it, if they can just get eyes on their target," said Jacks. He was warming to my idea. "Once they sleep off the engan."

"Kiyu, could you get a few people up over the Angel City walls? Like you pulled me and Zach out of the hole?" I asked. It hurt to say Zach's name.

"Sure," Kiyu said. "I can do it."

Jacks looked at Diego and the old man nodded.

"Select your team, Jacks, and do it tonight. You leave tomorrow at dawn. The Whispers are weakening quickly and we don't have much time."

———

JACKS SPENT some time conferring with Kiyu and the elders about my plan, but once I made it *very* clear that I intended to go along, I left him to handle the rest.

By dinnertime, Jacks was done with Kiyu, too, and I followed her back up through the sapphire-shadowed warren to her cave. I tried to memorize the way, but Kiyu's shapely ass kept distracting me.

"Julia... are you sure you really want to go back to Angel City?" she asked.

"Yeah. I never fit in there, but I still owe it to those people to help. If I can," I said. I tore my eyes off Kiyu's backside. "What about you? Last time you were there, you got shot and chased."

"You did that."

"Oh. Right." I ducked with Kiyu through the hangings and into her cave. "Still, it's going to be dangerous."

"I know. But I've been doing dangerous stuff for a while, Julia. I know the risks. Besides, I'm the best yang that we've got left. You need me."

"Yeah," I said quietly. "I do."

Just to look at Kiyu, she seemed so delicate. Jacks could probably break her slim body over his knee, but I knew it would never be that easy. Kiyu didn't give up and she didn't do things halfway. There was so much life, passion and power inside her.

Kiyu was making her way around the cave, shaking algae lights to life. I closed the distance between us and grabbed her shoulders. I leaned down and kissed her hard. I caught Kiyu by surprise and she gasped against my lips before returning my kiss in equal passion. I ran my hands up her shoulders, through her hair and then down again. I traced her slender arms and sides, felt the narrow curve of her hip. Her soft skin was finally under my fingers as we fought to shed our unwanted clothes without breaking the kiss. She smelled so good... salty as her desert, as her ocean, and sweet as her soft, kind heart.

Kiyu's small hands found my breasts and clutched eagerly. My nipples turned into hard buds at her lightest touch and I moaned as her palms grazed them. She led me through the blue shadows to the bedroom, then pushed me back until my legs hit the edge of her bed and I fell into the sheets. I didn't expect Kiyu to take the lead, but I had seen her in battle. She was fierce and as bright as flame. How could I have been surprised?

But I was no passive little flower, either, to sit still and wait for her touch. I pulled Kiyu down on top of me so I could feel her body against my own. Her tongue danced over mine, wet and hot, and her slender legs clamped around my thigh. I slid my hands along Kiyu's silky back as she writhed against me. I lifted my hips and wrapped my other leg around her to help her along.

Kiyu only took her lips from mine to cry out once, loud and long. When it was done, she looked up at me through dark lashes and smiled.

"I've been wanting to do that for so long now," Kiyu sighed. "You know what else I want to do?"

I had an impressive queue of playful and clever answers that Kiyu dashed to breathless moans as she kissed her way down my neck, over my collarbone and across my chest. She left little spots of pleasure where her lips touched me, like flowers blooming across my skin. Kiyu slipped gracefully off the edge of the bed and nudged my legs apart, then kissed me deeply once more.

Kiyu's lips and tongue stirred something deep in my core. I couldn't hold still. My back arched and I clawed at the rough blankets, trying to find purchase just to keep from being carried away. I fought for each gasping breath and finally managed to gulp down enough air to scream out as Kiyu kissed and caressed my body to a dizzying climax.

I collapsed into the bed, weak and limp, but it felt good this time. Right. Kiyu crawled over my trembling body again and wriggled her way into my arms. I slowly regained enough muscle control to run my finger up the delicate line of her spine.

"Stay here with me, Julia," Kiyu whispered into my ear.

Her hand slid over my belly, leaving heat in its wake. I reached down her slim body to find her wet and ready and silky soft. Kiyu kissed me.

"I think I finally found something beautiful, too," I told her.

ALWAYS EFFICIENT, Jacks had taken care of gathering our supplies during the night. So when Kiyu and I emerged from her cave the next morning, everything was pretty much ready to go. Kiyu went through the packs and pulled out a long, dust-colored cloak. The cloth had the slightly sticky texture of the Whitefinger's insulating resin. The cloak was faded, but otherwise in good condition, even if the hem was permanently dusted white with salt. Kiyu handed it to me and showed me how to work the fastening.

Jacks approached as I tied the cloak off under my chin. I wore my mended fatigues – now cleaned – with my knife on my belt and a full canteen. I'd taken the night-lens goggles and settled Zach's wide-brimmed hat down over my auburn hair. The hat was a little too big for me, but I couldn't let it go. Jacks looked me up and down, dressed as half Blackthumb and half Whitefinger. Finally, he held out the crossbow he had confiscated from Zach. Was that really only a week ago?

"Take this. You know nothing about using a spear," he said, then hesitated. "If you were going to stab us in the back like your partner, you would have done it by now."

It was better than being punched, but not by much. I guess that was acceptance.

"This is Sidney," Jacks said.

He whistled and motioned to one of the other Whitefingers. The man was taller than Kiyu, though only by a few inches, with curly hair and skin covered in brown freckles. I thought I recognized him from the communion. Sidney left Ahmet packing the last bags and walked over to me. He extended his hand and I shook it.

"I'm your yin. Lekan was my brother," Sidney said. "I'll finish what he started. I hear this is your plan."

"It's our only chance," I told him, then laughed. "At least, the only one I can think of. Don't suppose you have any ideas?"

Sidney smiled and shook his head. "Not that I think are any better than the one we've got. This Gregory, will he have a strong mind? How hard will it be to pull the activation codes from his thoughts?"

"Gregory?" I scowled. "The only trouble you'll have is finding a thought in his head at all."

Jacks called a start and we shouldered our packs. I groaned. They were incredibly heavy and crammed full of supplies, but Kiyu assured me that we would cache a lot of it on the way out for use on the return journey. If there was a return journey.

We climbed up the spiraling and crisscrossing warren ramps all the way to the top of the fissure. The whiteness of the Pacific Desert stretched out all around us. I fitted the goggles over my eyes and the Whitefingers tied cloth across their faces.

"Let's move," Jacks said.

————

I WAS PLEASED to note that I slowed the Whitefingers much less now than on the trek to Lago Warren. This time, I wasn't recovering from being high on engan, had a full stomach and my leg was mending.

If any dangerous mutants gave us shit, I was going to show my new team just how useful I could be.

I didn't get the chance, though, not for a while. Sidney was able to sense anything hungry or angry enough to be a problem long before we got close. Once, a warning rattle brought us to a halt, but the snake was a little thing, only a few feet long with no visible mutations. They could still be dangerous – it was a snake like this that had killed Lekan, after all – but Kiyu just picked it up from a distance and broke its neck. We ate the snake for dinner.

Kiyu and I slept close together and made love under the cover of our cloaks. We couldn't do all the things that we wanted to, but we were happy. I had been with other women before, but Kiyu was unlike any of them. She was so alive, so beautiful. So willing to risk her own life to save others.

On the second night out from Lago, I may have gotten a bit carried away. The next morning, Ahmet gave me a cross, bloodshot look. Kiyu and I kept a little quieter after that... but it was hard to feel very sorry.

———

IT'S a much swifter trip from Lago Warren to Angel City when you don't get lost, have a well-trained yin to warn you about monsters, and plenty of supplies. But on the morning of the fifth day, Jacks pointed out north, to the low line of black and bilious green shadows – a sandstorm. Ahmet doubted that it would hit until after we reached the Whisperward, but we ate breakfast on the move and increased our speed anyway. We didn't want to risk getting caught out in the open.

When we neared the husk of the original Angel City and could see the Whisperward walls, I slowed. The storm line had moved again. A lot. The clean perimeter of weathered rubble and standing ruins was gone. Now they were sandblasted and etched by wind.

There was at least one new fallen building that would change the skyline from the Whisperward. Everything right up to the walls belonged to the sandstorms now. How long did Angel City have left? A year? A month?

"What's our approach?" Jacks asked.

"With all of the refugees in the city, most of the Blackthumbs should be busy either keeping the peace or guarding the Stormsphere," I told him. "But with the storm line closing in, that's going to drive mutants right to the city gates when that sandstorm hits. There will still be Greenguard on the walls, maybe patrolling outside until that storm gets closer."

Jacks considered my answer and then nodded. We moved between crumbling bits of cover, running hunched over as we crossed the open spaces. Each time we stopped behind a weather-beaten section of wall, Sidney concentrated, listening and searching for any Greenguard's wandering thoughts.

"I feel fear," Sidney said.

"That doesn't sound like a Blackthumb," I said.

"That way," Sidney told us. "A lot of people. A lot of fear."

With his head down, the yin pointed toward the nearby Whisperward's western gate. Maybe there was someone staked out for the oncoming storm. I took the lead and steered us closer to the gate, trying to keep the leaning husks of old buildings between us and any watchful Greenguard. But even moving cautiously, it didn't take us long to find the fear that Sidney had sensed. I didn't need to be a yin to see them.

The gate stood open and a crowd of people gathered around it. But the uniformed Greenguard weren't letting them into the city. They were shoving the frightened throng *out*. Men and women clutched bundles and sacks of everything they owned. They were shouting and crying, but the crossbows pointed out at the crowd pushed them further into the dusty wasteland beyond Angel City's walls.

"What the hell are they doing?" Jacks whispered harshly.

"Pruning," I said. Acid burned in my throat and I felt like I was vomiting up the words. "There are too many people in the city. So Thorn is cutting the numbers."

A woman broke off from the mob and made a dash back toward the Whisperward. A Greenguard on the wall shouted an order and then a bolt was quivering in the woman's chest. She ran a few more faltering steps and then toppled face-first into the sand. A cry went up from the crowd, but the metallic glitter of arrowheads held them back until the Blackthumbs retreated behind the walls once more. They pulled the gates closed again, sealing Angel City.

My blood was on fire. This was *not* the Whisperward Zach tried to save.

"Julia!" Jacks hissed.

I had drawn my loaded crossbow without thinking.

"We have a mission," Jacks said. "If we do it, we can save them all. But if we fuck it up now, they all die."

I felt the urge to growl, but nodded and slung my weapon again. Kiyu put her hand on my arm and some of the tension faded. Jacks was right.

"Fine," I said. "Let's get over that wall, then."

WE CIRCLED around the north gate to the far side, where I knew that the ruins were thick and visibility from the wall was low. Jacks led us out from behind the leaning pillar of a concrete overpass to the lumpy foot of the city wall. Overhead, the sky had gone from white to a pale, washed-out green.

"Kiyu, get Ahmet up there first," Jacks ordered in a quiet hiss. "Sidney, I want to know if anyone's coming. I don't care if all they're thinking about is how much they need to take a piss."

Sidney nodded and Ahmet stepped up to the wall. He held his spear across his chest and whispered to Kiyu that he was ready. My girlfriend – yeah, I was pretty sure Kiyu was my girlfriend by now, though this wasn't exactly the time or place for the relationship talk – raised her hand and Ahmet lifted off the ground. His cloak didn't swirl in the wind; the cloth was pressed tight against his body by the grip of Kiyu's power. She deposited Ahmet at the top of the city wall and he waved down to us.

I went next, then Jacks and Sidney. Finally, Kiyu flew up and we crouched along the top of the wall while the Whitefingers un-screwed the pieces of their spears and tucked them away under their cloaks.

"Someone's coming," Sidney whispered.

I checked right and left, then spotted a pair of green-clad men mounting a ladder just down the curve of the wall. For now, their attention was on navigating the rungs, but at any moment, they might look up and see us.

"Everyone jump," Kiyu instructed.

I balked at the edge of the wall. It was thirty feet high and had nothing but hard-packed earth to break my fall and legs down below, but Kiyu gave me a shove. Everyone else just jumped over at Kiyu's command. Something caught me roughly a few yards off the ground and I jerked in the air. It was still a lot softer than the dirt, though, and Kiyu lowered us the rest of the way more slowly. We pressed ourselves against the base of the wall as the Blackthumbs reached the top. They would have to look straight down to see us.

We could have killed them, I supposed. We outnumbered the pair more than two to one, but I was glad that Jacks hadn't ordered it. In a way, those two Greenguard were just like Zach. They were only defending their homes under the guidance of the Gardeners, and I didn't want to kill them for that. Everyone who died was one less person we saved today. And each body increased the chances of the Gardeners realizing that Whitefingers had breached their city.

Jacks and the rest finished unscrewing their spears and hiding them away. I paused to make everyone rub dust into their cloaks and gloves, concealing the salt stains there. Nothing would get a Blackthumbs' attention quicker than actual white fingers.

As we slipped out away from the wall, I could see why Thorn must have ordered the pruning. The roads of Angel City had become camps, full to bursting with refugees. Tents had sprung up like greenhouse seedlings, choking the streets with people all trying to carve out a place of their own in this last refuge.

We slipped into the road and moved along the edges of the crowd, trying to blend in. They were thickest around the scale farms and cactus patches, of course. The banter of lively barter was too loud. Every voice was strained and a hundred shouting arguments raged all at once. The sellers were raising their prices in the face of dwindling supply and high demand. Everyone was hungry and frightened and felt cheated. A pair of uniformed Blackthumbs jogged across the square, pushing through huddled people to break up a fight that had started over some roast snake.

More Greenguard patrolled along the road, crossbows in hand. They stopped people – apparently at random – and forced them to kneel while one placed a hand on the frightened citizen's head. The Halo lit up, flickered and scanned, then finally turned green. With a shove, they sent the citizen stumbling away and began searching for their next subject.

"We can't let them test you two," I told Kiyu and Sidney, cocking my head slightly in the direction of the roaming patrol. "They can detect your abilities."

So we crept away from the Blackthumbs and I pulled Zach's hat low over my eyes. If any of them recognized me – and everyone in the Greenguard knew Julia the troublemaking traitor by now – then we were fucked for certain. I nodded to a side street at the edge of the market and we made our way toward it, trying not to hurry or look over our shoulders too much.

But I was checking back at the Greenguard, of course, when I ran smack into Sam Garza. I took a step back and shook my head clear, but by the time I realized who I was looking at, Sam recognized me, too.

"What?" he gasped. "But I thought they executed you!"

Sam looked at the cloak covering my fatigues, then at the others gathered around me. He might not have been able to tell they were Whitefingers, but I was sure that he didn't have to be a yin to feel the guilt I was projecting.

"Julia..." Kiyu warned. I glanced over my shoulder again and saw the Blackthumbs circling the market perimeter toward us.

"Climb," Sam whispered. He pointed to a ladder that led to the second story of a leaning gray-white highrise.

Jacks urged everyone up quickly and then threw himself down flat on the terraced ledge. The Greenguard stopped at the mouth of the street and saw Sam. They turned and pushed through the crowd toward him. Jacks swore softly and began pulling the sectioned spear out from under his cloak.

Sam leaned closer to a group of refugees sitting with their backs against the nearest alleyway wall and whispered something to them. I couldn't make out the words, but Sidney held up his hand to me and Jacks, shaking his head.

Sam thrust his hands into his pockets and turned away down the street, but the Blackthumbs whistled sharply and pointed to him. Sam stopped, eyes wide. One of the Greenguard leveled a crossbow at him while the other one appeared to be asking a question, to which Sam stammered an inaudible answer. The Greenguard didn't seem pleased with whatever he said, though. The one with the crossbow grabbed Sam by the shoulder and gave the dyer a rough jerk. Beside me, Sidney looked nervous, but his hand remained raised.

Wait.

Kiyu was as taut as a steel cable beside me. The Blackthumb forced Sam to his knees and the other placed a hand on his head. The Halo beeped and the floating image of Sam's brain lit up with scan lines. The halo-gram flashed green, flickered and then went dark. The two Blackthumbs exchanged a glance. The one wearing the Halo pressed the button again, but the halo-gram didn't reappear. The battery must have finally died in the ancient piece of technology. The other man yanked Sam to his feet once more.

"Go on, then," he said.

Grumbling, the two Blackthumbs made their way into the street again and back toward the Greenguard base. I grabbed the edge of the roof and swung onto the ladder, beating Jacks down to the road.

I tapped Sam's shoulder. His shirt was dark and clung to his skin with sweat. Sam flinched violently at my touch and spun to face me, but then he relaxed and stepped further down the narrow street.

"I didn't rat you out," he promised.

"Thanks." I looked at the refugees huddled along the alleyway. Every one of them dropped their eyes and refused to meet my gaze. "What about them?"

"I said I'd tell the Blackthumbs that they were dreameaters if they talked. They won't say anything. But what are you doing here?" Sam asked. "Do you know what's going on? They say the storms are at the city walls."

"They are," I admitted. "But we think we can help. You should get out of here."

"Wait, I want you to meet–" Sam stopped and looked over my shoulder again.

I spun, expecting to find more Greenguard, but Sam brushed past me toward a woman carrying a baby in a sling across her chest. She paused when Sam called out and he leaned over the infant, smiling broadly in spite of the tears shining in his eyes.

"That's not her daughter," Sidney said. I hadn't even realized that the yin was standing next to me. "She's Sam's baby girl. You saved her."

I shook my head. "No, not me. It was Zach. We were supposed to give her to the storm. But Zach just couldn't do it."

"Zach did that?" Jacks asked.

I stood up straight and looked the tall, scarred Whitefinger almost in the eye, but he said nothing else.

If I survived any of this, there would be time to meet the baby girl later. Before Sam could introduce me, we hurried out of the crowded street. I felt eyes on me everywhere and asked Sidney if he would be able to sense if someone spotted us.

"Maybe," he said uncertainly. "There are an awful lot of people here. It's... noisy."

As we closed in on the Greenguard base, the roads began to clear. Not because there were fewer refugees here, but because the patrolling Blackthumbs and their crossbows kept everyone away. We no longer had to squeeze between tents and people, but that meant that it was harder to conceal ourselves, as well. I led the Whitefingers toward the base at a brisk, business-like walk. Fast enough, I hoped, that we would look like we knew exactly what we were doing.

I didn't tempt fate by heading straight for the front gate, but circled the tall fence and its coils of sharp razor wire. I didn't see anyone in the training yard. All of the Greenguard were out working the city or guarding the Stormsphere, I guessed. The base itself should be nearly empty. Except for Gregory, if he was the lazy ass I suspected him to be.

"I don't sense any thoughts in the yard," Sidney said.

A pair of water boys made their way across the far end of the street, but they leaned together as they walked, gossiping. It was as clear a shot as we were going to get. Kiyu quickly flew us up over the fence, panting a little with the effort. When we landed on the other side, I unfastened my cloak and handed it to her. With any luck, my uniform would be enough to move unnoticed and unremarked until we made it to Gregory.

We made our way swiftly across the yard in the direction of the blocky concrete base, but two Greenguard were heading toward us from the front gate. Sidney cursed. He hadn't felt them coming from the crowded market... I shushed him and kept us moving. I waved to the other Blackthumbs.

"Hey there," I called as cheerfully as I could manage.

It was the same pair that we evaded as they scanned the market crowd. They had dawdled on their way to the base, probably reluctant to report the broken Halo, and we had beaten them back.

"What are you doing here?" one of them called out. "Who the hell are these people?"

They were uncomfortably close, but for the moment, the two Greenguard were focused on the Whitefingers and hadn't recognized me. Yet.

"They say they've got some information for Chief Gregory about the Whitefingers," I lied quickly. "They want to get some barter out of it."

I turned and motioned everyone toward the door, bringing up the rear with my crossbow pointed at Ahmet's back.

"Hey, wait! What's that?"

The Blackthumbs jogged to catch up with me. One of them was pointing to Ahmet's spear – the end had caught in the hem of his cloak. Ahmet darted a quick glance down and pulled the spear away out of sight, but it was already too late. The other Greenguard whipped their crossbows up.

"He's armed! Take him down!" one of them shouted.

There was no way we could simply walk into the base now. Kiyu and Sidney both threw their hands up in surrender, but the nearest Blackthumb's finger twitched on the trigger of his crossbow.

Shit.

I heard a thud, a shout and then everything turned into a storm of steel weapons and swirling cloaks. I whirled and fired. A body slumped to the ground. I heard another crossbow twang as I yanked the knife from my belt and went after the closest green shape. He ducked a jab from Jacks, who wielded his spear in pieces, smashing the blunt end into the other man's gut. I caught the Blackthumb with a slash to the arm that sent his empty crossbow sliding across the ground. He was still reaching for his own blade when the point of Jacks' spear emerged red and dripping from his throat.

I spun with my knife held ready, but Kiyu had already finished with the reinforcements from the Greenguard base. The doors had been smashed off their hinges and two bodies lay in crumpled heaps inside. One of them groaned and curled slowly into a fetal ball, but the other didn't move at all.

Sidney and Ahmet lay sprawled on the ground, though. Ahmet had a bolt buried between his ribs, probably right into his heart. Sidney had been shot in the side and blood bubbled from his mouth as he struggled to breathe. Jacks pulled him inside the base and tried to help Sidney sit up. The yin cried out in pain. I was no healer, but I could hear air whistling through the hole in his side. It didn't sound good.

"I'm fine," Sidney said. Blood ran down his too-white chin. "I can make it. Just help me..."

Jacks heaved Sidney up to his feet, slinging one of the yin's arms over his broad shoulders. Sidney coughed and blood poured from his mouth, soaking his shirt in red. He slipped off of Jacks' shoulder before anyone could catch him, fell to the ground and did not rise again.

"OH SHIT," I said.

"What do we do now?" Jacks asked. His big hands were crimson with Sidney's blood. "If we can't get the robot activation codes from Gregory, we'll never make it to the Whispers."

"This thing has gone pretty fucking stormy," I admitted. I closed Sidney's eyes. Which was harder than it sounds – the yin's body was already growing stiff. "But we can still get those codes. I told you that Gregory wasn't the brightest flower in the garden. We can still do this."

"I'm with you," Kiyu said. She reached out and squeezed my hand in hers.

"Are you sure?" Jacks asked. "If the Blackthumbs catch us now and figure out what we're up to, we can never try this plan again. We get just one shot at this, Julia."

"We can do it," I told him.

Jacks sighed. "Alright, let's go."

We worked our way slowly through the bright-lit hallways of the base. Jacks and Kiyu stared at the glowing bulbs in their re-cessed ceiling niches, but didn't ask any questions. I led with my crossbow as we rounded each corner and passed open doorways.

Jacks had reloaded a crossbow from the fallen Blackthumbs and carried it in one hand so he could keep his now-assembled spear ready in the other. Kiyu held her spear loosely, but it wasn't her weapon that the Greenguard needed to worry about.

But besides those we had already faced, we saw no one else inside. A single bright light tube still glowed in the stairwell leading down to the hangar, so we moved cautiously. I heard a double gasp from Kiyu and Jacks as I pushed open the doors and led them out through the ranks of silent robots. The machines stood like statues, but I couldn't deny the air of cold menace that hung over their folded limbs and darkened weapons.

"They're all deactivated," I whispered. "It's safe. Come on."

Kiyu took my hand and I pulled her along behind me. Jacks followed closely. He moved pretty quietly for such a big guy. We kept to the side of the hangar, in the shadow of the robots, just in case any Greenguard were on their way in or out of Gregory's office. I had been more or less right about the base being empty so far, but there were bodies outside now. As we moved out of the hangar and down the stairs, I heard voices.

"The High Gardener wants another thousand pruned from the city. Today," Gregory said. I hadn't missed that voice.

Gregory was answered with groans and gasps. A thousand in one day? There weren't enough Blackthumbs to do the job.

"Can't we wait until after the storm, sir?" asked another voice. At least someone still had a little respect for human life.

I held my finger to my lips and stood up onto my toes to peak through the tiny window set into the metal door. Inside, Gregory was pacing and rubbing his hands against his robes as he issued Thorn's orders to six Greenguard standing at attention on the other side of his desk.

"And what would be the point of that, Basinger? Every day – every *hour* they remain – these people consume more and more of our dwindling stores," Gregory said. "The safety of the Whisperward is paramount. The High Gardener knows that requires some sacrifice of life. I want one thousand people outside the city walls by nightfall."

I slung my crossbow and showed Kiyu six fingers. She pointed to herself and then motioned for us to wait. Jacks nodded and took up a position on one side of the door just like a Greenguard before charging into a suspected criminal's den. I ducked to the other side, holding my crossbow at the ready.

I grabbed the handle of the door, yanked it open and Kiyu jumped through. I was only a half second behind her, but Kiyu had already pinned the six Blackthumbs against the wall. Arms and legs were bent at odd angles and backs arched up painfully over slung crossbows. The Blackthumbs groaned and one of them screamed in terror at Kiyu. I wondered if he noticed the sweat streaming down her pretty, heart-shaped face.

Since Kiyu had taken such effective care of the Greenguard, I pointed my crossbow at Gregory.

"Nice to see you again, boss," I said.

"Reed?"

Gregory stumbled back into the filing cabinets, clutching at his robes. He darted his eyes to the Blackthumbs crushed against the wall. No help there.

"We need some information," I told him. "Maybe you can help us out. Give me the activation codes for the robots. Tell me how to use them and not only do you get to live, but I'll do you all a favor and save the whole fucking Whisperward."

"Thorn says you're a traitor. Tainted," Gregory said. It sounded like a sob.

"Now would be a really great time to start thinking for yourself, Gregory. The Whitefingers heard the Whispers crying out for help. I know Byron was trying to save them, but it's not working. The storms are at the city walls. The Whispers are dying and we can only help them if we get into the Stormsphere."

"The Tear of God is sacred. You wouldn't dare!"

Piety gave Gregory a moment of something like bravery. I almost felt sorry for him.

"Okay," I said. "Let's put it another way. You see that girl?"

I pointed and Kiyu gave Gregory her best chilling glare. To me, it still looked pretty cute, but he had just seen her sweep a half dozen men aside with her mind, so he was probably less inclined to kiss Kiyu and more inclined to wet himself. At least, I hoped so.

"She's what you call a dreameater, and what I call a total badass," I said.

Kiyu lifted all the pinned Blackthumbs with a thought, sliding them up along the wall so their legs kicked and dangled two feet off the floor.

"You can tell me the activation codes," I suggested, "or I can let her rip out what passes for your thoughts, one by one, until she finds what we need. By the time she's done, it's going to be a good thing Thorn already tells you what to think, Gregory, because you'll be drooling mindlessly down the front of your robes for the rest of your life."

I glanced back at Jacks. Kiyu wasn't that kind of psychic, but Gregory didn't know that. The big Whitefinger was giving me a lopsided grin.

"No, please!" Gregory begged. "I... I'll give you the codes."

———

WE LEFT Gregory and the Blackthumbs in his office, bound with their own handcuffs and gagged so they couldn't call for help. We backtracked to the hangar. I repeated the code to myself over and over again.

"Activate as many as you can," I said.

Jacks and Kiyu seemed a lot less unsettled by the robots this time. The ancient machines were somewhat less menacing now that we knew how to control them. I went to the back of one row and clambered up the folded mass of metal legs. The little plate was an inch below the robot's head, right where Gregory said it would be. I worked a fingernail into the seam and pried it open to reveal the square of buttons.

I pressed the numbers in the order Gregory had instructed and a deep hum started up in the robot's depths, followed by a series of mechanical beeps. I hopped off as it rose on spider-like legs and unfolded its weapon arms. A green light glowed in what passed for the machine's eye. I heard Kiyu give a cheer and then another green light kindled in the darkness.

I ran to the next robot in line. I entered the activation code three times, but nothing happened, so I leapt down and moved along the row. Kiyu and Jacks worked their way along the other side, cursing when they found a dud and shouting when another robot powered up. We moved between dozens of the robots, more than half the hangar. Twenty of the machines turned on, though three of these only sputtered for a moment before going dark again. But time was starting to worry me, so I went to the center of the hangar. Seventeen of the deadly robots were more than enough to get us where we needed to go.

"Mission parameters," I told the humming, green-glowing machines. Had I remembered what Gregory told us correctly? Well, I would find out soon enough. "Protection detail. Proceed north with us to the... the pea-dee-see. Only non-lethal neutralization of opposition authorized."

"Acknowledged," the robots responded in a chorus of shockingly clear, almost boyish voices.

They formed up around us and we marched through the base in a parade of metal and polymer. As we retraced our steps out into the training yard, the robots reacted, two of them moving swiftly and firing at another pair of Blackthumbs just coming through the gate. The two women fell to the asphalt. I checked their pulses and both were still alive, though unconscious. There was an acrid smell in the air that made me dizzy and I hastily retreated.

We moved out into the street. Our work had not gone unnoticed. More Blackthumbs charged up the road, followed at a distance by a curious crowd. A crossbow bolt hissed through the air at me, but then it vanished in a burst of red light. Six of the robots split off silently and fell back, covering our exit. They fired at the Greenguard and held the crowd at bay while the other eleven closed their protective perimeter around us.

I strode through the greenhouses, flanked by Kiyu and Jacks. The dimming gray-green sky cast the glass houses in shadows, but there were spots of bright color inside. The flowers. Food for the dying Whispers.

Silhouettes paced us on the far side of the greenhouses, but whatever the robots used to see, they were a lot more effective than eyes. One of them fired something smoking through the glass. Greenguard and a robed Gardener scattered, staggering and choking, into the road. Our mechanical guardians dispatched them in short order with small, bug-shaped projectiles that made the fallen Greenguard twitch in the dust.

The Houses were full of people. Jacks sent four more robots – two in each direction – to clear out the area. Seven left. I kept my finger on the trigger of my crossbow, but the bolt remained in the groove. I paused, closing my eyes as the robots fought their all too efficient way through another team of Greenguard.

But I couldn't hear the Whispers.

One of the robots malfunctioned suddenly as we cleared the Houses, sparking and sputtering. It fell into the dirt and we left it behind. Six left. But then we were climbing the rise toward the smooth black immensity of the Stormsphere. Still, I heard nothing, felt no alien thoughts among my own. Were we already too late?

"You two," I instructed, pointing to a pair of the robots. "Get to the Stormsphere. The pea-dee-see. Quickly!"

The robots moved swiftly. Four left. I broke into a run, but they were still outpacing me. Kiyu and Jacks hurried to follow. There were no refugees gathered in prayer around the Stormsphere. They were all gone and a few rust-colored stains on the concrete suggested that they had not gone willingly.

The shrine appeared at the top of the hill. And Thorn right in front of it, flanked by fifty Blackthumbs with crossbows cocked and loaded. The two robots I had sent ahead were dark and unmoving, down on their metal knees like attentive worshipers before the High Gardener.

The Blackthumbs raised their crossbows and our remaining robot escort swiveled toward them. There was a hiss and thump of displaced air and then more of the buzzing bug shots arced out, hitting five of the Blackthumbs in the chest or shoulders. They cried out and fell in a spasm of twitching limbs.

"Command override," Thorn announced with icy calm. He held up something that glowed with blinking lights. All around me, the robots made beeping sounds from somewhere deep inside and turned to face Thorn. "Deactivate."

The glowing green lights went out and the robots sagged to their metal knees with a few ratcheting convulsions. The remaining Greenguard switched their aim from the machines to me and my two Whitefinger companions.

Thorn stepped forward to rest a long-fingered hand on a deactivated robot. I tightened my sweating grasp on the trigger of my crossbow. I could take one of the Blackthumbs, or maybe Thorn, but then I was going to be bristling with bolts like a cactus.

"God entrusted the Gardeners with the old science," Thorn said. He held up his hand and showed me the metal cylinder he held. It looked a bit like the one that Zach had carried, but this was larger and had tiny buttons on the casing. "This has been an unforgivable waste of battery life. They are *my* tools, child. You were foolish to try to use them against me."

"Thorn, listen!" I shouted. "You're a prick, but I'm not here to fight you. We're here to help. The Whispers are dying in there! We have to release them!"

"Release them? The Gardeners put those pathetic creatures into the Tears for a reason, Reed," Thorn said.

"You knew!" I snarled. "You *know* what's in there!"

"It was the duty of the Gardeners to catch them and to care for them, Reed. Ours is the burden of knowledge."

"You don't know everything, you prick! They don't need better flowers or better food. They are dying because you've imprisoned them, Thorn. The Whispers are begging for help. They're dream-eaters and they've filled the world with their cries. Let them go!"

"Of course they're dreameaters," said Thorn. The High Gardener's voice was rising. "Nothing else could operate the Tears of God. But the damned things were too wild. They would never just... be still. We had to abandon our homes, follow them across the deserts like beggars. Never again!"

"But they're dying!" I shouted. Why didn't he understand? All of his pride, all of his stupid reasons wouldn't matter anymore if the Whispers fell silent. They would die and so would we.

"Then we'll use the Whitefingers and their dreameaters," Thorn said. The wind was rising, too, tugging at his black robes. "A needle to the right part of the brain to keep them docile, a little cactus and some crickets to keep them alive. So much easier than growing the flowers."

"You'll never take us," Jacks growled.

"We will do what we must. God gave the Earth to men, and to us command of the plants and the beasts," Thorn said. He leveled his finger at us. "Lay down your arms or die where you stand."

"Julia," Kiyu said.

She held out her hand to me and I took it, but kept my crossbow aimed at Thorn with the other. But my 'bow wavered when I felt something smooth against my palm – the plastic key card.

"Go," Kiyu whispered.

I fired. With a shout, one of the Blackthumbs crumpled around the bolt in his stomach. The rest swung their weapons toward me and fired. I threw myself to the ground, but the arrows shattered against Kiyu's sudden invisible barrier. Jacks shot one of the Greenguard down and then ran forward with his spear held low.

"Set them free!" Kiyu shouted at me. My favorite psychic raised her hands and Blackthumbs flew up into the air. "Save them. We can handle this!"

I jumped up and ran behind Jacks, pulling my knife. The Blackthumbs scattered as he barreled toward them. One of them didn't move fast enough and was skewered like a lizard kebab. Mottled green and brown and polished steel closed in around us.

Thorn bellowed orders to the powered-down robots, but everyone was shouting and even the High Gardener couldn't make himself heard. He whirled away, jabbing frantic fingers at the device in his hands.

"Keep moving!" Jacks grunted.

A bolt punched into his knee, but the big Whitefinger didn't fall. I pushed past Jacks, through the hole in the line of Greenguard and sprinted for the temple, but something as black as a storm cloud loomed up before me: Thorn and his damned robot controller.

There wasn't enough time to reload my crossbow. I swung it like the world's most awkward club and one steel arm cracked against the High Gardener's wrist. Thorn shrieked and the control fell from his spasming fingers. It bounced across the dusty concrete and I stomped down on it as hard as I could. I felt more than heard the metallic crunch under my boot. Another irreplaceable ancient artifact ruined, courtesy of Julia Reed.

Thorn drew himself up, imperious and commanding. "Enough. Stop this, child. You know not what–"

"Fuck you, Thorn," I said and punched the High Gardener in the mouth.

He fell back, spitting blood and teeth. I jumped over Thorn and ran to the temple. The offering tables were empty, but the sweet smell of nectar hung thick in the air. The Whispers that should have been a swelling rasp like the hiss of the ocean all around me were silent.

I'm coming, I thought as loud as I could. *I'm coming to set you free.*

I had no idea if they could hear me, but I repeated it like a prayer as I nearly slammed into the doors at the back of the offering shrine. I ran down the steps two at a time and between the Gardeners' edited murals. From the fields of milkweed at the top to the strange, needle-covered trees... The journey of the Whispers. That was what the Gardeners had painted over – the creatures they once revered and now imprisoned in the Stormspheres. What they had hidden away in the darkness.

I jumped down the remaining stairs and staggered to the slick black Door of the Stormsphere. I could barely see, but I found the little red light and swiped the key through the slot. For a heart-stopping moment, nothing happened, but then I realized the dark stripe was facing the wrong way. I flipped the key over and tried again.

The red light turned green and the Door glided silently open.

ON THE OTHER side of the Door, everything was white, so bright that I wanted to throw my arm across my eyes. But I could hear them – the Whispers, so faint that I could barely distinguish them from my own thoughts. I forced my leaden legs to work and stepped through the Door. The floor and walls were slick and pale, striped with narrow rows of glowing light. I was in a corridor just wide enough to spread my arms. The metal walls were cold to the touch.

Squinting, I crept down the blindingly white hallway. It was only a few yards long. I didn't have much time. Kiyu and Jacks were out there, trading their lives for this one chance. I had to hurry. But my knees felt like water and my mouth was dry. The Whispers were in here. They were waiting for me and needed my help.

The hall ended in a set of doors, panes of more shiny metal with another black panel. Words stood out in warning red above the door: Psionic Defense Center. PDC. Pea-dee-see.

There were smaller words printed underneath:

Emergency access
All personnel are subject to search
Please have identification ready

Emergency access? So this wasn't the front door. But I had never seen any other way into the Stormsphere.

I approached this new door slowly. There was another slot and I slid the key through. The light turned from red to green again and the corridor hummed. It was like being inside something alive. There was a soft whirring noise and the door behind me – the one I'd entered through – began sliding closed. I ran back, but not fast enough. The door thumped shut and the air in the hall hissed like an angry snake. A cold wind blew down on me, pulling at my hair and clothes. I pounded on the door and shouted for Kiyu, but only managed to bruise my fists on the metal as cool, dry air blasted me. But then the hidden machinery whirred again and something clanked beneath my feet. The wind stopped as the far door opened.

As much as I wanted to get out of the tiny hallway before I could be trapped again, I walked slowly. My pulse hammered in my ears as I stepped through the open door and into the Tear of God.

Inside the Stormsphere was a pillar of white. I don't know how long I stood there, staring uncomprehendingly. The scale was impossible to understand. There was nothing to compare that lonely streak of white to. It seemed at once huge, towering like a highrise, but then small enough to pluck down out of the darkness and hold in my hands. The white pillar floated before me, shifting and undulating like a mirage. Daring me to comprehend it.

Challenge accepted.

The pillar wasn't the only thing in the Stormsphere, I realized a moment later. I was moving forward, frightened and fascinated, drawn by the huge white... thing, but I hadn't plummeted down into the darkness below. I stood on a landing made of textured metal mesh, my hands resting on a thick steel railing. I thought it might ring the entire inner circumference of the Stormsphere, but it was hard to tell. More metal glinted in the distance.

Why could I see at all? I looked over the railing, down into the sphere. There were more ring-shaped landings connected by flights of metal stairs, and at least one above me. At the bottom of the hollow sphere, a cluster of bright lights pointed up at the tall, eerie white pillar. The air tasted strange, sweet and burnt and something else, something alive and something dead.

"Hello...?" I called out. "Can you hear me? I... I came. Like you asked."

My voice echoed through the darkness, off the floating pillar of white. It wasn't the only sound. There was a soft rustle. The Whispers. I could *hear* them, actually hear them with my ears. But there were still no words. What now?

The column floated in the center of the black Tear, tethered to the circular walkways. Not tethered, I saw, but connected by bridges of the same silvery mesh that I was standing on now. I made my way to the nearest one and began edging toward the white pillar. The bridge was plenty wide and hemmed in on both sides by sturdy, waist-high railings, but I was still dizzy as I walked. My boots rang off the metal. It felt like I was in some other world, some alien place, millions of miles away from the sand and salt and storms.

Reluctantly nearing the pillar, I realized that neither of my initial impressions had been correct. It *was* large, much taller than I was, but hardly an entire building. The white thing was maybe fifty or sixty feet tall and a bit less than that in circumference. And the shimmering effect was no mirage or even a polished shine. The pillar was covered in something. Something white that was moving restlessly, fluttering like pieces of paper in a breeze I couldn't feel. What was it?

I tripped, staggered and clutched at the railing, panting and swearing. When the icy sweat abated and my pulse slowed a little, I took a look at what had just tried to stop my heart. It was a shallow metal tray full of flowers, small bundles of pink five-petaled blossoms. Milkweed. The offerings.

No, I corrected myself. The food. For what, though? Milkweed was poisonous.

But the leaves and stems showed tiny marks where something had nibbled at them. Gingerly, I reached down and picked up one of the flowers. Something small and white wriggled across the petals. It wasn't a maggot or a worm... It had a collection of stumpy legs and arched antennae in the front. There was another, smaller pair in the back. At least, I assumed it was the back, not another head. I peered closer. The tiny thing wasn't quite white – there were faint, barely visible stripes of yellow and gray along its length.

"What are you?" I asked.

Was this thing the source of the Whispers? The pale little shape inched across the leaf toward my fingers and I dropped the milkweed with a startled gasp. There were more of the metal trays set up along the bridge. Carefully, I stepped over them. The Whispers were growing louder, but no more discernible.

I was only yards out from the column now. It was rougher, more textured than I had first thought – there were flat parts, panels that stood out at angles from the rest. Walkways, too, like miniature versions of those around the black inner skin of the Stormsphere... All covered in that shifting, shimmering whiteness. The layer of white crunched slightly under my feet as I reached the end of the bridge. It was flaky and as pale as ash. Had there been a fire?

I trailed my hands along the railings. The white layer wasn't very firmly attached. It broke off beneath my fingers at the slightest touch, falling. Until one of the drifting bits of white fluttered and flew, circling me on bone-colored wings. It soared a few faltering feet, clumsy and awkward, and landed on the back of my hand. I couldn't even feel the little winged thing's tiny feet on my skin. I held my breath and stared.

Six pale gray legs, antennae with teardrop-shaped tips. And the wings slowly fluttering against my hand, as soft as Kiyu's skin and as delicate as flower petals...

I knew what this was. I didn't know its real name, but I had seen something just like it before. In the desert, with a belly and brain full of engan, I saw the flutterbies, the beautiful wings in bright orange and black, edged in white spots. The shape was the same, but this flutterby was pale. Sick.

Help.

I heard the plea clearly in my head, just like my own thought, but just as obviously alien. I jumped back with a scream, but the winged insect flew closer again and landed on my temple this time, under the brim of Zach's hat.

More flutterbies took wing, all flying toward me. Hundreds of them. I threw my arm across my face, but they alighted on me. They were on my hands, my head and even the nape of my neck. The Whispers filled my ears, my mind. They were no longer soft, but the crashing of waves that deafened me. I was caught in a storm of white, thoughts that were not my own jolting through me like lightning.

Help us. Help us... We're dying. We must fly!

I saw the mural again, flashing through my mind. No... not the mural, but the journey that it depicted. Flying north, into the cold places. Eating and growing, changing from eater to flier, mating and dying. The new generation continuing the great journey, led by vital, primordial instinct. South to north, north to south and back again. The endless journey of life. But here, trapped in the darkness, they were dying.

These were the Whispers. The flutterbies. That name wasn't quite right, I sensed, but it was close enough. I felt it as hundreds of wings brushed my skin. I raised my eyes to the column. The flutterbies that had come to me were only a tiny fraction of the ones contained inside the Stormsphere. Thousands more covered the column like the salt crusted along the hem of Kiyu's cloak. Many of the flutterbies were too small, some with too many legs or too few, pale orange or gray stripes and bands across their wings in fading memory of their once-vibrant colors. Some flutterbies flapped their wings or crawled awkwardly along the curving surface. But more of them did not move. Dead.

I took another faltering step forward and heard their tiny bodies crunching beneath my boots. Only one in ten still fluttered their pale, weak wings. When I breathed, I thought I could smell sunlight and nectar.

"Can... can you hear me?" I asked.

Yes. We hear you. Hear us. Help us... Release us!

"How?"

The flutterbies crawled over my skin. One of them tickled my cheek with stunted white wings. They didn't know. They had only a vague understanding of the Stormsphere that was their home, their prison. This thing was a human creation.

They built this place to protect themselves. The thoughts came in strange, overlapping bursts. Only some of them were in words. The Stormsphere had always been for protection, but from other humans, not the storms. The storms came later. *Humans were afraid of each other.*

"They still are," I said.

I circled the pillar slowly. I tried not to step on any of the dead flutterbies, but it was impossible. They covered everything. There were bowls, too, on the walkway and crowded onto every horizontal surface of the flickering white column. Flutterbies crawled along the edges, occasionally falling down into the nectar inside. This wasn't right. This wasn't how they were meant to live.

This wasn't how *anything* was meant to live.

I stopped to inspect a shape molded into the side of the floating pillar. I waved my hand gently, scattering the still-living flutterbies. Some flew away to find other perches on the column, several landing on my shoulders or the brim of Zach's hat.

A person...! I jerked a startled step away before realizing that it wasn't an actual human, just a depression in the column shaped like one. I would have fit quite snugly inside. Reluctantly, I drew closer once more and delicately swept away the layer of dead, brittle white flutterbies. The surface beneath them was a shiny pale gray set with what looked like copper dots all along the centerline and limbs of the human-shaped hollow. There were more of them around the head, like some kind of helmet or crown.

"What's this?" I asked. I felt strange just talking to the whole communing swarm of colorless insects, so I addressed one of the larger flutterbies perched on the back of my left hand.

This place, this... machine... it was meant for the humans to use. Not for us.

"Why? What the hell is all of this for?"

I saw the answer in the flutterbies' shared mind, in our communion. There was a war. There was *always* war. The world burned. The Wrath not of God, but of men. Psychics died. I wondered if they died in communion, like the elders of Lago Warren.

The entire world burned, cities consumed by white-hot fire and men by engineered fevers. Even afterward, frightened humans executed their own psychics, the flutterbies thought. I thought. We remembered it together.

Their own psychics. And the Gardeners – keepers of the old science and the old prejudices – kept right on killing dreameaters generations later. I touched one of the copper nodes. This machine was built for human psychics.

There was no one left to operate these ancient machines, to put inside the cocoon. The... sphere. So humans roamed. They followed us. But then they caught us in nets and sealed us here in the dark.

I dropped my gaze to the flutterbies, salt-white and flaking beneath my bootheels. They were insects with short life cycles, even if their endless communion created an unbroken chain of memory. Their eggs hatched into tiny, psychic caterpillars that grew up into psychic flutterbies. Humans followed them in their journey until the Gardeners got tired of it all and captured the flutterbies in the Stormspheres.

"You were powerful enough to push back the storms even before the Gardeners imprisoned you here," I told the white flutterby on my hand. "Can't you just... bust out?"

The darkness resists us. It is a strong cocoon.

The thought felt slightly petulant and I couldn't help smiling a little. A cocoon...? So the great black sphere wasn't a part of the old machine. It was some kind of shield to protect the pillar during the ancient wars. And it did the job well, but now Thorn and the Gardeners had turned protection into a prison.

"There have to be controls for it somewhere around here," I said. "Where are they?"

On my hand, the flutterby's pale, mismatched wings drooped and I thought it might be embarrassed. The flight didn't know. They didn't understand human machines much more than they did human war. That made sense, I supposed. If they did, why would they need me to free them?

Something white drifted across my vision. A flutterby that had been perched on my hat was falling, wings beating slowly, weakly. I caught it in cupped hands. It lay on its back. I prodded it carefully over onto six tiny feet, but the flutterby only managed to crawl a few more inches and then went still in my hand.

Tears stung my eyes. The dead flutterby was just one of thousands, like the ones I crushed underfoot with every step. But they were small, gentle things. Dreameaters, certainly, but ones who had never hurt anyone, only protected humanity even after we imprisoned them in the Stormspheres. Powerful as their psionics were, surely the flutterbies could have threatened the Gardeners or held the Whisperward hostage to force their freedom. But I could feel their thoughts mingled with mine. Violence had never even occurred to the flutterbies.

All they wanted was to fly.

I didn't know how much time was left. The flutterbies were a tiny fraction of their former strength and I had no idea what was going on outside the sphere. How long did I have before Green-guard stormed in, sacred taboo giving way before violent necessity?

I searched all around the upper level of the column of white-covered machinery. There were more human-shaped alcoves for the original psychic operators, a half dozen of them up and down the length of the column. But nothing helpful in opening the spherical black shield. I climbed down a ladder, cringing as I smashed more dead flutterbies into ashy dust. I cleared off another panel, but there were no screens or switches or levers. I found one slightly recessed button, but there was no label or anything else. Now what?

I remembered the Halo and its single button. The whole thing was automated, the halo-gram its only interface. I held my breath and pressed the button on the column. The plastic panel began to glow and words appeared in the air, then vanished, replaced by the floating image of an eagle with a shield clasped in its claws. There were stripes and stars on the shield, shining in red and blue. Then the eagle vanished and I was staring at a detailed halo-gram of the Stormsphere. The image of the huge sphere was a faintly pulsing purple-blue.

Now if only I could... I reached out and touched the indigo shimmer and lines of text flashed into glowing life:

PDC barrier is currently engaged: 89% integrity

> System maintenance

> Diagnostics

> Disengage barrier

I slid my fingers through the third option. The short list disappeared, replaced by more text.

The PDC barrier has been engaged for the protection of all personnel and assets
Please confirm authorization before opening

Something slid out of the shiny, ancient pillar of machinery, a black bar with a slot down the middle. There were no red or green lights, but it looked like the same kind of lock as the one on the Door. I guess the long-dead humans didn't want some floor sweeper opening the shield and exposing their precious machine to enemy dreameaters. I just hoped that Kiyu's key was the right kind. It had gotten me this far...

I slid the white card through the slot and the halo-gram words changed.

Authorization confirmed

A deep hum started somewhere under the skin of the Storm-sphere. It grew louder and crested into a squeal of metal and the growl of machinery. A line split the darkness above me and for the first time in centuries, the two halves of the Stormsphere ground open like a waking eye. Storm-shrouded sunlight flooded into the sphere and I threw my hands up, blinded.

Freedom. Fly. Fly!

All around me, the flutterbies spread their wings, basking in the first sunlight they had ever known. One by one, and then in hundreds and thousands, they began to beat their ashen wings. Some couldn't fly at all and others managed only a few wobbling flaps before falling once more, but the rest rose up into the air. The Whispers were a roar in my ears as the flutterbies flew off my hat, my clothes, my skin. They were a cloud of white against the darkness, spiraling up into the stormy sky. They were so delicate and fragile, but the black clouds overhead parted before them, leaving only pale sky above.

Something fluttered back down to perch lightly on the tip of my nose. I wondered if it was the same flutterby I had been talking to, but I couldn't be sure. I had to cross my eyes to keep the little thing in focus.

Its gentle thoughts brushed mine, full of questions and answers and gratitude. I closed my eyes and stood there for a long moment, communing with the flutterbies.

Finally, the last little white shape spread its wings, flew off of my nose, and joined the rest of the flight. They circled over the Stormsphere once and then flew north.

"Julia!" called a voice.

I stood in a deep bowl in the earth, the upper half of the Stormsphere peeled open and exposed. The white column floated in the center, still and silent now. Kiyu skidded over the edge of the open sphere and down onto a walkway. Blood ran from her nose and one of her ears, as well as a dozen other wounds. The veins in her left eye had burst, turning it bright red.

"Julia!" Kiyu cried again. "Are you alright?"

"I'm here," I shouted.

I crossed the bridge to her and wrapped my arms around her. Kiyu kissed me and I thought of flutterby wings. Then we looked together up into the clear white sky.

"What were they?" she asked.

"Very forgiving," I said.

THE STORM PASSED HARMLESSLY over Angel City, dispersed by the flutterbies' passage, and thirty thousand people watched in awed silence. There had been violence and battles in the streets of the Whisperward, refugees and citizens against Blackthumbs, Blackthumbs against robots. There was damage and lives had been lost, but the opening of the Tear of God had struck the Whisperward dumb and the stillness persisted. For now, at least.

There were a lot of questions and for the first time, I was the one answering them instead of asking. There were fanatics among the Greenguard and the Gardeners, but with Thorn and Gregory cuffed and the robot activation codes in our hands, we could keep things quiet until a more lasting peace could be established.

It would take some time for the people of the Whisperward to accept that their angels had been a swarm of psychic insects all along, and that their continuing protection would require human dreameaters learning to work the strange white pillar of machinery. The flutterbies were too few and too weak to save us yet. But Thorn laughed bitterly when I told him that his threat would come to pass, that humans would operate the Stormsphere once more.

"You'll never control them," he sneered. "You can't trust dream-eaters."

"Watch me," I said, putting my arm around Kiyu.

Protection would have to come from the Whitefinger warrens for a while, but the Halos would be useful for finding more young dreameaters in Angel City. There was still a lot of hatred for the psychics, but the Blackthumbs were good at following orders and now those orders were to protect the dreameaters that they once hunted. It wouldn't be easy, but the people of the Whisperwards would learn acceptance.

They had to. Without the psychics, none of us were going to survive.

I thought often of Liam, how I wished I had protected him. If he could have gone to the flutterbies back then, when he heard them crying for help, when this all began... Too many good people had died for the wrong reasons. Kiyu held me while I cried for them.

They asked me to lead the Greenguard, of course. I think I laughed. I recommended Jacks for the job, once he was recovered from his wounds. Which wouldn't take long, I suspected. Jacks was a tough bastard. I would have been a terrible leader and he was far better suited to the job. Besides, the flutterbies and I had made an agreement and I intended to live up to my end of the bargain.

"There's another generation of caterpillars still down there. A lot of them are sick and a lot of them will die, but the rest will grow their wings and join the journey," I said. I leaned back and let the gentle wind tug at my hair. Was it my imagination or did it smell sweeter? "But the world has changed a lot since the Gardeners first captured them. The flutterbies can't just return to their migration like nothing's happened."

"What will you do, then?" Kiyu asked.

We sat on the roof of the Greenguard base with a magnificent view of the open sphere and its pale, floating contents. With the black shield still lowered, there was no need for the shrine or the key cards now. Everyone could see the gleaming white tower. We would need to rename that thing... *Stormsphere* just didn't make much sense anymore.

"There are other Whisperwards out there. The machines inside the Stormspheres still work. The flutterbies needed to be free, but even they can't survive on freedom alone. Everything has to eat and there's only desert beyond the cities."

"What do you mean?"

"The Gardeners were right about one thing," I said. "We really do need the plants. We need the flowers and the Gardeners' expertise in raising them."

"Do you think Thorn will help?" Kiyu asked.

"He's a prick, but Thorn's got decades of experience managing the greenhouses. We could use his help, but if he won't work with the flutterbies, we'll talk to Martin or Torres. Maybe one of them followed Byron's research. We still need the flowers."

Kiyu leaned against me and I put my arm around her. She kissed my cheek while I held her close. I still had to run the plan I had hatched with the flutterbies past Diego and the Gardeners, but I was fairly certain that they would agree. We all wanted to live, after all. The world was a dangerous enough place without fighting each other.

"The flutterbies will need somewhere to go," I told Kiyu. "Not to be imprisoned, but to rest. To eat and lay their eggs. The forests and fields that their migration used to protect are gone. But the Gardeners know how to take care of plants. We'll keep growing the flowers for the flutterbies, and we can open the greenhouses to them. To everyone. In time, with the flights banishing the storms along their migration paths, the gardens will spread. There could be forests again. But we need each other to make this work."

"Together, we can make the world beautiful again," said Kiyu.

I nodded. "But someone needs to tell the other Whisperwards what happened here. We can't just execute psychics like Liam Fox.

No one should have to die like that. We've got to open the Storm-spheres and the gardens. It's going to take some convincing. There will be a lot of questions and people who don't want to listen."

"Wind City is a long way off," Kiyu said. She tipped my hat back to kiss me. "And it's a dangerous trip."

"I don't know. It won't be so bad," I told her, "as long as I have a partner."

For more books by
Erica Lindquist & Aron Christensen,
visit us at **LLStories.com**

www.ingramcontent.com/pod-product-compliance
Lightning Source LLC
Chambersburg PA
CBHW020911130726
47904CB00006BA/1833